# She put her left hand on his shoulder and held up her right hand.

He seemed baffled, but silently took her hand and pulled her close. She couldn't read his expression. Confusion? Anger? What the hell was he doing here anyway?

His gray eyes never left hers, even when other people patted him on the back and told him how good it was to see him. They seemed genuinely surprised and happy at his presence, but he paid them no attention. He just stared at her as they moved to the music. His body was tight with tension under her fingertips.

Looking into his eyes made her dizzy. She closed her own to regain her equilibrium, and her fingers absently traced the rough scars that scrolled under the dark tattoos on his arm. No wonder the tats had seemed three-dimensional.

When she opened her eyes, Cole was still staring as he moved her across the floor. She felt a sudden urge to sink her fingers into his thick, tobacco-colored hair. This was crazy. She tried to pull away, but he wasn't letting go.

The song came to an end, and still he didn't release her. Sh_____ whatever dem_____ immobile in th_____

"So...your ex-fi\_\_\_\_\_

Dear Reader,

I start my writing process the same way for every book—with the opening scene. Once I have an opening that sets the mood I want, I let the stories spin out from there. The funny thing is, the story doesn't always end up where I expect! I love the opening scene of *She's Far From Hollywood* with Hollywood diva Brianna Mathews driving through the Carolina countryside arguing with herself in the rearview mirror. When I wrote that, I expected this to be a light romance between city and country, but the characters took me so much deeper.

Writing Bree and Cole's story sometimes made me laugh out loud, but it also brought me to tears more than once. I hope you enjoy reading about their journey as much as I enjoyed writing it.

Having this, my debut novel, published by Harlequin Superromance is a dream come true for me, and happily there's more to come, so stay tuned! Dreams don't happen in a vacuum, and none of this would have been possible without the loving support and understanding of family and friends.

Wishing you forever love,

*Jo McNally*

PS: My research into PTSD revealed an average of twenty-two veterans commit suicide every day. And while I really do believe love can conquer anything, love can't always do it alone. Please reach out to maketheconnection.net or one of many other organizations out there ready to assist. A portion of the proceeds from this book will go to support programs for veterans.

# JO McNALLY

---

## She's Far From Hollywood

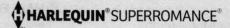

**H** HARLEQUIN® SUPERROMANCE®

Recycling programs
for this product may
not exist in your area.

ISBN-13: 978-0-373-64015-7

She's Far From Hollywood

**Printed in U.S.A.**

**Jo McNally** lives in coastal North Carolina with one hundred pounds of dog and two hundred pounds of husband—her slice of the bed is very small. When she's not writing or reading romance novels (or clinging to the edge of the bed), she can often be found on the back porch sipping wine with friends while listening to great music. If the weather is absolutely perfect, Jo might join her husband on the golf course, where she tends to feel far more competitive than her actual skill level would suggest.

She likes writing stories about strong women and the men who love them. She's a true believer that love can conquer all if given just half a chance.

You can follow Jo pretty much anywhere on social media (and she'd love it if you did!), but you can start at her website, www.jomcnallyromance.com.

I'm lucky enough to know what forever love looks like. My husband of twenty years is my hero, my lover, my cheerleader, my coach and my very best friend.

To John. I love you.

# CHAPTER ONE

BRIANNA MATHEWS HATED North Carolina.

Seriously.

She *hated* it.

She'd left the cosmopolitan appeal of Charlotte a couple of hours ago, and now it was just field after field of...what? Corn? Tobacco? Cotton? What did they grow in North Carolina, anyway? Cotton, right?

Some of the fields looked like golden-green grass and were undulating prettily in the wind. Was that wheat?

*...amber waves of grain...*

Wasn't wheat a grain?

She cursed softly behind the wheel of her rented red Mercedes. She was completely out of her element driving through farm country, and she laughed at her reflection in the rearview mirror.

"You're a long way from Hollywood, girlfriend."

This seemed like such a good idea last night. But last night she was still in the civilized world.

She'd been happily ensconced at her cousin Amanda's palatial stone castle, Halcyon, in the Catskill Mountains of New York, sipping pink champagne at Amanda's baby shower. Then she got the news that upended her tidy little world. The consensus was she needed a place to stay that was out of the public eye. Amanda's best friend, Caroline, offered her mother's rural farm as the perfect place to avoid both paparazzi *and* crazed stalkers.

"'Go to North Carolina,' Caroline said. 'You'll be safe there.'" Bree glared at her reflection as she continued her one-sided conversation. "'Mom has a cute little cottage you can use.' Didn't that all sound so delightful last night at Halcyon? And look at me now. Driving down country roads in the middle of nowhere. Me! Miss California!" She shook her head. "I haven't been here three hours and I'm already talking to myself. How am I supposed to last a month?"

According to Caroline's scribbled directions, the small town of Russell should be coming up anytime now. Thank the good Lord for that. This was not how her life was supposed to turn out. She was not supposed to be driving past feed mills and dusty double-wides that had signs in their front yards advertising things like Steve's Stump Grinding and Bob's Deer Processing. She didn't even want to know what "deer processing" was.

No. North Carolina was *not* her life. Her life was back in Los Angeles. She *owned* that freakin' town. Clerks in the shops on Rodeo Drive knew her by name. The waiters at the finest restaurants knew which tables she preferred, and had a Sapphire martini waiting for her before her ass hit the chair seat.

Then it all went to hell. And now she was driving to East Bejesus, USA. To *hide*. The whole situation ticked her off royally.

*Village of Russell, North Carolina*
*Founded 1820*
*Population 249*

She nearly wept with relief when she saw the faded wooden sign. Russell looked like so many of the other towns she'd driven through since leaving the Charlotte airport, except it was even smaller than most. *Downtown*, for lack of a better word, consisted of five or six buildings, washed out and faded in the scorching-hot summer sun. It looked like the set of a movie out of the 1950s, with aged and dusty brick storefronts. The Methodist church at the edge of town was the largest building, with the exception of the towering metal silos gathered directly across the street. It was midafternoon on a Monday, and the streets were quiet. A few pickup trucks were parked along the side of the road. Four in front of the farm supply store. Two in front of the bank. And one particularly dirty one sat in front of the only restaurant in town. A sign identified the business as The Hide-Away, and there was a neon beer sign in the window. She grinned at the irony—it was just what she was looking for.

She hadn't eaten anything since that reheated egg and biscuit concoction she bought at the airport, and she could most definitely use a drink. Caroline told her to stop in town and ask for directions to "Miss Nell's house," and the restaurant was as good a place as any to do that. Apparently Caroline's mom was so well-known in town that last names weren't necessary. Bree uncharitably wondered what it took to become famous in a place this small. She pulled the Mercedes into a spot next to the enormous black pickup truck caked with dried mud. Her car was as out of place in this dirty little town as she was.

The Hide-Away was dark and cool inside, with the blinds narrowed to block the heat of the sun. As her eyes adjusted, she saw an old-fashioned wooden bar that ran down the right side of the room, complete with a massive etched mirror on the wall behind it. The wooden bar stools had seats of well-worn dark leather. The place was straight out of a John Wayne Western. Dining booths lined the left wall, with more tables in the back of the room. A wide accordion door was pulled across an opening that seemed to lead to whatever business was next door. She didn't see any other patrons, and she wondered for a moment if the place was closed. Then she saw the good-looking man standing behind the bar.

He gave her a warm smile, and she relaxed. Somewhere around his late thirties, he wasn't overly tall, but he was muscular. Not Hollywood Beach muscular, where the muscles came more from steroids than actual exercise. No, this man had the lean, sinewy muscles that came from real physical labor. Dark brown hair fell across his forehead, stopping just above golden-brown eyes.

She slid onto the first bar stool she came to, settling down with a dramatic sigh. The still-smiling man wiped his hands on a thin towel and nodded toward her.

"How y'all doin' today, ma'am?"

*Ma'am?*

She was only twenty-nine years old. Well… okay, she'd be thirty-one in six months, but very few people on this earth knew that. Still, no-where *near* being a "ma'am" to anyone. She bit back her protest when she met his kind eyes, and reminded herself that she was in the South, after all.

"Would you like a menu, ma'am, or just something cold to drink on this hot afternoon?"

She finally remembered her manners and returned his smile. "Both, please. I'd like to see a menu. And I'd absolutely love to have a chilled white wine. Do you have a Sancerre?"

She flinched when she heard a sharp snort of derision to her right. A man sat in the shadows just a few feet away, at the short end of the bar. He was close to the wall, and there was a shot glass of amber liquid in front of him. She couldn't see his face because of the camouflage ball cap pulled low on his forehead. His jeans were worn thin and covered with dirt and something that looked and smelled worse. She wrinkled her nose. His Western boots were crusted and cracked. He wore a sweat-stained dark green T-shirt that stretched snugly across his broad chest. Dark tribal tattoos wound their way down his left biceps, looking three-dimensional. His hands were rough, with dirt plainly visible under his short fingernails. A day's growth of stubble covered what little she could see of his jawline. If she saw this guy in LA, she would have assumed he was homeless, or perhaps a day laborer. And he'd just snorted at her.

She pulled her shoulders back and sat up straight, but the bartender spoke before she could.

"Don't start, Cole." So the bum had a name. Cole sounded like "coal," which was basically dirt. It fit.

"Come on, Ty," Cole said with a gravelly voice that made her breath hitch for some weird reason. "A Sancerre? You really think this lady drove to Russell in her fancy red car to eat one of your famous Hide-Away burgers? Clearly she's lost. Give her directions and send her on her way."

The man behind the bar, Ty, leveled a glare in Cole's direction. She still couldn't see Cole's face under the brim of his hat, but the two men were having some sort of unspoken conversation as they stared at each other in stony silence. Finally, Ty turned back to her, slipping his easy smile back in place.

"Ma'am, for white wine we have chardonnay and also pinot grigio, mostly because that's what my wife likes."

She liked the way his soft Southern accent made "wife" sound like "whahf."

"Your wife has excellent taste. A glass of the pinot would be perfect, thanks."

Her nemesis in the corner spoke up again. The angry rumble of his voice made her skin tense and tingle, setting her on edge. "You better tell her what vintage it is, Ty, and maybe offer to take her on a tour of the wine cellar. And don't forget to let her sniff the cork."

He turned his head subtly in her direction. She could see the hard outline of his chin, but she still couldn't see his eyes.

Arrogant jackass.

Ty's voice was no longer gentle. "I won't say it again, Cole. Shut up or go home." He turned back to Bree and looked chagrined. "I'm sorry, ma'am. My brother's being more surly than usual. And he was born surly, so that's saying something."

Her eyes went wide. "You're *brothers*? Really?" She made a point to smile at Ty. "But *you* seem so nice…"

Ty laughed as he poured the wine, but Cole just grunted and stared back down into his glass.

"Cole's my baby brother. He's not always as bad as he seems this afternoon. I'm Ty Caldwell."

She took his extended hand and shook it. She was sure no one in this little burg had ever heard of her. "Nice to meet you, Ty. I'm Brianna. You can call me Bree."

Her stomach rumbled, making her laugh. "You know, a burger sounds absolutely divine right now. Could I have one, medium rare?"

She glanced in Cole's direction. She shouldn't engage with him, but she just couldn't resist.

Tossing her hair over her shoulder like she used to do for the cameras, she raised a brow coquettishly. "That is, if my order meets with your approval?"

He turned slowly and, for the first time, raised his head to look straight into her eyes. The effect was momentarily paralyzing. His eyes were blue-gray. And they were hard. Flint hard. His features were sharp and handsome, but they seemed to be chiseled into ice. Every muscle line was tight and tense, like a cat waiting to pounce. The corner of his mouth twitched into a semblance of a smile that never reached his eyes.

"Ma'am, I don't give a flying fu—"

"*Jay*-sus, Cole!" Ty seemed stunned by his brother's actions. But Bree was grateful to have a target for all the anger she'd been nursing for the past twenty-four hours.

"Well, forgive my confusion," she said with saccharine sweetness, "but just a minute ago you were so terribly concerned about what I ordered. And if you think for one minute that tossing profanities around will make me faint dead away, think again. I can out-curse the best of them. I doubt you qualify as the best in any category."

His eyes narrowed dangerously, but he didn't speak. Her anger gave her a rush of adrenaline, and her lips parted as she took a deep, steadying breath. His gaze flickered down to her mouth, and his chin turned to granite.

Ty looked back and forth between Bree and Cole in stunned silence as the atmosphere crackled with tension. Then he started to laugh.

"Brother of mine, I do believe you've just met your match. Miss Bree, I'll be happy to go make that burger as long as you two promise not to kill each other out here."

Cole's eyes met hers, and she didn't flinch from his hard glare. She nodded. "I promise. Thank you."

Cole just turned back toward his drink with a grunt. That seemed to be his favorite form of conversation. Ty looked between the two of them one last time then nodded, apparently satisfied no crimes would be committed in his absence. He turned and walked through the swinging door that led to the kitchen.

Bree picked up her wineglass and silently cursed her trembling hand. It was just adrenaline and exhaustion, but it made her look weak. She raised the glass for a sip and slowly set it down again. The base rattled against the gleaming wood. Cole snorted again, and she lost it.

"Look…" She spun and pointed her finger at his rock-solid chest. She saw a flash of surprise in his eyes, but he hid it quickly and returned to his usual glower. "I've had a miserable few days.

I'm tired, I'm hungry and I'm angry." She left out "terrified," because she thought he'd enjoy it too much. "I'm in the middle of nowhere. On *purpose*. But I at least expected a little freakin' Southern charm. Is that too much to ask?"

This time his grin almost reached his eyes. He seemed amused by her outburst.

"Yeah, well, I ran out of charm a while ago," he said, lifting one eyebrow. "Maybe around the same time you did."

She sat back and her mouth dropped open. Then she smiled thinly and lifted her glass in his direction in a mock toast. "Touché."

He nodded and turned back to his drink, swirling the liquid absently. She caught a movement near his feet and saw a dark-haired dog lying close by his bar stool.

"Are dogs allowed in restaurants in North Carolina?" She tried not to sound snobbish about it, but really, was it sanitary?

"This one is, in this restaurant."

"He's yours?"

"*She* is."

The dog was beautiful, with a sleek coat. Her ears stood up and she stared at Bree intently.

"What's her name?"

"Maggie."

"What breed is she?"

"Belgian shepherd."

"Is she friendly?"

"Most times."

The guy wasn't exactly a conversationalist.

"May I pet her?"

"Nope."

"Why not?"

He finally raised his eyes to hers. "Because she's not a damned pet, that's why. She's a working dog, and she's working. Leave her alone."

A working dog? Did she sniff out seizures? Was Cole disabled in some way that he needed a dog for balance or fetching things? She couldn't see any crutches or canes nearby. He turned back to his drink with another grunt.

Unintentionally, she spoke her thoughts out loud. "Well, if she's supposed to be making you human, you'd better return her, because it's not working."

He started to turn toward her again, and Bree drew back. She may have poked this bear one time too many. But the kitchen door started to open, and Cole stilled and went back to the intense study of his drink.

Ty walked through the doorway and checked the atmosphere in the room before he turned to Bree.

"Your burger will be ready in a few minutes, ma'am. So where are you headed?"

She stammered then steadied her voice.

"Um… I'm actually headed right here, to Russell. I'm…vacationing for a few weeks. I wanted some peace and quiet, you know? I was told to stop in town and ask for directions to Miss Nell's farm."

"Miss Nell? You're renting Nell's cottage? For *vacation*? In *Russell*?" Ty shook his head and chuckled. "Well, that'll be quiet, for sure. Where you from?"

"Southern California."

Cole let out another snort. She sent him a dark look.

"What?" she snapped.

He just shrugged and avoided Ty's warning glare. Ty turned back to Bree.

"Would you like another glass of wine?"

She stared at her empty glass.

"Gee, Ty, I wouldn't want to offend your brother's sensibilities by ordering more wine. Maybe I should try what he's having."

Cole let out a sharp, humorless laugh. "You'd hurt yourself, honey."

Oh, no, he didn't. "Let's make one thing clear. I am *not* your honey." She impulsively reached for Cole's glass. His hand shot out so quickly she didn't see it move until he grabbed her wrist. His fingers were as hard as his eyes, and she gasped at the feel of his calloused skin on hers.

Ty's voice dropped to a growl. "Cole, I'll

throw you out the door myself if you don't let her go. What the hell is wrong with you today?"

Cole pierced her with his eyes, and he didn't let go. His voice was low and threatening.

"Don't start something you can't finish... *honey*."

They glared at each other, then he released her hand and pushed it away, causing some of the golden liquor to slosh over the rim of the glass onto her fingers. She kept her eyes locked on his as she lifted his glass to her lips and emptied it. His eyebrows rose just enough that she knew he was surprised, even if his expression remained carved in stone. Both men probably expected her to have a coughing fit or some other girlish reaction, but they were going to be disappointed. She welcomed the burn as the strong drink warmed its way to her stomach. After setting the glass on the counter, she slowly licked the spilled whiskey from the tips of her fingers. Cole's nostrils flared just a bit at that move.

"Not bad." She shrugged, and Ty laughed.

"Day-um, woman. You may *look* city, but you sure act and drink country!"

She grinned and looked down at what she considered to be casual traveling clothes. She was wearing a pale green broomstick skirt with ballet flats and a simple ivory knit top. Her dark red hair was long and straight, enhanced with several hundred dollars' worth of extensions. In Russell, North Carolina, she probably looked like a cover girl.

She was just starting to respond when the door from the kitchen opened again. A teenage girl walked through it, carrying a plate holding a delicious-looking burger. Bree guessed she was around fifteen; pretty in a wholesome, cheerleader sort of way. She had long blond hair and lightly tanned skin, with big brown eyes. Those eyes snapped to a halt when she saw Bree.

A lot of things happened very quickly in the next few seconds. The girl nearly dropped the plate, but Ty caught it just as the burger was ready to slide to the floor.

"Emily! Watch what you're…"

Emily was reaching for something in her back pocket as her eyes grew even wider.

"Oh. My. God. You're Bree Mathews! Right here in The Hide-Away! Oh, my *God*! No one's going to believe this!"

Bree saw the iPhone in Emily's hand. The girl was raising it to take a photo. An image of Bree blasted out to the internet would ruin her plans to hide here in Russell. She jumped to her feet and reached for the phone with a distressed cry. Cole stood and grabbed Bree's wrist, yanking her back and closer to him. Ty snatched the phone from Emily's hand. They all stared at each other in confusion, panic and anger.

Ty was the first to speak. "Emily! What is wrong with you? Is it a full moon today or what? Everyone's going full-bore crazy around here! And Cole, for the last time, get your effing hands off that woman!"

Bree was close to his side now, and the heat emanating from his body took her breath away. His grip was rough, just short of painful. He glared down at her then back at his brother.

"She grabbed for my niece and I damned sure want to know why."

Ty nodded in understanding. "I get that. But everyone's safe now, so let her go."

Cole looked down at Bree, and her face flamed with humiliation. This day was turning into one hot, glorious mess. He slowly loosened his hold on her, and she took a step away, rubbing her wrist.

"Emily." Ty looked at the girl who was clearly his daughter. "What on earth is wrong with you, girl?"

Emily's eyes were still bright with excitement, and her voice was breathless and quick.

"Daddy! This is Bree Mathews! She's *famous*! She's from *Hollywood*! And she's standing here in our restaurant!" The men clearly had no idea what she was talking about, and the words started tumbling out of her mouth. "Oh, my God! Don't you know? She was Miss California and a runner-up to Miss America. Then she married Damian Maxwell, the actor from that big hit TV show about high school from a few years ago, *Drama in the Halls*. Remember? He played the hunky coach? And then…" The words were coming fast and furious as Emily recited the timeline of Bree's life. "Then his show was canceled and he and Bree went on the reality show *Hot Hollywood Housewives*. She was supposed to be the 'good girl' of the group, and the other ladies were so mean to her. By the third season, Damian was doing drugs on camera. When she caught him with Jessica Darling, one of the other wives on the show, Bree had an epic meltdown."

"Emily," her father said, trying to intervene. But his daughter was on a roll.

"She flipped an entire table on its side in a restaurant. It was awesome! Anyway, even though she divorced Damian, they tried to keep her on the show for another season, but she refused. Now she plans events and stuff for famous people, and she wrote a cookbook, and I heard she might get her own show on Bravo. Some people hate her because they say she ruined Damian's career. He hasn't had a hit since she left him, but of course that's not her fault. Daddy, she's *famous*. And she's standing right in front of us!"

Emily finally stopped for air. Bree dropped her head, wishing the floor would open up and swallow her whole. Three decades on this earth, and her entire life had just been recapped in breathless detail by a teenager in less than a minute. And the highlight was that she flipped a table over in a crowded restaurant. That was what people thought of when they saw her. What did that say about her choices? About her values? About *her*?

"Are you filming something here? Is that why you're here?" Emily was bouncing up and down now. "You are, right? You're filming? Why else would you be in a place like Russell? Oh, wow…"

This was her chance to protect herself, and Bree took it. She plastered on her best pageant smile.

"Yes. Yes, we're filming here. But it's a huge secret. That's why I didn't want you to take the picture. No one can know about it, or it will all be ruined. I'm just here checking things out, but if the press finds out, we'll have to find a new location to go to. I didn't think anyone would recognize me out here…"

Cole snorted. Again. "So you didn't think we had television? Or the internet? Or teenagers?"

Damn his arrogance.

"Look, it was all very last minute, and I didn't know the show was popular in rural…in the country…places like this…" She closed her eyes, trying to think of a way not to sound offensive. But she never thought anyone would recognize her here in the boondocks.

Emily was still focused on the idea of a film crew arriving. "You're doing a 'Bree in the country' kind of thing? That would be so funny! Maybe we'll have a dance here at The Hide-Away and you could film it! Daddy, you'd let me waitress, right? I could be on TV!"

Ty looked at Bree in confusion, and she figured she'd better settle his daughter down a bit.

"I'm sure we can figure out a way for a pretty girl like you to be part of the show." The girl beamed at the compliment. "But it's critical that no one, not even your very best friend, knows that I'm here right now. Seriously, I'll have to leave and never return if word gets out. You know how it is once news starts spreading on social media. The press will be here in a heartbeat, and I can't have that…"

"I promise. Cross my heart and hope to die. I won't tell anyone if you'll promise that my friends and I can be part of the show. I didn't get the photo of you before. Y'all moved too fast."

Ty swiped his finger across the screen on Emily's phone, which he still held. He nodded.

"She's right. No picture. And she won't ever be taking pictures of *anyone* without asking permission first, right?" He gave his daughter a stern look and handed her phone back to her.

"I'm sorry, Daddy. I promise. I just lost my head…"

Bree smiled. "It's all right, Emily. Just remember to keep my secret, okay?"

Emily nodded, hugged herself and danced back into the kitchen.

Bree grabbed the hamburger in front of her. A girl had to eat, right? She took a large bite of it and sighed. This burger alone might make up for the lousy day she was having.

She wasn't at all surprised to hear another grunt from Cole.

"You proud of yourself, Hollywood? Lying to a nice kid like that?"

She was too ashamed to have any fight left in her. She wiped her mouth with a napkin before answering, and her voice was barely a whisper.

"No. No, I'm not proud at all."

Ty's voice was low. "Then why did you do it?"

She closed her eyes and took a deep breath, blowing the air out slowly through her lips. She didn't care about Cole's opinion, but Ty deserved the truth. She raised her head and met his puzzled gaze.

"I thought it would be kinder than telling your daughter that someone out there wants to burn me alive. Because that's what the truth is. I have a stalker, and the whole situation has taken a bad turn. I'm trying to lay low for a while until they can find him. Nell's daughter, Caroline, is my cousin's friend, and she suggested I come here."

Her gaze dropped back to the bar, and the room fell silent. Ty turned and took a bottle from a shelf. He poured the golden liquid into a shot glass and slid it into her hand. She downed it with one swallow, welcoming another burn. She looked up and nodded, and he refilled the glass. But this time she took just a sip before taking another bite of her burger.

"Someone's threatening to kill you?" Ty asked.

She shrugged. "Or worse. He says he needs to 'cleanse me by fire' to remove my sins and make me worthy. He broke into my beach house Saturday while I was gone and burned all of my clothes, because he thinks I dress like a whore." She took another sip from the glass. "And he sent a threatening message to my cousin's home in New York while I was there, even though I hadn't publicized the trip. So now I'm on the run."

She tried to give Ty a smile, but felt her mouth

trembling, and bit down on her lower lip to steady it. Cole, who'd been still and quiet at her side, inhaled sharply. She looked over, but he turned away, staring at Ty. Once again, the brothers carried on a silent conversation. Cole shook his head abruptly, but Ty just glowered at him. Cole's shoulders slumped and he nodded as he took a step closer to Bree. He lifted his chin toward the shelves behind the bar.

"Give me a hat" was all he said.

Ty handed him one of several Hide-Away ball caps for sale above the cash register. Cole moved behind her and put his hands on either side of her face, making her gasp. He pulled her hair back and through the opening of the cap, creating a ponytail as he pushed the hat low on her head. Before she could protest, Ty started to explain.

"If Emily recognized you, someone else might. Cole will take you out to Nell's place in his truck. He lives out that way. That fancy car is no way to lay low in this part of the country. My guess is half the town already knows there's a ninety-thousand-dollar Mercedes parked at The Hide-Away. Leave me the keys and I'll pull the car around back, then take it home after dark and put it in my barn. I'll see if my wife, Tammy, can take you shopping for something a little more… casual. We'll tell people you're a college friend of Caroline's. Everyone loves Caroline Patterson…er…McCormack. She's married now, right? She married that guy from Boston?"

Bree nodded, feeling stunned. "Yeah, they got married in Barbados. Look, why are you doing this? You don't know me, and *you* don't even like me." She looked over her shoulder at Cole. His close proximity was making her nervous.

Cole arched an eyebrow at her. "Call it that 'Southern charm' you were looking for. We help people in trouble down here." His mouth twitched again. She decided that was the closest thing to a real smile the guy had. "Even people we don't like."

# CHAPTER TWO

COLE CALDWELL STOLE a sideways glance at the redhead as he drove out of Russell. She was pressed up against the passenger door, with Maggie curled up on the seat between them. While the dog generally rode with her nose pressed snugly against Cole's leg, today she lay facing their guest. Her head rested on Bree's thigh, and Bree was absently scratching Maggie's ear.

Traitor.

Despite the ridiculous layers of makeup, Brianna Mathews could easily be the most beautiful woman he'd ever seen. Pulling her hair up under the cap revealed her long, slender neck, fine-boned face and those deep green eyes. Her skin was like porcelain. She was tall, almost as tall as he was. And she moved with a natural grace that said she was confident and very aware of herself. The whole package was sexy as hell.

Too bad she was such a flaming, toxic viper.

The lady could peel paint off the wall with those angry eyes of hers. And her sharp tongue could probably flay a man alive. Cole shifted in his seat, suddenly uncomfortable and surprisingly aroused by that thought. He sure as hell didn't want anything to do with this woman or any other woman for that matter. And it seemed the feeling was mutual. He grunted to himself, earning him another one of her icy glares.

"What?" she snapped.

He shook his head in the closest he'd come to amusement in a long time. Baiting her temper was as easy as shooting very big fish in a very small barrel.

"Oh, nothin'. I'm just picturing you settling into Nell's hundred-year-old bungalow. All by yourself. No Starbucks. No fancy parties to attend. No television cameras. Girl, you'll die of loneliness out here."

She turned to stare out the passenger window. Her voice was quiet.

"It's better than dying in a pool of blood."

Well, hell. She'd just managed to turn him into a complete jackass, hadn't she? No, actually he didn't need her help with that. He'd done it all on his own. After a year of feeling pretty much nothing but anger, he now felt guilty. He winced at the sharpness of it.

"Sorry." There's a word he hadn't said in a while. "I wasn't making light of your..."

"Situation? My very interesting situation?" She dropped her head back against the seat of his pickup then turned to look at him. "We don't exactly bring out the best in each other, do we?"

He snorted. "Apparently not."

Awkward silence filled the cab as he made a few more turns. The roads got progressively smaller and the fields got bigger. He slowed the truck as they approached a yellow farmhouse with a wide front porch. There was a wooden farmstand next to the road with a simple sign that read Nell's Produce. He glanced over at the stand as he pulled into the gravel driveway. It looked like Nell had a good selection of tomatoes and blueberries today. He snuck another look at Bree and bit back a smile at her wide-eyed expression.

A faded red barn stood behind the house. Chicken and geese wandered the yard. The pigpen was off to the left, and he could see Nell's big sow, Spot, sunning herself there with her piglets. Two old workhorses were standing in a small paddock to the right, head to rump, swishing their tails rhythmically to keep the flies away. In the fields behind the barn, his own beef cattle were grazing. He leased the pastures from Nell, and she kept an eye on the cows and calves for him. Nell's huge garden stretched along the far side of the house. She grew enough vegetables to keep her stand well stocked. What she didn't grow herself, she sold on consignment for area farmers. People drove for miles to buy from Miss Nell, because they knew she sold the best locally-grown produce. She served up her unique country wisdom, homemade sweet tea and amazing baked goods to her customers, most of whom she knew by name.

A rangy hound of indiscriminate origin trotted toward the truck, baying loudly, but his tail wagged in greeting. Cole stepped out and scratched the dog's ears. Maggie sat up in the truck and watched alertly, staying silent.

"Hey, Shep, how are you, old boy?" He looked back at Bree, who seemed to be in some stage of shock in his truck. "Are you going to sit there all day?"

She looked down at the dog and hesitated.

"Don't worry about Shep. He's more welcoming committee than watchdog."

Bree slid across the seat past Maggie and stepped down out of his side of the truck. The woman was acting as if she'd been dropped in the middle of a dangerous jungle instead of a quiet North Carolina farm. Her ironclad confidence slipped just a little, and her face paled. She was clearly out of her comfort zone here. He should have enjoyed it, but instead he was troubled to see her lose that cloak of brittle anger.

"Well, as I live and breathe!" a woman's voice cried out from the front porch. "Colton Caldwell!

What's up, darlin'? You get thirsty for some of my sweet tea on this blistering day? I didn't figure to see you till the end of the week. That miserable old cow of yours won't be ready to drop her calf for a while yet."

Nell Patterson's face was weather-worn, and her hair was more gray than brown, but her slender body moved with the sure strength of someone who worked hard for a living and didn't give a darn what anyone thought of her. She was wearing cotton shorts and a white blouse, with a bright yellow apron tied around her waist. It struck him as the tall, sturdy woman stepped off the porch that the way Nell carried herself was very similar to Bree's. Two strong, but very different, women. They'd either kill each other or be friends forever. Nell spotted Bree at his side, and her brown eyes went wide with surprise.

"And you brought *company*! And isn't she a pretty thing? Introduce me to your girl, Colton."

He gave her a crooked smile and shook his head. "She ain't *my* girl, Nell. She's yours. This is your new tenant, Bree Mathews."

He watched with grudging respect as Bree stifled whatever terror she was feeling about the farm. She painted on a bright smile and stepped forward to extend her hand to Nell. "It's so nice to see you again, Mrs. Patterson. We didn't have much opportunity to talk at Caroline's wedding, but she's told me wonderful things about you. I appreciate you letting me use your cottage under the circumstances…" Her formal words and tone were swallowed in a bear hug from Nell.

"Oh, I remember you! You planned their wedding reception, didn't you? Caroline called me this morning and told me why you're here. Don't you worry, honey. We'll keep you safe." Nell held Bree out at arm's length and looked sharply between her and Cole. He could see her wheels turning, and he didn't like it one bit. What kind of scheme was she putting together in that very clever brain of hers? "But of course, this is a mutually beneficial arrangement."

Bree looked confused. "I'm sorry?"

"Oh, didn't Caroline tell you? I need someone to help me with the farm. It gets so busy in the summer, and I just can't handle it all on my own." Cole frowned. Nell was the most capable farm woman he'd ever known, and she abhorred offers of assistance.

Bree started to protest. "Oh, Mrs. Patterson, I'd love to help, but I'm afraid I know nothing about farming. I'm a city girl through and through. I know how to *cook* vegetables, but I know nothing about *growing* them. As far as I'm concerned, they magically appear at Whole Foods Market. And animals…well, animals and I don't get along all that well…"

"First, call me Nell or Miss Nell. And second, don't be silly. You can learn to grow and pick veggies, and you'll get along just fine with all the animals. Why look, Shep likes you already." They all looked down to where Shep was lying close by Bree's feet. Damned if the dog wasn't looking up at Bree like she was an angel or something. Maggie sat in his truck with the same adoring expression. What the...?

Nell continued. "The cottage is just one hay field away, so you go get yourself settled, and we'll talk more tomorrow about what you can do to help around here."

Cole coughed back a snort, and Bree spun to slice him with her angry eyes. He raised his hands in surrender.

"I'm sorry! I can't help being amused at the thought of you sloppin' hogs and picking tomatoes and feeding those one-ton horses over there." He nodded toward Pete and Ruby, Nell's elderly and famously gentle horses. Bree's back stiffened, and he knew he'd struck home with his not-so-subtle suggestion that she couldn't possibly be a farmer. But just look at her, for heaven's sake.

"Are you saying you don't think I can do it?"

"Isn't that what *you* just said?"

She put her hands on her hips. "I said I didn't know anything about farming. I didn't say I couldn't do it if I wanted to." She turned to Nell, and he couldn't miss the stubborn set of her chin. The woman didn't seem capable of turning down a challenge. "Nell, I look forward to learning more about your farm."

Oh, this was going to be fun.

"Cole, honey." Nell dropped something in his hand. "Be a dear and drive Bree over to the cottage, will you? Here's the key. You know your way around the place and can show her where everything is." Before he could object, Nell turned back to Bree. "I stocked the fridge with plenty of food, and there's a dish of my beef stew there for you to heat up for dinner tonight. There are clean linens on the bed. You must be exhausted. And don't worry about not having a car, honey. I'm sure Cole will give you a ride anywhere you need to go."

Bree started to say something, then closed her mouth. She'd just been bulldozed by Miss Nell, and Cole knew exactly how she felt.

BREE WAS USED to waking up in unfamiliar surroundings. She'd traveled nonstop as Miss California, and again as the wife of Damian Maxwell. When she joined the cast of *Hot Hollywood Housewives*, they were constantly being shuttled off to exotic locations to spice up the show. There were trips to Paris, Hawaii and even the Australian outback on a ridiculous survival challenge. She'd probably slept *away* from her beloved Malibu home as much as she'd slept *in* it.

But she still wasn't prepared when the predawn light filtered through the thin cotton curtains and nudged her from a restless night's sleep in Nell's cottage. She sat up and blinked in confusion. Even the outback accommodations were fancier than this place. The bedroom barely managed to contain the queen-size iron bed and a dresser.

She stood and stretched slowly, sighing at the feel of her satin nightgown sliding against her skin. The luxurious fabric was a welcome reminder of her *real* life, which should be taking place right now far, far away from this country cottage. She'd packed the fancy sleepwear for her trip to her cousin's baby shower over the past weekend. It was entirely appropriate to wear as a guest at Amanda and Blake's historic home, or even at the lakeside resort they owned next door to Halcyon.

Here in this rustic whitewashed cottage? Not so much.

But she didn't have a lot of wardrobe choices, since whatever she'd packed in her weekend bag was pretty much all she had left for clothing. She ran her hands down the expensive material and shook her head. It was ironic that the one thing she'd fought for throughout her adult life—indeed, the driving force behind nearly every decision she'd made—was her desire for security and stability. And now that she'd finally achieved it, some psycho had snatched it all away by torching her clothes and forcing her out of her home.

She jumped when her phone chirped in her purse, indicating an incoming text. The alarm clock on the bedside table showed it wasn't even 5:30 yet. She grabbed her Hermes bag and dug around inside for the phone. Her personal phone had been left behind in Gallant Lake to prevent anyone from tracing her location. This was just a throw-away burner phone and only a handful of people had the number. She couldn't imagine which member of that small club would be awake at this hour.

R U awake?

The text was from her cousin, Amanda. Bree grinned and was quick to type a response.

Barely. Why are YOU awake?

Instead of a responding text, the phone rang in her hand.

"Bree! How are you, sweetie?"

"Amanda, what on earth are you doing up at this hour? Did your ghost rattle some chains in the hallway or something?"

Amanda, normally such a level-headed woman, insisted the castle she'd remodeled for hotelier Blake Randall before marrying him was haunted by its original owner.

"Very funny. It's not the original Madeleine that's the problem. It's her namesake. This baby kicks me awake earlier and earlier every morning. If she's not born soon, I won't be sleeping at all."

Amanda not only believed that a ghost named Madeleine haunted Halcyon, she'd also insisted on naming her unborn daughter after her. A feisty five-foot-four, her cousin had been miserably uncomfortable at her baby shower, with the baby occupying a beach ball-size bump directly under her breasts.

"Yeah, well, little Maddy isn't due for another month, so you'd better start grabbing naps during the day to get your rest." She left the bedroom in hopes of finding some coffee, and almost swooned at the sight of a small coffee-maker sitting on the counter. She popped in a pod of Sumatra Dark and inhaled the rich aroma as her mug filled.

"Now you sound like Blake. He'd make me stay in bed twenty-four hours a day if he could."

"That sounds like your husband, for sure. Is he home yet?"

"He won't be back until next week. He wants to visit all of the resorts one last time before Maddy arrives. So tell me, how are you really doing? Did you get settled in without any problems?"

"Well, I don't know if I'd call it problem-free, but yeah, I'm here in my temporary prison." She sat on the blue plaid sofa and told Amanda about her arrival in Russell yesterday and the drama at The Hide-Away, as well as her introduction to Nell and the rustic cottage she was now calling home. She made her disdain for the rural setting very clear.

"Nell has horses and cows and…and *pigs*." Bree jumped to her feet in agitation and walked to the front windows. Soft fingers of wispy fog moved across the fields like chiffon as the sun slid up over the horizon. There was a large white farmhouse across the road. It was her only visible neighbor other than Nell.

In the distance beyond the white house, a man on a tractor drove through the fog into the endless field of young plants. The wheels of the tractor kicked up a cloud of dust, and the man pulled his cap lower over his eyes. Oh God, she was living in the middle of a Norman Rockwell painting. She spun and returned to the overstuffed sofa, sitting down with a huff of frustration.

"Oh, come on, it can't be *that* bad." There was laughter in her cousin's voice.

"This isn't funny! I just walked the length of the living room in four steps. *Four!* It takes more than that to walk across my *closet* in Malibu. I've been here less than twenty-four hours and I'm already feeling like a caged animal. How am I supposed to last three or four weeks?"

There was a brief moment of silence before Amanda answered. "No, it's not funny. You need to remember why you're there in the first place. You're safe, and you're giving everyone time to track down the monster who's stalking you. I don't want you to be the next Nikki Fitzgerald."

Bree swallowed hard. It was a little over five weeks ago that Nikki, a pretty up-and-coming actress, woke to find a crazed "fan" in her Hollywood Hills bedroom. He raped her, stabbed her repeatedly and then slashed his own throat at the foot of her bed. The gruesome murder-suicide made headlines around the world and sent a convulsion of fear through Hollywood. That was the moment Bree started to take her stalker a lot more seriously.

"I'd trust Caroline and her husband with my own life," Amanda continued, "so I certainly trust them with yours. This is what they do for a living."

Andrew and Caroline McCormack ran a security firm that provided protection for celebrities and politicians around the world. When Caroline heard about the stalker at the baby shower, it was her idea to send Bree to Nell's. Bree leaned back against the cushions of the sofa and closed her eyes.

"I'm not sure we really thought this through. There must be other options. Instead of being cooped up in this miniature farmhouse, why couldn't I stay in a luxury resort somewhere? Surely your husband has a suite open in one of his places?"

"Of course you could have gone to one of Blake's resorts, but the celebrity websites all have standing offers to employees of hotels to leak information about famous guests. Blake does his best to control that sort of thing, but this is your *life* we're talking about. Besides, this nut case knows we're family, so he surely knows about all of Blake's properties. Everyone agreed the best solution was for you to go somewhere totally off the grid where *no one*, including the stalker, would think to look."

"Yeah, but I was still recognized an hour after I arrived." She cringed at the memory of Emily's reaction in The Hide-Away. "I should have left right then."

"Yeah, probably not your best idea to rent a ridiculously expensive car and park it in front of a bar in the center of town in the middle of the afternoon. Why not just hire a marching band to announce your arrival while you were at it?"

She held her phone away and looked at it in surprise. Her cousin wasn't usually so…blunt. Amanda noticed her silence, and rushed to apologize.

"Oh, damn it, I'm sorry! I swear it's the hormones talking. I have no filter anymore. I've turned into that crazy pregnant lady who's laughing one minute, crying the next and throwing a tantrum after that. Everyone is tiptoeing around me."

Bree sighed. "No apology necessary. You're right. I *was* an idiot yesterday, sweeping into town like I did. And then I made a scene by arguing with that guy in the bar. You know how I fall back on that snob routine when I'm nervous."

Her skin tightened at the memory of the one man who didn't take her crap for one second. Cole Caldwell had ripped through her carefully crafted persona with a couple of grunts and well-aimed insults.

"I get it," Amanda said softly. "I know all about defensive walls and how to build them."

Bree nodded. Amanda's childhood had been dark and painful, and she'd buried that trauma deep until she'd met Blake Randall last summer, along with his orphaned nephew, Zachary, whom they'd now adopted. They lived in Blake's century-old castle in the Catskills, along with that romantic ghost Amanda credited with their happiness. She'd married Blake six months ago, but they'd gotten a bit of a head start, and she was now eight months pregnant.

"Bree? Are you there?"

"Yeah, sorry. Just daydreaming." She stood again, feeling restless. "This isn't where I belong. I know that sounds awful and pretentious or whatever, but I don't *belong* here. I mean, Caroline's mom seems like a nice woman, but there's a vegetable stand in her front yard. She bakes pies and bread. We have nothing in common."

"Wait. She cooks? Didn't you just write a whole book about cooking?"

"The title of the book is *Malibu Style*, and it's about *entertaining*, not just cooking. Somehow I don't think Nell would be interested in swapping recipes for my famous caviar and gruyere canapés."

"You'll never know until you ask. Maybe your

next book will be about country style and bread-baking." Amanda started to giggle. "Sorry, I just had a mental image of you posing for the cover in a ruffled country apron over your designer evening gown!"

They both laughed at that and ended the call with promises to stay in touch as they each counted down the next few weeks: Amanda to deliver her baby girl, and Bree to return to her real life in California.

After a shower and a bowl of cereal, Bree pulled on a pair of skinny jeans and a T-shirt from Gallant Lake, advertising her cousin's resort.

Beyond the compact kitchen, the rest of the cottage consisted of one more bedroom, a small bathroom with a claw-foot tub, the living room and the front bedroom she'd slept in. The living room opened to a covered front porch facing the road. While the decor wasn't awful, it was... simple. It reminded her of the plain suburban home she'd grown up in back in Corona, California. That might be why it made her slightly uncomfortable. It represented everything she'd been trying to run away from since her eighteenth birthday.

There was a small bookcase in the back bedroom, and she pulled out a well-worn paperback. The cover featured a bare-chested man with long, dark hair, clutching a red-haired woman in a green velvet gown. A rearing horse in jousting gear was in the background, in front of an imposing castle.

"If I'm going to be here alone for the next few weeks, I may as well enjoy a trashy romance novel." She grimaced, partly at the book and partly at the realization that she was once again talking to herself. Out loud.

The brave heroine was just beginning to succumb to the brooding charm of her medieval captor when Bree was startled by a knock at the door. She was surprised to see it was almost noon. Her cheeks flushed in embarrassment for losing herself so completely in a bodice-ripper, as if she'd been caught being naughty. She tucked the paperback between the cushions of the sofa and went to the door. On the porch stood her biggest fan in the entire town of Russell, North Carolina: young Emily Caldwell. Emily grinned and raised her hands.

"I don't have a camera, I promise! My mom and I are having lunch over at Miss Nell's, and we thought you might want to join us. She made sweet tea and we're having pimento cheese sandwiches on the porch. I promise not to act like a starstruck idiot today."

The girl's humor and friendliness touched Bree unexpectedly. She had no idea what a pimento cheese sandwich was, but she suddenly wanted one more than anything. If she didn't find a way to socialize while she was here, she'd lose her mind. Or end up addicted to historical romances.

"I'd like that, Emily. I'd like that a lot."

# CHAPTER THREE

NELL PATTERSON SAT in her rocking chair and sipped from a tall glass of cold sweet tea. Emily was seated on the steps leading to Nell's front yard, her hand idly scratching Shep's ears as the old dog snored by her side. Emily's mother, Tammy, was on the porch swing with Bree, humming softly to herself as a light breeze brought some blessed relief from the sweltering humidity of the afternoon. The four women had fallen into a comfortable silence after hours of nonstop talk and laughter.

Nell had quickly dispensed with everyone's initial awkwardness during lunch by asking thoughtful questions and showing genuine interest. Bree found herself giggling at the stories Nell told about the farm animals and some of the customers who came to her fruit and vegetable stand. Tammy talked about her job as a teacher and the bar that was Ty's pride and joy.

After a bout of shyness, Emily opened up and shared a story about the sophomore class pulling a prank on the high school principal, filling the floor of his pickup truck with ping-pong balls that came bouncing out when he opened his door. Tammy rolled her eyes and winked at her daughter, and Bree felt a pang at the look shared between mother and daughter. It reminded her of times she'd shared with her own mom. The memory was like a paper cut on her heart, unexpected and sharp in its sting.

Bree was reluctant to join in, worried that talking about her Hollywood life would sound pretentious. Which made her wonder if perhaps it was. She sighed.

Tammy turned. "You okay over there?"

"Just feeling a little overwhelmed at the moment."

"You have friends here. You know that, right?" Tammy rested her hand on Bree's leg. "Ty told me everything while we were on our way back from Fayetteville." Ty and Tammy had returned her rental car early that morning. Bree glanced down at Emily, but Tammy went on. "Emily knows, too. I appreciate that you tried to shield her from it, but she's almost sixteen and more mature than she may have seemed yesterday. It must be scary for you, going from your life to...this."

"Please don't take offense, Tammy, but I'm a fish out of water here." She liked these women. They were so different from women she'd met in Hollywood, who tended to view all other females as adversaries and threats. A simple dinner party there was often nothing more than a prettily disguised battle, with winners and losers clawing for social status.

She didn't feel the need to be on guard while sipping tea on Nell's shaded front porch, moving slowly back and forth on the swing. There was no sense of competition, no furtive glances to see what the others were doing or wearing.

Tammy laughed softly. "Why would I take offense? I'd feel just as out of place if you dropped me in the middle of Hollywood."

"Sweetheart, you're doing fine," Nell said. "You broke bread with us today, and we had some good laughs and told stories and passed an afternoon together."

Bree nodded. "Yes, but it's day one of what could be several weeks. What am I going to do? I hardly have any clothes, and I'm afraid to go shopping for fear I'll be recognized. I'll go stir-crazy if I don't keep busy, but how can I do that if I don't do something to look…different?"

"Are you saying you want to change your looks? Like a disguise?" Emily's interest in the conversation had shifted back into gear. "We could take you to Aunt Melissa's and she could change your hair! And Mom and I could go shopping for clothes for you. We could give you an alias. It would be perfect!"

"Who's Aunt Melissa?"

"My sister," Tammy said, looking thoughtful. "She has a hair salon over in Benton. She'd never tell a soul. It might just work…if that's what you want. And I could run up to Fayetteville and pick up clothes for you…"

"No!" Emily was almost bouncing with excitement. "*I* want to be the one who picks out her clothes! I want to make her a country girl!"

Nell shook her head. "Emily, you know full well that clothes don't make a country girl. It's the living that does it." She'd been watching Bree carefully all through lunch, and there were moments when Bree distinctly felt as if the older woman was sizing her up.

"You're right, Brianna—you're going to go stir-crazy if you don't keep yourself busy. I told you yesterday that I needed some help. Get yourself over here in the morning and help me pick vegetables and clean the barn. If we have time, I'll show you how to bake some of my bread you like so much. New clothes are fine, Emily, but make them working clothes. Miss Mathews is going to learn how to farm."

"Oh, Nell, I don't think so…" She tried to come up with an objection, but her mind went blank. It wasn't like she had anything else to do.

"You don't need to think. You just need to show up and let me teach you how to *be* a country girl, not just *look* like one."

Within an hour they had a plan in place. Tammy would take Emily to Fayetteville to shop, using a couple of the untraceable gift cards Bree had purchased at JFK before flying to North Carolina. Since Emily would be shopping at Target instead of Escada, Bree was pretty sure no one would recognize her in her new clothing. But just in case, they would make a clandestine visit to Tammy's sister's salon on Saturday before it opened, so Bree could get a new look.

Bree was far more relaxed that evening when she walked out onto the front porch of the cottage than she'd been that morning. She'd never expected to spend so much time laughing, or to actually make *friends*. She took a sip of wine and leaned against one of the tapered pillars supporting the porch roof. The sultry air was thick with the luxurious scents of nature: a heady blend of sweetness and earth and spice and green. The color actually seemed to have a scent of its own here in the South. A background chorus provided by an assortment of insects, frogs and birds serenaded the otherwise still countryside. Unlike the screeching seagulls of Malibu, the birds in North Carolina actually *sang*.

Southern California tended to be a perpetual assault of noise. There were always a few annoying photographers shouting at her from the outer gate of the beach house, trying to catch her doing something "newsworthy" that a magazine would pay good money to publish. She might be stuck here in Podunk, USA, but at least she didn't have to worry about paparazzi hiding in the hedges. She could stand outside with a glass of wine and enjoy the solitude, and not hear a single man-made sound. It was a rare moment of peace for a woman normally so driven by the demons of her past that she never took time to savor a respite like this.

She pushed away from the pillar and turned toward the house. A dog barked, and her eyes followed the sound. A dark-colored dog ran around the corner of the big white house across the road. There was a man walking slowly into the enormous field that stretched along the road as far as she could see. He was dressed in jeans and a dark T-shirt, with a ball cap pulled low on his forehead. It was the same man she'd seen on the tractor early that morning. Looking down, he moved slowly along the edge of the field, stopping occasionally to kick at the dirt with the toe of his boot. Once in a while he'd bend over and examine one of the young green plants growing in long, neat rows. His movements were sure and measured, and he appeared totally absorbed in what he was doing. There was something about his lean build and the way he moved that captured her full attention.

Bree walked over to the top of the steps for a better view, and the dog began barking more insistently, looking in her direction. The man, still a good distance away, turned to the dog then raised his head to see what the dog was barking at. That was when the breath vanished from her lungs. She'd know the hard lines of that face anywhere. She could feel his gray eyes on her, even if she couldn't see them beneath the shade of his hat.

*Cole will take you out to Nell's place in his truck. He lives out that way...*

Cole Caldwell was her neighbor.

Before Bree's brain could fully absorb what that meant, Maggie bounded down the driveway and across the road. She'd never been a fan of dogs, but she knelt on one knee to greet the happy girl. She was a pretty thing with those expressive brown eyes.

"A little early for drinking, isn't it?" Bree's head snapped up. Cole was standing in the middle of her yard. He'd stopped there as if that was as far as he dared go, which made her smile just a little as she rose to her feet.

"That's rich coming from the guy who was drinking at a bar in the middle of the day yesterday."

"Yeah, well, I'm a man." He made a point to look her up and down, taking in her bare feet, jeans and T-shirt. Women in the South tend to act more like ladies."

"Sorry to offend your Southern sensibilities, but I'm afraid I left my hoop skirt at home."

His eyebrow arched and she saw a touch of admiration there. The two of them had scathing sarcasm down to an art. She bit back a smile of triumph and turned to the door to leave him standing there, but Maggie's soft whine stopped her. She looked down and couldn't resist scratching the dog's ears one more time.

"Maggie hasn't seen anyone at the cottage in a while, and she seems to like you for some reason." His expression made it clear he couldn't understand the dog's logic.

"You never mentioned you were going to be my neighbor." The words tumbled out without warning, and she knew they sounded like an accusation.

His stoic expression never changed, even as he shrugged a shoulder in dismissal.

"Didn't see a need to. Doesn't change anything. You're Nell's guest, not mine."

He gave a sharp, short whistle and Maggie

immediately trotted back to his side, leaning against his leg and closing her eyes as his fingers moved against the top of her head. Some of the ever-present tension seemed to leave his body when he touched the dog. Bree wondered what made him so uptight all the time. Then she shook off the thought. She shouldn't care about a guy who had been nothing but rude to her. She lifted her chin.

"Yes, well, I think we can all agree that the chances of me being *your* guest are slim to none. What were you doing walking in the field?"

"My job."

"Which is…?"

He heaved a heavy sigh and his eyes met hers with the force of a sledgehammer. She almost took a step back, just from the intensity of his angry stare.

"Seriously? I'm raising a crop. Checking the soil, inspecting the plants for insects and disease. Just another day in the life of a farmer, Hollywood."

She didn't miss the not-so-subtle jab of that ridiculous nickname. He'd made it clear yesterday he thought she was some prima donna who'd faint dead away at the thought of a little hard labor.

"I was just trying to show an interest, *Plowboy*." Two could play the nickname game.

He looked as if he was going to reply, but stopped. He started to turn away then turned back toward her with a fierce expression on his face.

"I saw you with Nell, Tammy and Emily this afternoon, laughing it up on the porch like you belonged there." Her back stiffened at his insinuation that she *didn't* belong. "Everyone around here loves Miss Nell, and you'd do well to remember that. I don't want you bringing any trouble to her or to my family."

Bree bristled. "Are you suggesting I have some ulterior motive?"

"I don't know *what* to think or what your real motivation is. For all I know, cameras are going to come swooping in here at any minute." He took a step closer, his eyes icy gray and threatening. "You don't really strike me as the victim type, so maybe you're just pulling some kind of publicity stunt. I don't know, and I don't care, as long as you don't bring embarrassment to the people I care about."

He thought she was making up the story about being stalked? That she was here as some kind of *joke*? This man really was a jackass of major proportions.

"Do you have a computer, or is that too twenty-first century for you?"

"I have a computer. And no, you can't borrow it."

"I wouldn't dream of it." Her hand rested on the knob of the front door and she looked over her shoulder at him. "If you really think my story is some kind of joke, type in the name Nikki Fitzgerald and see what you find."

"I have better things to do with my time than to look up Hollywood gossip."

His cool dismissal made her want to stomp her feet in frustration.

"Fine." She spat the word at him. "You did your good deed and delivered me to Nell's. Why don't you just go home and leave me alone?"

He stared at her hard for a long, silent moment. Then he gave another careless shrug.

"No problem, Hollywood. I'm gone."

He turned away without another word. Maggie looked over her shoulder at Bree and gave a quick wag of her tail, then trotted away at Cole's side. Bree watched them walk back to the big white house. A porch wrapped around all four sides. Did he live there alone? I wasn't like she knew anything about the man. She went into the cottage to find more wine. Maybe he was married to some unfortunate woman and had a houseful of grumpy, gray-eyed children. Instead of making her feel better, the thought soured her mood even more.

# CHAPTER FOUR

BREE SAT DOWN on the grass in front of Nell's house Friday afternoon with a loud sigh that morphed into an even louder groan. Every muscle cried out for mercy. Scratches covered her arms and legs, exposed by her denim cutoffs, which had been created when Nell took a pair of scissors to Bree's three-hundred-dollar designer jeans. Her sweat-soaked lavender tank top was borrowed from Tammy. Her white running shoes were brown with dirt. Her skin was taking on a surprising golden hue already, despite the sunscreen she slathered on every morning and again at lunchtime. Her acrylic nails were cracked and broken. Three were missing entirely, exposing her real fingernails to the air for the first time in years. Rivers of sweat drifted aimlessly down her back in the stifling humidity.

She'd already learned a lot in just a few days working on Nell's farm. The work had to be done, regardless of sweltering sun or pouring rain or protesting muscles. Animals needed fresh bedding every day. Eggs had to be gathered. The piglets liked to have cool mud to squirm around in. Even though they were out to pasture, cattle needed to be fed and checked routinely. Vegetables needed to be picked at the exact moment of perfect ripeness. And weeds grew like…well, like weeds. Weeds were evil and must be destroyed. She leaned back on her arms and looked up through the thick canopy of leaves on the tree above her. She'd been weeding Nell's enormous vegetable patch for two hours now, and she still wasn't finished.

"Darlin', you look about done in. Why don't you call it quits for today? You can finish the weeding tomorrow." Nell was walking toward her with a tall glass of her famous sweet tea. She started to hand it to Bree then frowned. "Oh, honey, you should get up off the grass. You're sitting right next to a fire ant nest."

Sure enough, there were already several dots of six-legged misery crawling on her right arm and hand. She jumped up with a squeal and started brushing them away, but they were already biting her. She frantically danced around, slapping and cursing at the tiny pests who bit with the ferocity of lions. When she was free of them at last, she looked up at Nell and saw laughter dancing in the older woman's eyes.

Bree started to laugh out loud. "It's *not* funny! I already have welts on my arms from those little devils! You told me not to sit on the grass, but I was too tired to walk to the porch."

"Child, it's too hot to be out here weeding in this sun today. You need to slow down. It isn't a race, you know. Those weeds aren't going anywhere." Nell looked at Bree's dirty, shattered fingernails and smiled. "You don't have to keep trying to be the best farm woman ever."

Nell was always telling her to slow down, but Bree didn't want to. She needed to be too busy to think about where she was and why. Too busy to think about the guy who wanted to kill her. Too busy to think about the difference between women like Nell and Tammy and the supposed friends she had in Malibu. Too busy to think about the man with the gray eyes who was riding his tractor in the field across the road from her right now. And she needed to make herself tired enough to sleep through the quiet, lonely nights.

She took a long draught of the teeth-clenching sweet tea. It was amazing that something so sweet could be so refreshing on a hot day. It was an even bigger surprise that she was truly enjoying these long days of hard work and easy laughter, and the warm friendship she was developing with Nell. They'd baked together in Nell's kitchen yesterday, and she already had a deep respect for the woman's skills. Nell muttered something, and she looked up to see her staring across the road. Bree followed the direction of her gaze and saw Cole in the distance, driving his tractor across the field behind the barns. She stiffened, and Nell noticed.

"He's a good man, honey. I know he's a hard man, but he has his reasons. You don't know where he's been. What he's seen. He was hurt serving in Afghanistan, in more ways than one. He's doing the best he knows how."

Bree choked down the urge to ask all the questions that were right on the tip of her tongue. She didn't need to know. Didn't care. Instead, she changed the subject.

"What time is dinner, Nell?" While they were baking pies yesterday, Nell had suggested the two women should share their evening meals. Nell stared at her for a minute before answering, and she had the distinct impression that the older woman knew she was intentionally avoiding any conversation about Cole.

"Not until around six. Why don't you go take a shower and a nap?"

"I want to take care of the barn first, then I'll go shower. I'll save the sleeping for tonight." Nights were her most difficult time. The darkness of the countryside was almost smothering, and she jumped at every noise she heard. Her dreams were a restless mix of lurking danger and slate gray eyes. The more tired she was, the better chance she'd sleep through the night undisturbed.

COLE WALKED ACROSS the country road and up the front path to Nell's house Friday night with Maggie trotting at his side. It wasn't unusual for Nell to invite him over for dinner, but this morning was the first call she'd made since her new tenant arrived. He'd started to politely decline, but then she'd asked him for help. There was a board on the horse corral that was split, and she wanted him to replace it. He would never refuse Nell. He owed her too much. He couldn't bring himself to ask that Bree not be invited, but he was sure crossing his fingers that she wouldn't be here.

He'd avoided Nell's place all week just so he didn't have to see the sharp-tongued redhead. And he'd had plenty to do, with the young soybean crop needing pesticides to fight off an invasion of stink bugs. That kept him busy on the tractor all week. He'd seen Bree around the farm the past few days, and he had to admit she was working pretty hard for a city girl. But he still wondered when she'd give up on her little adventure and run back to California.

He didn't see her stretched out on the porch swing until his foot landed on the top step of

Nell's porch. Her soft lips were parted and her chest, under a gauzy leopard print top, was rising and falling slowly. She was sound asleep. One arm rested across her stomach, but the other had fallen off to the side, her fingertips trailing on the floor. Her dark red hair was swept to the side, partially covering her face. There were new cinnamon-colored freckles sprinkled across her cheeks, brought out by hours in the sun. Unlike the last time he'd been this close to her, she didn't seem to have a drop of makeup on. Her porcelain skin was beginning to take on a soft honey hue. The only hint of sunburn was on the tip of her nose, where he could see just a bit of peeling red skin.

A soft voice behind him made him jump. Usually so hyperaware of his surroundings, he hadn't even heard Nell come outside. She looked at Bree fondly as she rested a hand on his shoulder.

"She's about wrung out, poor child. I told her not to worry about those last three rows to be weeded, but she's a stubborn one. Takes everything as a challenge." Nell glanced up at him. "She's a good girl, Cole, and she's a hard worker. I like her." The last three words were said with some force, as if Nell was warning him to be on his best behavior. He nodded.

"I assume she's having dinner with us?"

"Of course. Bree and I are teaching each other all kinds of recipes and having a great time doing it. There hasn't been this much laughter in the house since Caroline moved away."

It came as a bit of a shock to realize Bree's laughter was something he'd really like to hear. So far, he'd only seen her hissing and spitting like a feral cat. Of course, that might have something to do with him. Nell nudged his arm. "Wake her up and bring her inside, Cole. Dinner's about ready." She was gone before he could protest.

He meant to wake her without startling her. Really, he did. But the swing rocked unexpectedly when he put his hand on the chain, nearly sending Bree to the floor and causing her to sit up with a jolt. Their eyes met, and he couldn't help but admire the fire he saw flaring up in her emerald glare. She was like a wild horse just looking to be tamed, and he wanted to be the one to tame her.

*What?*

He scolded himself for thinking such a stupid thing. Her voice sliced into him, driving home exactly how stupid it was.

"What the hell are you doing here? What do you want?" She blinked rapidly, trying to catch her bearings.

"I'm an invited dinner guest, Hollywood.

Sorry for startling you, but dinner's ready." He couldn't resist giving her a jab. "And real farmers don't sleep while the sun's still up."

She stood, her back ramrod straight. In flat sandals and skin-tight black leggings, she was only a few inches shorter than him. What little she lacked in height, she made up for in spirit.

"Don't give me that crap." Her lips curled in anger. "I've worked my butt off since I got here. Now excuse me, but I'm going to see if Nell needs my help with anything. I didn't know we were having company tonight, but it figures you wouldn't turn down a free meal." She brushed past him with her head held high, looking like freaking royalty as she slammed the screen door closed behind her.

Well...*damn*...

It seemed as if all their conversations ended with her storming off mad as a hornet. But she sure put on a fine show while doing it. He followed her into the house in bemused silence.

Dinner was more relaxed than he'd expected. Bree and Nell had obviously become close in their short time together, and he finally got a glimpse of Bree's softer side as she interacted with his neighbor. Nell told him about Bree's lessons in farming, laughing as she described Bree's first few failed attempts at pushing a wheelbarrow full of horse manure up the ramp to be dumped behind the barn.

"I swear, I think this woman filled every wheelbarrow load two or three times as they kept spilling, but she didn't give up! And then she went into the pigpen and found out how good Spot is at the sneak attack. Bree ended up sitting waist-deep in the mud, surrounded by squealing piglets! My God, the look on her face…"

And that was when it happened. Bree's cheeks blushed pink under the freckles, and she laughed out loud. Her green eyes were sparkling and clear, just like the sound of her laughter. She rested her hand on Nell's arm.

"Nell, stop it! Pretty soon you'll be telling him about me getting stepped on by that stupid horse, and then I'll be forced to tell him what happened when you tried to fold a napkin into a swan. It looked more like a phallic symbol!" The two women were both laughing hysterically now, with Nell wiping tears from her eyes. Bree glanced across the table at him, and for once, she didn't put her armor up. She just smiled at him as her laughter faded into giggles.

Brianna Mathews was a drop-dead gorgeous woman when she smiled, and damned if he wasn't attracted to her. The feeling was unexpected and unsettling. He hadn't been attracted to a woman in a long time. It was more than lust or the need to scratch a long-overdue itch. He wanted to *know* this woman. He sat back and frowned in confusion. Why now? And definitely why *her*?

She saw his dark expression and stopped mid-giggle, as if remembering she wasn't supposed to be smiling at him. There was a split second of awkward silence before Nell jumped in.

"Emily told me you were in beauty pageants, Bree. What got you started in that?"

She clearly wasn't comfortable talking about herself, but she opened up under Nell's gentle nudging. She told Nell—she was back to avoiding looking his way—that she entered her first teen pageant at her mom's request. Her mother was ill, and Bree wanted to please her. She made it sound like money was tight, and she'd started doing more pageants to earn scholarship money and prizes. Her mom died on Bree's eighteenth birthday, and Cole couldn't miss the shadow of pain that crossed her face when she said that. Half his meal was cooling on his plate, and he didn't care. He was too absorbed with her story and the swirl of emotions in her eyes as she spoke.

She quit the pageants, but then some pageant coach tracked her down and convinced her to try for Miss California. She won that and was a runner-up in the national competition.

"So is that where you picked up this stalker of yours?" Nell's question was said kindly and with concern, but the effect on Bree was immediate. Color drained from her face, and her fork clattered noisily against her plate.

"Oh, honey, I'm sorry…"

"No, Nell, it's okay to ask. After all, that's why I'm here." Her smile was tight and forced, but he had to give her credit for trying to make Nell feel better. "That didn't start until recently. Unfortunately, Hollywood breeds weirdos. At first it was just letters in the mail signed 'Your Loving Husband,' and I knew they weren't from my ex. The letters referred to specific events or outfits, making it clear that he was watching me. He said I needed to remember that my appearance reflected on him, too. He started texting photos of me that he'd taken with a cell phone, and he'd give me his opinion on whether my clothing was 'appropriate.' I changed my number, but he had the new one in just a matter of days and started again as if nothing had happened. He said I should start acting more—" she glanced across the table at him "—more like a lady." Cole winced, remembering his comment to her a few nights ago. "There were odd phone calls that I figured were from him. It was only in the past month or so that I felt someone might be watching my house."

"Your *house*? While you were there?" Nell put her hand on Bree's. Cole's own hands were clenched tightly.

She frowned. "I thought I was imagining it at first, because it was just a feeling that sometimes I wasn't alone. But he confirmed it when he sent a picture of me inside the house, taken from outdoors. He was looking through the windows somehow. And then, after Nikki Fitzgerald…"

"Oh, Lord, that poor young thing," Nell said.

Cole was really regretting not looking up that damned name, because he had no idea why the heavy silence fell on the table. As if she felt the weight of it, Bree suddenly stood and started grabbing plates.

"I've forgotten my manners, Nell. This is hardly appropriate dinner conversation. Let me get that dessert."

While they enjoyed Nell's blueberry pie and talked about the farm, he glanced at Nell and was surprised to find her staring straight at him. She raised an eyebrow and he realized he was leaning forward, toward Bree, as if he was hanging on every word. He frowned and pushed himself back into the chair.

"I'd better get to work on that fence before it gets dark." His chair scraped across the tile floor as he rose abruptly to his feet. "Thanks for dinner, Nell. It was great, as always."

She had an odd smile on her face, as if she was holding back some sort of joke. She nodded at him and winked. What the hell was *that* about?

"Come on, Bree, let's take care of the kitchen while Cole does his chores."

Bree didn't answer, but she collected the dessert plates and followed Nell. Maggie trotted behind him out the back door as he headed to the barn for a toolbox and a fresh fence board. Old Shep started to join them then thought better of it and stretched out on the back steps to the house.

Twenty minutes later Cole slid the newly sawed board into place at shoulder height and leaned against it, holding it against the post while he fished for two more nails in his pocket. The board started to slip and he cursed as it dropped. But it was caught and lifted back into place. He looked up to see Bree on the other side of the fence, holding up the board and giving him a crooked grin.

"Farmers help each other, right?"

He looked at her long fingers supporting the rough-cut 1x8. Most of her fingernails were chipped and devoid of polish. Three nails were broken, one nearly to the quick. There was an angry blister on her palm. His eyebrows rose. Nell wasn't bluffing when she said Bree had been working hard. But instead of complimenting her, he fell back to his standard snarl.

"You should have gloves on. You'll be full of slivers." He lifted the hammer.

"Yeah. You're welcome. Glad to help." Sarcasm dripped from those pretty lips. Wait. He wasn't supposed to be thinking about her lips. Those full, rose-colored lips that had haunted his sleep every night this week. The lips he was staring at right this minute. The lips that were now moving, speaking to him.

"Take your time, Cole. I'll stand here all night if you need me to." Her forearm trembled, and he realized she was holding the full weight of the ten-foot board.

"Sorry," he said automatically. Damn it, that wasn't the first time she'd gotten him to say that word since she arrived, and the thought annoyed the daylights out of him. He swung the hammer, making quick work of the final two long nails that now held the fence firmly intact. Bree shook her hand, wincing. He grabbed her wrist, sliding off one of his leather gloves to examine her palm. A dark half-inch sliver was visible just under the tender skin at the base of her thumb.

"I tried to warn you..." he muttered, half to himself. He held her hand firmly and fished his jackknife out of his pocket. With one swift move, he opened the knife, set it under the tip of the sliver and pulled it out. When a dot of blood appeared, he was surprised how much it affected him. He brushed the blood away with his thumb, still holding her hand in his.

"Go inside and have Nell put something on that so it doesn't get infected." He saw the angry red bites on her forearm and rubbed his fingers across them. "Fire ants?"

"One of my many lessons in farm life this week. Look before you sit down in the yard to rest, because there might be an ant hill there." She slowly pulled her hand out of his, and he felt a surprising pang of loss. "And today's lesson is…wear gloves. And apparently naps are for sissies."

The corner of his mouth twitched toward a smile. "Nah. Naps are okay. For old people and womenfolk, anyway."

She grinned, and his body warmed. "And which category are you putting me in?"

His eyes slid down her body. The gauzy top and snug leggings didn't leave much to the imagination. Before he knew it, he was saying his thoughts out loud. "You're all woman, Brianna. All woman."

"I won't be for long if I keep this up. Look at my hands. And my skin. I haven't had this many freckles since I was a kid. The sun is doing a number on me…" Her eyes met his and she stopped talking, as if she just now realized what he'd said. "Wait…did you just say something *nice* to me?"

This conversation was heading in a dangerous direction. He forced the growl back into his voice.

"What? By calling you a woman? Isn't that how you make your living?" She stepped back and paled. But wasn't it the truth? Pageant queen? Hollywood trophy wife? He wasn't going to feel guilty for stating the obvious.

Her voice settled to a steely level. "Right. I knew I must be mistaken about that 'nice' business. Are we done here?" She nodded to the fence.

He barely managed to stop himself from apologizing yet again. Instead, he bent to pick up his tools and walked away without saying another word. He was pretty sure he heard her call him a jackass under her breath. So be it. She wasn't wrong.

When Cole got home, he paced the floors in agitation.

That woman. That woman. That *woman*.

Just being in her presence was enough to send his pulse jumping. She challenged him and pushed him and ticked him off. And that was the problem in a nutshell. She made him *feel* things. And Cole Caldwell didn't want to feel. He didn't want to let his emotions out of the cage he'd stuffed them into. They were safe and controllable when they were confined. Bree Mathews was anything but safe and controllable. She was too big a risk. Too dangerous for a man who used to face danger as part of everyday life.

When he'd reached for her hand and held it... well, something happened. Something that felt profound, which was ridiculous. Her hand in his felt soft and smooth and perfect. And those freckles she complained about? He thought they looked like gold dust scattered across her ivory skin. In the bar on Monday afternoon, he thought her complexion was artificial, a product of cosmetics and Hollywood magic. But tonight she was scrubbed clean and glowing from a week in the sun. Tonight her skin, unencumbered with artificial enhancement, was perfect. He wondered what the parts of her body that he hadn't seen looked like. Did she have freckles in hidden places? Did she have porcelain skin everywhere?

He kicked an ottoman and sent it sliding across the hardwood floor. She was making him crazy. Thank God she was only here temporarily. Once that stalker was arrested, she'd be back home in Hollywood.

Maggie settled onto her bed by the front door with a heavy sigh and stared at him with large, dark eyes. Most of the time she spent her nights outside on the porch, reminiscent of their days in Afghanistan when she'd stand watch outside the tents. Old habits died hard, even for dogs. But tonight she knew he needed her close.

# CHAPTER FIVE

BREE STOOD IN front of the mirror in the ladies' room at The Hide-Away on Saturday night and laughed out loud. She looked nothing like the Malibu Barbie who'd walked into this same bar on Monday with long red hair and expensive taste in wine.

Her hair fell in feathered curls around her face. Tammy's sister had carefully removed all her extensions that morning, then cut, colored and layered her hair so that the soft, natural curls came back. The ombre coloring was an edgy mix of her original dark red fading into soft cinnamon, with champagne blond on the tips. The length barely brushed her shoulders after it was cut, but she'd taken a curling iron to it tonight so it fell just below her ears in a jumble of messy ringlets.

Her outfit was the result of Emily's shopping spree at Target. Instead of linen and silk, she wore a short denim skirt with a red gingham shirt tied at her waist. The shirt was unbuttoned, revealing a white tank top decorated with the glittering outline of a galloping horse. Her earrings were long, swishy tassels that dangled the length of her neck and ended in tiny gold horseshoes. Tall Western boots finished the authentic country look.

She'd laughed when Emily pulled the bright red boots out of the shopping bag. Not only were they *red*; they were also adorned with gold metallic thread stitched into a phoenix design. They made her feel brave and sexy. With her fresh crop of freckles, she was a new, sassy, all-natural Bree.

She turned back and forth, staring at herself in the mirror. Being recognized seemed unlikely after this transformation, which was why she'd agreed when Emily suggested they come to The Hide-Away for dinner. She thought she'd feel like an actress playing a role wearing this little country bumpkin outfit, but instead, she felt relaxed and energized.

A week ago she wouldn't be caught dead looking like this. What if some paparazzi snapped a photo? Cole's words had stung last night, but he was right. Her looks were her living, and she spent a good hour every morning plastering on her identity before walking out of her bedroom. But now...well, now she looked far more genuine than Malibu Bree had ever looked or felt, even with the silly multicolored curls.

"You gonna come eat with us or what?" Tammy rapped on the restroom door.

"Yes, ma'am! I'm on my way." She quickly applied some sheer lip gloss. It was the only makeup she was wearing. She'd insisted Melissa pluck off what remained of her fancy acrylic nails, and she'd tossed out all of her cosmetics except sunscreen and moisturizer. The best way to look the opposite of the famous Bree Mathews was to ditch all the phony stuff. That thought made her pause again. Nearly everything about her in California had become phony. How exactly had that happened?

She stepped out into the dark, noisy bar and gave Tammy a thumbs-up. The Hide-Away was as different tonight compared to Monday as she was. The wide accordion doors she'd noticed that first day were now opened wide, revealing an adjoining room larger than the bar itself, filled with tables, chairs and an elevated stage at the far end of the dance floor. Tammy had explained that Ty and Cole were partners in the bar. They'd purchased the neighboring business a few years ago and used the space to expand the bar on the weekends and for special occasions. Friday was karaoke/jukebox night, although Tammy said their second-hand equipment was sadly outdated. On Saturday nights they had local bands come in. Their reputation was growing, and the place tended to fill up not only for meals, but also for a fun time afterward.

They found Emily sitting in the corner booth farthest away from the bright lights over the stage. She jumped up and gave Bree a hug.

"Oh my God, you look so hot! I told you those boots were perfect for The Hide-Away!"

It was true; nearly everyone was wearing boots.

"I'm so glad we came here tonight, Bree... I mean, Anna!"

That was the alias they'd decided on—Anna Lowery—using the second half of her actual name and her mother's maiden name. A new name for a new woman. Tammy slid into the booth across from Bree and next to her daughter, her hazelnut hair pulled back into a ponytail.

Ty delivered three plates of burgers and chips to the table, shaking his head. "Tell me again why you decided to come out dining and dancing when you're supposed to be in hiding?"

"Oh, Dad, who could possibly recognize her now? *I* wouldn't even know who she was if I didn't watch it all happen today." Emily grinned proudly. "And the clothes I picked are perfect, don't you think?"

Ty looked at each of the three women, stopping to give his wife a warm gaze that seemed to contain an unspoken question. Tammy barely nodded, and Bree remembered the silent conversations that went on between Ty and his brother. The Caldwells were men of few words, but plenty of communication. He shrugged and walked away with a final word to his daughter.

"You just remember that your friends can't know anything about 'Anna' being here. I don't want to see a bunch of high school kids trying to sneak into the bar tonight."

"I promise, Daddy! I'd never do that to my good friend, *Anna*." She giggled as Ty continued to walk away, still shaking his head.

They talked about the events of the day as they devoured their burgers. Tammy looked down at Bree's legs and started to laugh. "You are rocking those boots, girl."

"I suppose I should have worn something less flashy if I wanted to stay under the radar, huh?" She frowned at her outfit.

"Bree, it's not the clothes that are going to get attention. Trust me, there'll be women here wearing a lot less than you are." Tammy shook her head. "It's the body beneath those clothes that will have the boys jumping to dance with you. They won't have a clue that you're hiding some secret identity."

Bree started to answer but stopped when a noisy group of women walked in from the bar. They were led by a striking woman with waist-long raven hair and brilliant blue eyes. Tall and slender, she wasn't walking as much as she was strutting, gazing around coolly as if she owned the place. She was wearing a snug blue knit dress that showed every curve. When she turned to say something to one of her friends, it was obvious she was wearing a thong under the thin fabric of her dress. So was Bree, but she wasn't advertising it like this girl was.

The brunette was the country version of the woman Bree had been in Hollywood—the queen of the room. She admired that kind of confidence, but her admiration faded when the dark-haired woman made eye contact with her. She sighed as the woman's eyes narrowed and her nostrils flared. She looked Bree slowly up and down, and obviously tagged her as an adversary. Bree had seen that look all the time at parties in LA. There was nothing some beautiful women hated more than seeing *another* woman in the room who might steal their limelight.

The woman left her group and walked boldly to their booth. For a minute Bree thought she'd been recognized, and she took a deep breath to brace herself. The woman's heavily made up eyes didn't leave Bree's face, but she spoke to Tammy.

"Great to see you, Tammy. Hi, Emily. Who's your friend?" Bree couldn't help but notice that

Tammy's whole body had stiffened. These two weren't friends, and that came as a relief, because, while Bree didn't know this woman, she certainly knew the type.

"Amber." Tammy's voice was cool. They not only weren't friends, but sweet Tammy clearly didn't like Amber one little bit, either. "This is Caroline's friend Anna. She's staying at Nell's cottage this summer."

Amber's eyes went wide and she kept her gaze fixed firmly on Bree, but continued to speak as if she wasn't there. "Caroline? Oh, how lovely. I adore Caroline. Anna looks familiar, though. Have we met?"

There was a quick inhale of breath around the table, but Tammy jumped in to deflect the conversation.

"I don't remember you and Caroline being all that close in high school, Amber."

"Don't be silly. Caroline Patterson and I have always been great friends…"

"Caroline *McCormack*, actually." Bree's voice was a lot more level than her heart rate.

"Excuse me?" Amber finally addressed her directly.

"Caroline's last name is McCormack. She was married recently. I don't recall seeing you at the wedding, considering you're such good friends."

Bree knew how to put it in bitch-mode when

required. Tammy was trying to hold back a smile. Emily didn't bother making the effort, and just looked up at Amber with a big grin. Amber paled slightly under all of her heavily applied makeup.

"Oh, of course. Yes, I wasn't able to attend, but she'll always be a Patterson to everyone here in Russell. Isn't that right, Tammy?" Amber's mistake was in recruiting the wrong ally.

"Actually, I think of her as Caroline McCormack now. I heard she married a charming man, and Anna tells me they're madly in love with each other. They run a business together."

Amber stuttered for a moment then gathered herself together and walked away with a brittle nod to join her posse of friends at a table near the dance floor.

"Holy cats, what was *that*?" Bree started to laugh. "I thought we only had vipers like her in Hollywood!"

Tammy shook her head. "Amber and I used to be friends in school, but she hurt someone I care about. She thinks she's better than Russell, but she won't leave town long enough to prove it."

Emily spoke up. "She broke Uncle Cole's heart."

Tammy poked her daughter in the ribs with her elbow. "Emily, be quiet!"

Bree had already learned quite a bit about

Cole's past today when Tammy and Emily brought her new wardrobe to the cottage. While Bree tried on outfits, Emily, clearly enamored with her uncle, made a point of stressing that he was single. Bree had guessed as much, figuring there wasn't a houseful of grumpy little gray-eyed children after all. Emily had the openness of a teenager with no filters, and she'd rattled on for quite a while about Cole before her mother finally shushed her.

He'd done three tours in the Middle East and had been injured several times. The last time was the worst, and ended his career. Emily proudly proclaimed him a hero. Bree didn't doubt that, but Tammy's troubled expression told her there was more to the story.

Bree couldn't stop herself from asking the question. "What happened between Amber and Cole?"

Emily answered in her characteristic jumble of hurried words. "Uncle Cole and Amber got engaged before he left the last time, and then she dumped him. She dumped him by *email*, after he'd been injured. There he is in a hospital in Germany, and he gets an email from her saying she's found someone else and wishes him the best. But she found someone else long before that—turns out she'd been cheating pretty much the whole time he was gone…"

"Okay. That's enough gossip for tonight, Em," Tammy cut her off.

Bree leveled a cold look at the back of Amber's head. She shouldn't care if the woman hurt a man who insulted her at every turn. But right now the thought of someone breaking Cole's heart made her blood boil just a little.

After they finished dinner, Tammy's sister stopped by to pick up Emily for an overnight babysitting job. Tammy and Bree were ready to party, country-style. The band was setting up and the room was packed. There were families and older couples in the restaurant area, while the bar sported a younger crowd of singles. Amber and her friends pulled several tables together on the opposite side of the floor.

The band leader's sandy hair was pulled back into a ponytail, and he had piercing blue eyes. His smile was brilliant, and he kept aiming it at Bree. As she returned to the table with another glass of wine, he walked over. Tammy jumped up and hugged him then introduced him.

"Anna, this is our good friend, Mark Stenson. We all went to school together. His band plays here two or three times a month. Mark, this is Caroline's friend, Anna. She's staying in Miss Nell's cottage."

Mark took her hand and held it in both of his. He leaned forward and flashed her a dazzling smile. "I remember Caroline Patterson. Sweet kid. And she clearly has sweet friends, too." Oh, he was smooth, all right. "I hope you enjoy our music tonight, Anna. Maybe you'll share a dance with me later?"

Mark seemed harmless, and he was a friend of Tammy's, so she went along with his flirting. "Now Mark, are you telling me you can sing *and* dance? I'm so impressed!"

He stepped closer and whispered in her ear. "If that impresses you, wait till you see what I can do in the backseat of my truck…"

She laughed and swatted his shoulder playfully. "Oh, no, you don't! I'll be staying away from all those big old pickup trucks tonight."

"Don't be afraid, Anna. I'll be very gentle." It was easy to see from his expression that he was joking with her. He chatted briefly with Tammy then joined the guys on the stage. The first song was "Hey Girl." Mark looked straight at Bree as he started singing in his gravelly voice. Tammy laughed at Bree's blushing face. Amber was shooting daggers at her from across the room. Mark crooned about how fine she looked. It was pretty cool to have a hot guy sing a song right at her.

The next number was a fast one about country girls shaking, and the dance floor filled with people. Tammy grabbed her hand and they danced to that song and the next three fast ones. Then the music slowed again. A tall, skinny boy—truly, he looked about nineteen—stepped up to Bree before she could sit.

"Ma'am, may I have this dance?" He gave her a shy smile. She glanced in Tammy's direction, and Tammy gave her a "he's safe" nod. His name was Danny Miller, and he and his daddy owned a hog farm south of Russell. He'd sure like it if she'd come down and let him show her around sometime. Bree Mathews would have looked down her nose at Danny Miller and brushed him away in disgust. But she wasn't Bree tonight. She was Anna Lowery, and Anna gave Danny a warm smile and let him spin her around the floor to a two-step.

After Danny, it was Harley Benson who rocked out with her to a song about rednecks. After Harley, it was Arlen Howard. Then Ty joined her for another two-step. She and Tammy danced a few fast songs, with various guys from the bar joining them. The night flew by and the drinks went down quickly. She danced to songs about small towns, rednecks, tequila, bonfires and red Solo cups. There were no expectations. No judgments. Just people having fun on a Saturday night.

The band was a few songs into their third set when Mark stepped down from the stage and took her hand, tugging her to her feet. He pulled her in and started to sing a sweet love song, "Hey, Pretty Girl," right to her. She laughed and leaned into him, suddenly feeling the effects of all the wine she'd had. Mark was singing just inches from her face. She reached out and put her hand on his arm. His blue eyes darkened.

Tammy jumped to her feet at the exact same moment Mark looked over Bree's shoulder and his eyes went wide. The energy in the room tipped from relaxed to highly charged in the blink of an eye. Before she could turn her head to see what was happening, hard hands grabbed her waist from behind. She knew who it was without looking, but she had no idea what Cole Caldwell was doing here.

He tugged her back against his hard body and spoke to Mark, who'd stopped singing. "Sorry, Mark, this one's mine." She wasn't sure if he meant the dance or her, and neither made any sense. For one tense moment she was afraid there was going to be a fight, but no. Mark smiled slowly and shrugged his shoulders, raising his hands in surrender.

"I didn't know, man. It's good to see you, Cole. Damned good to see you." He stepped back to the stage and Bree spun in Cole's arms, ready to give him a piece of her mind for being such a caveman. As she opened her mouth, Mark addressed the room.

"Ladies and gentlemen, let's give a big round of applause to our very own Cole Caldwell, a genuine war hero. It's been way too long since we've seen him here with his friends."

The tension grew in Cole's eyes as everyone started to clap their hands and cheer. His jaw was tight, and a muscle in his cheek was pulsing dangerously. She started to ask what was wrong, but this time was interrupted by Amber, who'd suddenly appeared at their side, cooing at Cole.

"Oh, honey, it's wonderful to see you out. And you look so good…" She started to reach her hand toward him and he flinched. Bree moved between them and faced Amber.

"Amber, you need to walk away."

Amber ignored her, and her hand continued its path and brushed across Cole's shoulder. Bree heard his sharp intake of breath and felt another surge of defensiveness.

"Didn't you hear? Cole just told Mark that I was his, so why don't you run along…" Cole's fingers dug into her side, and she leaned back against him. Amber pulled her hand back, but Bree suspected it was only so she could strike out at her. She braced for it but kept her expression calm. It wouldn't be her first cat fight in public; the only thing missing was the cameras.

"Amber!" Ty swept up and wrapped his arm around the brunette's waist, pulling her away with a laugh. "You haven't danced with me all night, girl, and I love this song." He sent a sharp look to Mark, who immediately picked up the song he'd been crooning to Bree minutes ago. Amber was caught off guard and allowed herself to be drawn away, leaving Bree and Cole standing in front of the stage. Other couples came onto the floor. Anxious to get through Cole's wall of silence, she arched a brow, forcing herself to smile.

"Well, Cole, my dance card's been pretty full all night, but I guess I can make time to dance with my neighbor. Shall we?" She put her left hand on his shoulder and held up her right hand for him to take. He seemed baffled, but silently took her hand and pulled her close. She couldn't read his expression. Confusion? Anger? Why on earth was he here?

His eyes never left hers, even when other people patted him on the back and told him how good it was to see him. They seemed genuinely surprised and happy at his presence, but he paid them no attention. He just stared at her as they moved to the music. His body was tight with tension under her fingertips.

Looking into his eyes made her dizzy. She closed her own to regain her equilibrium, and her fingers absently traced the rough scars that scrolled under the dark tattoos on his arm. No wonder the tats had seemed three-dimensional.

When she opened her eyes, Cole was still staring as he moved her across the floor. She felt a sudden urge to sink her fingers into his thick, tobacco-colored hair. This was crazy. She tried to pull away, but he wasn't letting go. The song came to an end, and still he didn't release her. She needed to free him from whatever demons were holding him there, immobile in the center of the dance floor.

"So…your ex-fiancée seems nice." She used the sarcasm lightly, hoping to coax a crooked smile from him. His left brow rose.

"I'm curious how you know her name." Ah. The man speaks at last.

"Hey, she approached me. Marking her territory or something. It's a girl thing."

"And she just blurted out that she used to be engaged to me?"

Bree shook her head. "No, your niece filled in the blanks."

His head tipped to the side and he looked at her as if she were a puzzle that he hadn't quite figured out. His shoulders were just beginning to relax when an older man walked over and grabbed his hand, pumping it up and down.

"Thank you for your service, Colton. You did

a damn fine job over there, and you represented Russell well, son. It ain't your fault those others died. You did the best you could."

Cole's eyes closed slowly, and his words came through clenched teeth.

"If I'd done the best I could, they'd all be alive now."

The old man looked at Bree sadly, shook his head and walked away.

COLE GROUND HIS teeth together and held his eyes tightly closed, working hard to keep what was left of his composure. The phone call from Nell that evening had caught him completely unprepared. He figured she was going to tell him one of the cows had dropped a calf. Instead, she needed another favor. Nell rarely asked for favors, especially at ten o'clock on a Saturday night.

"Honey, I was going to go back into town to pick up Bree, but I'm just not feeling well. Do you think you could drive to The Hide-Away and bring her home?"

"What do you mean, you don't feel well?" Nell Patterson never admitted to illness or injury. "Are you okay? Do you need anything?"

"Oh no, I'm fine, darlin', but bless your heart for asking. I'm just tired." She sighed. "I can drive in after her if you can't do it…"

"No, of course I can." He just didn't want to. "But why is she expecting you to chauffeur her around town? And isn't she supposed to be hiding from the public?" How typical of little Miss Hollywood to be so selfish.

"Don't be mad at her, Cole. She and Tammy wanted to enjoy the band and have a few drinks. No one will recognize her. So you'll go get her for me?"

He'd never refused Nell before, and he wasn't going to start now. Nell Patterson was his lifeline in more ways than anyone knew.

"Yeah, fine. I'll bring your tenant home safe and sound, Miss Nell."

"I knew I could count on you, honey. Thank you."

He sat outside the bar for more than twenty minutes. The windows on his truck were down, and he could hear the band playing. It was Mark and the boys, and they sounded good. Cole sighed. He hadn't been in the bar on a Saturday night since he got back to Russell ten months ago. It looked crowded, and that was going to be a problem. He'd have to leave Maggie in the truck because she'd draw too much attention. The evening had cooled off enough that she'd be fine, but it meant he'd have to walk into the packed bar alone and look for that pain in the ass, Brianna Mathews. He used his anger at her to propel him inside.

Ty almost dropped the whiskey bottle he was pouring from when he saw Cole walk through the door. His face lit up, and Cole groaned. People were going to look at this as some kind of homecoming. Damn that redhead. He gave Ty a terse nod and tried to keep walking, but he was quickly surrounded by people he used to know. Harley. Danny. Billy MacIntyre. Arlen Howard. They were good guys. They hadn't seen him in ages. He shook their hands and tolerated the back thumps they gave him. He was as polite as he could force himself to be as he looked around for Bree's dark auburn hair. It was crowded and loud in here and he just wanted out.

He finally made it to the doorway of the dance hall, as he and Ty had laughingly dubbed it four years ago. His mouth twitched into a half smile. Some things never changed. There was Mark, holding some pretty girl's hand and crooning a love song to her. The ladies always swooned when he did that, and this one was no exception, leaning forward, slightly tipsy. Cole looked around the room for Bree, assuming she'd be hiding in some dark corner, looking down her nose at this small-town Southern crowd.

Then his eyes snapped back to where Mark was standing. The woman he was singing to had a mass of curls that barely tickled her neck in a tangle of colors that Cole didn't recognize. But there was something familiar about her. The sculptured neck and those legs…those long, gorgeous legs in that too-short skirt and those flame-colored boots. The strong arms peppered with golden freckles and fire ant bites.

Oh, hell no. Before he knew it, his hands were on her and he was pulling her away from his friend like a Neanderthal. Mark looked angry for just a moment, then he grinned at Cole and backed away, avoiding the beat-down Cole was seriously thinking of putting on the man who'd once been his best friend. Which left just him and Bree standing on the dance floor. Amber tried to latch on to him for some reason, but Bree chased her off as if she was protecting him, which made no sense.

When she turned to face him, it had been the most natural thing in the world to pull her close. He hadn't had a woman in his arms in over a year, and the feeling nearly knocked him to his knees. She smelled like flowers and fresh air, and he found himself breathing deep to take it in. People kept talking and patting his back, but he ignored them all.

Bree's hand traced the ridges of his scars under his thin T-shirt. Everywhere her fingers brushed felt like an electrical current going straight to his heart. He tightened the arm he had wrapped around her, and his fingers rubbed the small of her back. Her green eyes went wide and dark with some emotion he couldn't, or didn't want to, identify. He felt as if he'd fallen into some very deep water here, with no way to get out. When the music stopped, she started teasing him again. He knew she was trying to relax him; he just didn't understand why. She almost succeeded, too, until Marv Wilson walked up and started yammering about dead comrades.

He took a deep breath and opened his eyes. The walls of The Hide-Away seemed to be closing in on him. People here thought he was a hero, and he was anything but. It was suddenly difficult to breathe. He looked at the smiling faces surrounding him and felt a surge of panic.

Too close. Too crowded. Too loud. Too dangerous.

What was he doing here? What was his mission? How could he escape?

His eyes locked on Bree's worried face. That was right—*she* was his mission. Get her and get her home. That was his objective. He grabbed her wrist roughly and tugged her forward as he pushed his way through the crowd. She let out a yelp of surprise then followed without another word. People parted before him like the Red Sea, and he knew how fierce he must look. He didn't care. Fierce was good. *Anger* was good. It was the one emotion that felt familiar and safe.

He burst out the front door and took a deep draught of the night air as he propelled her toward the truck. His voice came out in a snarl. "Get in."

She spun and put her hands on her hips. "What are you talking about? I'm not going anywhere with you."

His blood was boiling now. "You get in the damned truck right now, you selfish little princess. Nell asked me to bring you home, and that's what I'm doing."

Her visible rage at his first sentence cooled at his second. Her brows knit together in confusion.

"*Nell* sent you? Why?"

"Because she was too tired to act as your chauffeur, that's why."

She still looked puzzled.

"But... I told her Ty was going to take me home..." She thought about it for a moment, then her eyes brightened. She shook her head and smiled.

"I think we got set up, Cole."

"Set up?" As usual, this woman wasn't making sense.

"I think Nell's trying her hand at matchmaking. Having us both to dinner last night? Asking you to pick me up tonight?" She gave a little laugh that sounded like a refreshing breeze through chimes. "Sadly, she's a poor matchmaker if she thinks you and I are going anywhere as a couple. I'm sorry. You didn't look very comfortable in there. You can head on home. I'll be fine and I'm not done dancing..." She started to turn away, but he grabbed her arm. He still felt frighteningly out of his depth.

"The hell you're not. Regardless of her motive, I told Nell I'd bring you home, and that's exactly what I'm doing." He started to pull her toward the truck again, but she dug in her heels.

"Cole, you're being stupid. I'm staying right here."

Defiance didn't work on a mission. Defiance could lead to disaster, and he couldn't tolerate that on his watch. Orders had to be followed to keep everyone safe. He yanked her forward and grasped her by her shoulders, glaring down at her.

"The mission is getting you home. You don't get to change it. I have to complete the mission, don't you understand?" Somewhere in his head, he knew he sounded like a lunatic. But if he didn't complete his mission, something terrible could happen.

She opened her mouth to protest then stopped. Her eyes locked on his. He felt as if she was looking right into his soul. He wanted to break away, but he couldn't. They stood there like that for what seemed like a very long time.

Ty's voice cut into the tense moment. He was standing at the front door of the bar, and he sounded angry. And worried.

"Let her go, Cole, and step away."

Bree shook her head. "No, Ty. We're okay. Cole's going to give me a ride home." She rested her hands lightly on his arms, and he felt his grip on her shoulders relaxing. Damn it, he didn't realize he'd been holding her so firmly. It must have hurt, but she hadn't complained.

"You should stay here, Bree," Ty said. "When he's like this, he's better off away from people."

Cole blinked. Ty made it sound as if he was some kind of dangerous animal. Was that what he'd become to his own brother? Something shuddered deep inside him. Was that what he'd become, period? The light touch of Bree's hand patting his arm broke him out of his dark thoughts.

"Not tonight, Ty. Tonight he needs to take me home." His heart thumped erratically. She understood the importance of the mission. How could she possibly know? She looked to Ty and flashed him a reassuring smile. "We'll be fine. Tammy can drop my purse at Nell's tomorrow. Good night." She calmly stepped back, and he released her without hesitation. She walked to the passenger door of his truck, opened it and gave Maggie a hug. Cole looked at his big brother and nodded.

"It's good, man. I'm good." He took a deep breath. "It just got too close in there. But I'm good now." He sounded like he was trying to convince himself, because he was. He and Ty stared at each other in silence while Bree climbed into the truck and closed the door.

Ty looked to the truck where Bree was sitting and shook his head.

"I can't figure out whether or not she's good for you."

"Yeah. Me neither. G'night."

He turned and got into the truck with the woman he was beginning to suspect would either be his salvation or his destruction.

# CHAPTER SIX

THE RIDE HOME was silent and thick with tension. By the time Cole got in the truck with her, Bree felt like she'd been on an endless emotional roller coaster. From the happiness of dancing with everyone and being serenaded by Mark to the drama of Cole bursting in and laying claim to her in the middle of the dance floor. From the defensive confrontation with Amber to the intensity of dancing in Cole's tight embrace.

He'd clearly been a bundle of nerves and anger by the end of the dance, but she couldn't tell where the anger was directed, and she didn't think he could, either. Maybe that was what created the panic she saw in his eyes just before he grabbed her and dragged her outside. He'd been desperate out on the sidewalk, rambling about having a "mission" to complete. His grip on her arms was just short of painful.

Any reasonable woman would have been afraid. And she had to admit to a flutter of fear when he grabbed her…until she looked into his eyes. She'd expected his usual cynicism and anger, that cold Cole gaze that could slice through her. But what she saw tonight was something she never expected. Those gray eyes betrayed his sheer, unadulterated terror. That naked fear nearly broke her heart, and she wanted nothing more than to make it go away. If he needed her to go home with him in order to complete some critical mission in his mind, then that was what she'd do.

He was apparently as worn-out as she was, or perhaps still struggling with his demons, because he didn't say a word on the drive home. He gripped the steering wheel so tightly that the veins stood out on the backs of his hands and forearms in the dim glow from the dashboard. His eyes stayed firmly fixed on the dark road ahead, as if it took real effort to not look in her direction. She absently ran her fingers through Maggie's thick fur as the dog lay between them on the seat. She couldn't think of a single thing to say to break the silence. Should she try humor? Ask him questions about his past? Talk about some neutral topic like the weather? She remained silent, afraid of making the wrong choice.

When he pulled into the driveway next to the cottage, he still wouldn't look at her. But he finally spoke.

"Bree…" His voice cracked, and he pressed

his lips together in frustration. He was silent for a moment then shook his head. His voice hardened. "I'll stay here until you're inside. See you 'round."

*See you 'round?*

After grabbing her and dragging her out of a bar filled with people, after she defended his freaking honor and had more faith in him than his own *brother*, that was all he had to say? She sighed. She'd never understand men in general, and she surely would never understand this man. Just trying was giving her whiplash.

"Yeah, right. See you 'round." She opened the truck door, and Maggie whined. Bree turned back with a small smile and scratched the dog's ears. "Good night, Maggie Mae. You're a sweetheart." Maggie stood and barked as Bree closed the door and walked away from the truck. Cole kept the truck idling until she closed the front door of the cottage and flicked on the lights, then he backed out and headed over to his own driveway. She watched the taillights head toward the big farmhouse and wondered what he'd do with himself once he got inside. Alone and uptight, stressed and haunted. Her heart softened. There was more to Cole Caldwell than met the eye.

"Girl, try not to kill the tomato plants along with the weeds." Nell chuckled. "The idea is to let the producing plants live. You've been whacking away at those weeds like they kicked your dog."

Bree stood in the garden and stretched, placing her hands in the small of her back and arching backward.

"Sorry, Nell. I'm just a little uptight."

She was still agitated about her confrontation with Cole at The Hide-Away. They hadn't spoken in the days since, but she'd seen him on his tractor that morning, circling the edge of his field in the hot sun.

"Are you still mad at me about Saturday?" Nell asked.

She smiled and reached out to grab the older woman's hand. "Oh, Nell, I was never angry with you. I just don't think Cole appreciated your matchmaking attempts. He was so uncomfortable in the bar. It hurt me just to look at him."

Nell looked solemn. "Come on, Bree, let's quit for lunch. I've got soup simmering on the stove, and it should be almost done." The two women walked toward the yellow house. "You know I never meant to hurt Cole, but being uncomfortable once in a while isn't a bad thing. He can't just lock himself up in that house and rage at the world for the rest of his life."

"You and I know that, but I don't think he does." Bree held the screen door open for Nell.

"The funny thing is, I think he wants to let go, but he's…afraid. I never thought I'd use that word for Cole, but he seemed so…afraid… Saturday night. Afraid of the crowd. Afraid of the attention. Afraid of me."

She fell silent as she remembered the way his muscles trembled when she started tracing the scars on his shoulder. That brief moment of softness in his eyes when she teased him after they danced. She gave herself a firm mental shake as she stepped into the kitchen. She had to stop obsessing about the man.

Nell lifted the top off the pot, filling the room with a delicious aroma. She stirred the soup with a wooden spoon and nodded.

"Sometimes when people go through hard times, they find comfort in certain emotions, and it's hard to let go of them. When my husband died years ago, I was so angry. He was a hellcat, but I loved him with everything I had. We tried for so long to get pregnant, and then Caroline finally came along. I begged him to quit autoracing, but he just couldn't do it. He was killed on a dirt track. We were up to our eyeballs in debt, and he'd left me here on this farm alone with a broken-hearted daughter. Caroline cried all the time, but me… I was just so *angry*." She looked at Bree and sighed. "I was mad at Everett for dying in his stupid stock car. I was mad that the sun came up the next morning and the world kept turning. I was mad that my anger didn't change a damn thing. God forgive me, I was mad that Caroline would cry herself to sleep every night and I couldn't cry with her. I was mad at everyone who stopped by and thought they could help. Lord, I clung to that anger for weeks. Months."

Her shoulders sagged and she covered the soup before sitting at the kitchen table. Bree joined her there and reached over to hold Nell's hands. Nell stared at their entwined fingers for a long time then blinked back tears when she looked up.

"And then one day I realized how foolish I was being. My anger had become my security blanket, and it may have made me feel safe, but it was a crutch. It was holding me back and hurting everyone around me, especially Caroline. I had to start living again. It was scary. And hard. So hard." Her voice faded off, but she started to smile as she spoke again. "It was worth it, though. Life was still waiting for me. I learned to tuck my grief away for quiet times when I could, and still do, embrace it now and then. But I had to *live*. I had to find joy again. And I did. I found it in my church, in my friends and in my family." She sat up straighter. "And Cole needs to find his way back to living again. He's just putting up a bigger fight than I did. But he'll get there."

"I'm sorry for your loss, Nell. You've done more than live. You've thrived." It was all Bree could think to say. They sat for a moment in silence before she continued, digging into a part of her past she rarely visited. "I was angry after my mom died. I wanted her to have the very best, and we simply couldn't afford it. My dad was an auto mechanic, and I was mad at him for not making enough money to save her from cancer." She took a deep breath and shook her head sadly. "I vowed never to feel that way again. I thought if I only had enough money, enough things… then I'd feel safe. That's why I fought Damian so hard during the divorce to keep the house. He *wanted* it, but I thought I *needed* it." It surprised her that now she was doubting that need.

"And your dad? Are you still mad at him?"

"No. We worked things out after Damian and I got divorced. Dad never liked Damian or our over-the-top lifestyle, but I think deep down he understood my need for the security I thought it brought." She gave Nell a crooked grin. "And look at me now. I've got my mansion on the beach, and here I am hiding from some nut who wants to kill me. I'm less safe now than I was the day my mom died."

The two women sat in silence for a long time,

while the sun beat down on the farmyard out-side the windows. The muffled hum of a trac-tor in the distance told them that Cole was still working hard in the heat of the day. Finally Nell stood and filled two bowls with vegetable soup. Bree sliced some of the cornbread they'd made the day before.

As they sat back down, Nell grinned at Bree, effectively shaking off their serious conversa-tion. "So, girl, what do you say we do some more cooking this afternoon instead of working in that hot sun? How'd you like to learn how to make yeast bread and some sticky cinnamon buns today?"

She quickly agreed, eager to learn more of Nell's cooking secrets. Bree loved to cook, which was how she'd moved into catering and event planning after her divorce. It was awkward ca-tering parties in Hollywood where she used to be a guest. She didn't like the way people looked down at her, or worse, pitied her. But she was a total foodie, and she was developing a real pas-sion for the back-to-basics country cooking that Nell embraced.

The woman's gentle strength and easy style were an inspiration. Every day, Nell taught her a new skill, from making Southern sweet pea salad to how to peel a tomato. Every night, Bree was writing notes and recipes. Nell pulled down a sack of flour from the pantry and started scooping it into a bowl while Bree poured a packet of yeast into a cup of warm water. The two women were developing a comfortable routine here in the kitchen.

"Is Maggie still visiting you at night?"

Bree grinned. "Every night since Sunday. She shows up around eleven and leaves before dawn. I don't know why she does it, but I have to admit I'm sleeping better with her there."

When she first heard the scratching at her door late Sunday night, she'd nearly jumped out of her skin. She was on the sofa reading her romance novel, and Sir Haverly had just entered lovely Rhiannon's bedchambers at night. The unexpected sound from her porch made her drop the book, and she gingerly opened the door. Maggie bounded inside and made herself comfortable on the sofa where Bree had been sitting.

Her first thought was that Cole had to be outside, but she saw no sign of her neighbor in the darkness. She tried to shoo Maggie back outside, but the dog wouldn't budge. She slept at the foot of Bree's bed that night, waking her with a cold nose against her face before the sun rose. Bree let her outside and watched the dog trot happily across the road to Cole's place. The whole episode was an otherworldly experience that she didn't expect to be repeated.

But the next night brought Maggie back to her door a little after ten-thirty. Once again the dog stayed close to Bree then slipped away before dawn. Surely Cole was aware of Maggie's nocturnal visits. If he was concerned about it, he would have let her know by now.

"I've never known Maggie to leave Cole alone at night." Nell gave her a grave look as she reached for a pitcher of tea. "Maybe she thinks you need her more than he does."

"I can't imagine why. She's been protecting Cole all these years, so why switch over to me now?"

"Maggie wasn't Cole's dog in Afghanistan. She was Scott's. He and Maggie served under Cole. Scott was killed in the roadside bombing that sent Cole home for good, and Maggie was injured. He and Ty tracked her down after he got home." Nell filled their glasses with tea. "She's not a trained therapy dog, but she seems to know when people need her."

Soon they had three braids of kneaded dough rising for the second time under a floured kitchen towel. Bree looked down at her scribbled notes, covered with buttery fingerprints, and smiled in contentment. The smell in the kitchen was intoxicating, and she reached for just one more pinch of raw dough. Nell slapped her hand with a laugh.

"Girl, you eat any more of that dough and you're going to have one epic tummy ache." Nell opened the door of the refrigerator and looked back over her shoulder. "You need to get out of the kitchen. Why don't you take a jug of sweet tea over to Cole? The boy must be roasting out there in the sun."

The steady chugging of his tractor was closer now. He'd been mowing the edges of the vast fields of young soybeans, which she knew because she'd been sneaking glances at him from the kitchen windows. She looked at Nell in suspicion, but Nell just laughed.

"It's not unusual for me to take him tea or lemonade on a hot day, or for him to stop by for some. You're a lot younger than me, and you can make the walk easier in this heat than I can. You don't have to dance with the man, just give him some tea." Nell filled a short, stout thermos with a handle on it. She tossed a few ice cubes in before closing it and handing it to Bree. There was really no reason for her to refuse, and she knew he needed to drink something if he was going to stay out there in the sun.

"Fine. But don't do any more with the breads until I get back." She took the thermos and grabbed her wide-brimmed hat from the table.

"Honey, this dough's got another hour to rise. Take your time."

Nell winked, and Bree just shook her head as she left. That woman was still trying to get her and Cole together, but it wasn't going to happen. He was way too complicated and she was not in the market. Bree walked across Nell's baked-dry yard and headed up Cole's gravel driveway when she saw the tractor turning back toward her. She stopped, shielding her eyes against the sun with her arm while she watched him. He didn't see her at first, too focused on looking back at the mower behind the big tractor. When he finally looked forward, he lifted his head with a start. He was still half a field away, but she felt his eyes burning into her. He was wearing jeans, which must have been sweltering hot, and a T-shirt, along with his ever-present ball cap. She raised the thermos, and he lifted his hand in a brief wave of acknowledgment as the mower clattered noisily behind him.

COLE ALMOST DROVE the tractor and Bush Hog straight into the ditch when he saw Bree standing there in his driveway. Only the sound of stones pinging off the whirring mower blades brought him back on course. She raised a thermos and he knew it contained Nell's homemade sweet tea, but that tea had nothing on the sweetness of Bree's sun-drenched body.

She was trouble. She was pushing and pulling him out of his safe, dark corner of life, and he wasn't ready. Her floppy yellow hat fluttered in the hot wind, and she raised an arm to block the sun from her eyes. Her denim shorts exposed long, tanned legs, and a bright pink top clung to her curves.

She was…no, it couldn't be…she was *bare-foot* in the grass along the drive. He saw her pink sandals abandoned a few feet away. The sight of her toes wiggling in the grass reminded him to shut down the mower before he pulled the tractor to a halt next to her. He was just thinking she couldn't possibly be any more enticing when he noticed a smudge of flour on her cheek. She was fresh out of the kitchen. Standing on his land. Barefoot. With a thermos full of cold tea. This had to be what heaven looked like.

He put the tractor in neutral and stared down at her. She raised one eyebrow and shook the thermos.

"Don't you want to come down and get some?" She had no idea how much he wanted to do just that. Her face flushed pink when she realized what she'd said, but he cut her off before she could clarify.

"Nope. I want you to come up here and bring me some." Both her brows shot high. "Some sweet tea, that is." He reached back and yanked his T-shirt over his head, using it to wipe the sweat from his face and arms, then he slid it back on, placing his cap back on his head. He held out his hand to her. She looked the tractor over, her gaze resting on the towering tires. "Come on. There are steps, and there's plenty of room. Unless you're too scared?"

He grinned as her eyes went from wide and doubtful to narrow and determined. Nell was right—the girl couldn't pass up a challenge. She shrugged in an attempt to appear nonchalant, and approached the tractor cautiously. When she remembered she was barefoot, she turned back, but he stopped her.

"Those slippery sandals will be more dangerous than your bare feet. Come on. I won't let anything bad happen to you. I promise." She raised her eyes to his, and he realized what he'd just said. His pulse jumped. It was true. He'd never let anything bad happen to her. She started to smile as she handed the thermos up to him. He set it on the platform where his feet were resting and leaned down to take her hand.

"Use the steps there. Don't step on that—it's hot. That's it. No, don't grab that handle; you'll start the mower. Just take my hand." She was obviously trying to avoid doing that, but she finally put her hand in his. She let out a squeal as he yanked her up sharply, and she landed with a gasp next to him on the tractor seat. It wasn't really meant for two, but it was wide enough that they could make it work. He was breaking so many common sense farming rules right now.

He reached down for the thermos and opened it, guzzling the refreshing tea and praying it would help settle his spinning thoughts. He could keep *her* safe, but who was going to protect him? When he finally lowered the container to take a breath, her eyes were sharp with humor.

"No, I didn't want any tea. Thanks."

"Oh, hell, I'm sorry. Here—there's plenty left." He tried to hand her the thermos.

She bumped him with her shoulder. "I was kidding. You must have been dying of thirst out here. How can you work in this heat?"

He frowned at her. "I'm used to it. But do you have sunscreen on? Are you okay?"

"I'm good, just a little amazed that I'm sitting here." She looked around. "So is this the 'big green tractor' Mark was singing about the other night?"

"Yeah. Hey, about Saturday… I'm sor—" She cut him off before he could once again apologize to her. Her fingers pressed lightly on his lips, stopping his breathing along with his voice.

"Don't. I've been scolding Nell about that all week."

He just nodded in response and drained the container of tea, sighing as the cold drink hit his stomach. His body needed the hydration. He was feeling more in control, as long as he didn't look down at the rounded cleavage right there at the top of her shirt.

"So, are you going to give me a ride or what?" Her cheeks flamed. "Damn it. Why does farming talk sound so dirty all the time?"

And that was when it happened. He heard an unfamiliar sound and realized it was coming from him. He was laughing. Out loud. He couldn't remember the last time *that* happened. But he couldn't stop. His head tipped back and he laughed some more. It felt…good. She just stared at him in shocked silence, until he finally had to ask, "What?"

"I've never heard you laugh. Or seen you really smile. I didn't think you were capable of either, to be honest. But they both look good on you." She tipped her head back, holding her floppy hat in place with one hand, her emerald eyes locked on his in that way that made him feel like he was under interrogation lights. When she did that, he was afraid he'd just give her anything she wanted. He leaned back and managed to squelch his smile.

"Yeah, well, it doesn't happen often, so don't get used to it. Now hang on. I'll take you 'round the field and drop you at Nell's." She looked for something to grab onto as he started to put the tractor into gear. He gestured for her to rest one hand on the fender and the other on the back of the seat behind him. She braced her feet on the platform, carefully avoiding where his boot-clad feet rested on the clutch and throttle. The tractor moved forward with a jolt and she laughed as she was thrown back against him. Her wide-brimmed yellow hat sailed off her head, and her hair whipped across her face. This may have been a really bad idea, he thought as he pushed the lever forward to engage the mower.

But her enthusiasm was infectious as they headed down the side of the field, bouncing gently as the mower roared behind them. He found himself biting back a smile as he watched her on her perch. They headed beyond the barns, and she turned to shout a question at him.

"How much of this is yours?" She gestured ahead to the endless rows of soybeans sloping downward away from them.

"All of it. All the way to the river and a few miles along the road."

"There's a river?"

He nodded and shouted back. "It's nothing big, but it has some nice fishin' and swimmin' holes." The tractor rocked to the side as they moved over the uneven ground, and she fell into him, grabbing at his waist with the hand that had been on the seat. She left it on his side, clutching his T-shirt to balance herself.

"You mean like Mayberry? With a rope swing for jumping in the water?"

He nodded then glanced down at her. "Want to go swimming?"

She shook her head quickly. "No! I don't like being in the water, especially when I can't see the bottom."

"You live in Malibu and you don't swim in the ocean?"

"Nope. I like looking at it, but I can't swim." She shrugged. "It's my one phobia, and yes, I know it's a doozie for a California girl."

"You don't know what you're missing. Jumping into the water on a hot night with a bonfire blazing on shore and your friends there...well, it's just about perfect." His thoughts wandered. Where had that memory come from? When he glanced down at her, she looked horrified.

"You jump in that murky water in the *dark*? Are you crazy? What if there are rocks, or snakes? Don't you have snakes down here?" She shuddered and somehow ended up even closer to him. He was pretty sure a groan escaped his lips, but she didn't seem to hear it. "So was this your father's land?"

"My great-granddaddy built the house I live in now." He glanced back at the big square farmhouse.

"You and Ty grew up here?"

"Yeah. He still owns a share of the farm. And I own part of the bar. We're partners in both." He didn't mention the trust fund created from his grandfather's tobacco crops.

"Where are your parents?"

"Right now? Probably on the golf course or at the beach. They went to Hilton Head for a vacation a few years ago and never really came back. They love it, but it's not for me. I don't get golf."

Her green eyes were laughing at him. "Yeah, I don't really see you as the country club type."

Look at him, making small talk on a tractor with a pretty girl from Hollywood. He changed the subject as he headed the tractor back toward the road.

"What are you and Nell baking?"

"How'd you know we were baking?"

"You've got flour on your cheek."

She raised her hand to brush it away just as the tractor hit another rut. Without her hand on the fender, her body snapped sideways and she started to slide. Before she could let out much more than a squeak, he wrapped his arm around her waist and pulled her back.

"Whoa, girl! Safety first. Besides, the flour looks good on you."

She raised her head and stared at him in surprise.

"Wait a minute. Are you saying something nice? Or are you just setting me up again?"

He disengaged the mower, making things quieter so they didn't have to shout at each other. He guided the tractor up Nell's driveway and brought it to a halt.

"Let me reword that. Seeing flour on your face is funny. I'm guessing getting dusted with flour is another first?"

She rolled her eyes dramatically. "Cole, I wrote a book on entertaining. I know how to cook, and I occasionally even use flour in my recipes. I'm not a total bimbo just because I live in California."

It was an unwelcome reminder that her presence here was temporary. He'd be a fool to allow anything to happen between them, no matter how tempting it was. He gave her a hard look.

"Yeah, well, the jury's out on that one. I haven't seen enough evidence to make me believe you aren't any more than that."

She lifted her chin and pulled herself free from his grip. "You really are an ass, Plowboy."

He choked back a laugh. She was one brassy broad. And he knew she was just getting started.

Before she could rip into him again, he gripped her forearm and swung her out from her seat, lowering her toward the ground as far as he could. When he released her, she only dropped a few more inches to land on her pretty bare feet. It happened so quickly that she just stared up at him as if she couldn't figure out how she ended up down there.

"Don't look so surprised, Hollywood. If you ask me, you need a little more man-handling." Her face flushed red again. It was so easy to get her hackles up. "Tell Miss Nell I'll be over tomorrow to help put up hay. I think Arlen and his dad are bringing by a few wagons of horse bales." He forced himself not to smile when she put her hands on her hips.

"The last thing I need is any of your man-handling, Cole Caldwell. *Or* any of your help. I'll take care of the hay. You just stay over at your own place and leave us alone." She turned and started to stomp away when he called out.

"Hey, Hollywood!" She spun to spit more words at him, but he flipped the empty thermos in the air before she could speak. She was surprised, but she caught it easily. She frowned and looked at her feet.

"My sandals…" She'd left them on the side of his driveway. "My hat…" It had fluttered to a resting spot somewhere in his bean field. He grinned.

"Sorry, Miss Mathews, but if I'm not welcome *here*, then you aren't welcome at my place. Your sandals and hat are mine. But don't worry—as soon as you call for my help tomorrow, I'll return them to you."

She glared at him, her eyes smoking with anger. "Those shoes will rot before that happens. Keep them, you jerk." And with that she was gone, stomping off in her naked feet toward Nell's house. Hopefully she'd miss that big fire ant nest. He rested his elbow on his knee and watched her in admiration. Whoever ended up taming that woman was going to have one heck of a prize.

## CHAPTER SEVEN

IT WAS A little after noon the next day when Cole left The Hide-Away and headed back to the farm. He and Ty met once a month to review the books from the bar and the Caldwell farm. They had the type of partnership that could only work between family members. The farm was primarily Cole's responsibility. The bar was Ty's. And they shared the profits from both. A monthly stipend from the family trust fund helped round out their budgets. They damned sure weren't rich, but they weren't poor, either.

Today they debated the pros and cons of installing an improved sound system and karaoke setup at the bar. It was a big investment, but they knew it could bring a lot more business. Cole wasn't convinced the slow summer season was the best time to make the move, but Ty argued they'd be able to set it up before the cooler weather moved in.

Cooler weather sounded pretty good right now, with the heat index already over one hundred degrees. The humidity was so intense that he did something unusual. He rolled up the windows and turned on the air-conditioning in his truck. Maggie seemed to appreciate it as she stretched out across the seat next to him with a sigh. Regardless of the temperature, he had to get home and change the wheel bearings on that old John Deere. A farmer's work didn't stop for weather.

Nell's place came into view, and he spit out a curse when he saw several trucks and wagons behind her house. He'd completely forgotten that Arlen and his dad were delivering hay to Nell's today. He pulled into her driveway, then swung the truck onto her front lawn to leave the way open for Arlen's vehicles. Grabbing a pair of leather gloves from behind the seat, he ushered Maggie out of the truck and started striding toward the barn to help.

"I wouldn't go any closer to that barn if I were you."

Nell was sitting on the shaded porch where she could watch the activity in the farmyard. But right now she was watching only him.

"Ty and I had a meeting and I completely forgot about the hay, Nell. I'll get up in the loft right now..."

"I don't think so."

"Excuse me?"

"Honey, you seem to have forgotten a conversation you had with Miss Mathews yesterday. Unless you have her shoes and hat in your possession, she made it clear that your assistance was not needed."

Cole's jaw dropped and he stared at Nell as if she was speaking a foreign language. She couldn't possibly be telling him that he was unwelcome because of something that redhead said.

"Nell, you can't be serious. Arlen and his dad can't put that hay up without some help. Hollywood's probably off doing her nails somewhere, so I'll just…"

"You'll just come up here with me and watch. Bree's doin' fine on her own."

Cole obeyed Nell without thinking, stepping up onto the porch. Maggie settled next to Shep in the shade. And then Nell's words connected. Bree was doing fine?

He looked at the barn where one of the wagons was parked. The hay elevator was chugging away, slowly moving bales of hay from the wagon up to the loft. Bree was standing in the doorway. It had to be like an oven up there in this heat. She was wearing denim shorts and a yellow tank top, with her spice-colored hair pulled up into a short ponytail. Even from this distance, he could see the sheen of sweat that covered every inch of exposed skin. Her cheeks were bright red. Her shirt was soaked through and clung to her body. At least she had the good sense to wear gloves.

Nell interrupted his perusal. "She told me this would be like a session of hot yoga, whatever that is. Apparently she has a personal trainer in California who's a professional kickboxer. No wonder she can work as hard as she does."

A large bale of hay reached the top of the elevator, and Bree leaned out and grabbed it, wrapping her fingers under the baling twine. She hesitated as if she was digging deep for strength, then yanked the bale off the elevator and turned away, moving out of his sight. A minute later she was back, breathing heavily and waiting for the next bale to come into reach. The routine was completed again and again as he stood there in awe of her.

It wasn't unusual to see Southern women helping out with farm work. But he never thought he'd see *Hollywood* doing this. Sure, she'd been weeding and cooking and cleaning a few stalls with Nell, and that was impressive. But putting up hay was actual *work*. In brutal conditions.

She came back to the doorway and placed her hand on the door frame to steady herself. She looked down at the wagon and said something to Arlen's father, George, a wiry little guy with the strength of ten professional wrestlers and a temper to match. George wouldn't care that she was a woman—he wouldn't hold back on the foul language and insults if she started complaining. The old guy looked up and pointed at Bree, shaking his head. He was probably ripping into her for something, and Cole stiffened. Maybe he should get out there and protect her.

And then Bree *laughed*. She threw her head back and laughed out loud, yelling down an insult at the old man. Did she just call George an "old fart"? George was laughing right along with her. She'd managed to win over George Howard, one of the toughest old birds in the county. They shared another laugh and then George sent more hay up into the loft. She took the first bale and spun out of sight again.

She was up there sweating bullets in a sauna because the work needed to be done and she was too proud to ask him for help. Damned if that didn't turn him the hell on. And that made him angry. He most definitely did *not* need to be feeling any attraction to Brianna Mathews.

Nell was speaking again. "She really is something, isn't she?"

He gave her a hard look. "Yeah, she's something, all right. Did you know she's trying to steal my dog?"

He cringed at the look she gave him. He sounded like a whiney ten-year-old, and he could see from Nell's eyes that she was thinking the same thing.

"So, you've noticed Maggie's nightly visits?"

"I caught her trotting over there Monday night. And last night, too. Bree must be feeding her or something."

"Honey, that dog's been going to the cottage every night since Sunday." He started to protest but she held up her hand to stop him. "It wasn't anything Bree encouraged. In fact, she tried to send her home, but the dog won't leave. She sleeps on the bed, and Bree said she feels safer with Maggie there. Safe enough to take long soaks in the bathtub at night."

Well. There was an image he didn't need in his head, and he had a feeling that was exactly why Nell had mentioned it. While he struggled to *not* think about Brianna Mathews naked in a tub, Nell kept talking, never taking her eyes from his face.

"Maggie's never done that before, even when that pretty little schoolteacher rented the cottage this past winter. She must figure Bree needs her there."

He just nodded without answering.

"I know it's killing you not to help put up the hay," Nell said. Little did she know that wasn't the only thing killing him right now. "Take some cold water out there with you. Remember that

Arlen and George know her as Anna. And don't expect her to be happy to see you."

"Yeah, yeah, yeah. And that would be different how?" He opened the cooler that was sitting next to Nell's chair and pulled out an armful of cold water bottles.

He was going to wait until Bree turned away with a bale of hay before heading across the lawn, but she didn't come back to the door. Instead, Arlen was there taking bales off the elevator and tossing them back into the loft. Cole sighed in relief as he tossed a bottle to George on the hay wagon. Bree must have come to her senses and decided to leave the hot loft, which meant Arlen would need an extra set of hands up there. He didn't pass her on his way inside the barn, but maybe she'd gone out back to cool off under the hose.

But that, of course, would have been the smart thing to do, which meant that Brianna Mathews hadn't done it. Instead, she was stacking the heavy bales deep inside the loft. When he got up there, the hay was four bales high, and she was standing on that level. Arlen threw a bale up to Bree, and she moved it into place on the sixth row, too focused to notice his arrival. It was even hotter up here than he'd imagined, and the heat combined with the hay dust made it difficult to breathe.

Or maybe it was the sight of Bree, drenched in sweat yet moving smoothly and powerfully as she stacked hay, that made it so tough for him to catch a breath. Arlen saw him there and acknowledged his arrival with a nod, and Cole finally snapped out of his stupor.

He threw a bottle of water to Arlen, who took it with a grin and raised it in a mock toast. Arlen turned to the door and made a slicing motion across his neck, telling his father to shut down the elevator for a break. Bree noticed the sudden silence and turned, finally seeing him standing there. He wasn't surprised when her hands landed on her hips.

"I told you yesterday we don't need your help, so beat it, Plowboy."

Ah. She was ticked off. It was his favorite flavor of Bree. He bit back a smile as she stood there glaring down at him. He tossed a water bottle up to her, and she was smart enough not to refuse it. While she was drinking, she couldn't be yapping at him. He turned to Arlen.

"Why don't you help your dad down on the wagon? I'll stay up here."

"Wait…" Bree started to object. But Arlen didn't waste any time leaving the loft. He crab-walked down the elevator to join his father, leaving Cole and Bree up there alone. He

looked at her and waited, knowing she wasn't
done with him.

"You're such a pain in my…" She stopped and
took breath. "I can handle the loft by myself.
Go home."

"Look, forget about yesterday, okay? It's a hot
freakin' day and the job's gotta get done, so let's
just get to it."

She finished drinking her water, and he
thought she was going to ignore him. Then the
hay elevator hummed back to life, and so did
she. Her eyes fixed on him and she wiped a riv-
ulet of sweat from the side of her face.

"Fine. Just stay out of my way and don't talk."

He shrugged and turned to grab the hay bale
that tumbled off the elevator. Talking always led
to trouble with Bree anyway, so he had no problem granting her wish.

BREE GLARED AT the back of Cole's head. He was
such a jerk. Sure, they'd shared a lighter moment
yesterday on his tractor, but, as with all their
conversations, it soon descended into him saying something infuriating. He actually seemed
to enjoy it when she stomped away from him in
a rage. It was as if baiting her was some kind of
game to him. Even now she could tell from his
smirk and the way he watched her out of the corner of his eye that he was amused by her anger.

*Jackass.*

They settled into a tense but efficient routine. Cole took the bales off the elevator, carried them across the loft and threw them up to where she was standing, four rows above the floor. He never said a word as he tossed the bales up to her level with the ease of someone who'd done farm work all his life.

She was walking the bales up another level and stacking them at shoulder height. The closer she came to the metal roof of the barn, the hotter it got. Her body shifted into autopilot, and she kept pushing forward. The sooner this was over, the sooner she could leave Cole Caldwell's annoying presence and step into a nice, cool shower. She was pushing a particularly large bale over her head when her arms started to tremble with exhaustion. She stepped back so she could use her whole body to shove the stubborn bale into place.

The bale she stepped on wasn't fully anchored. As it tilted under her weight, the one she was lifting settled back against her arms, and she came to the sickening realization that she wasn't going to be able to fight gravity for both herself and that damned bale.

The bale under her foot tipped farther, the one in her hands tumbled free and she was falling. But not for long. Arms like iron gripped her and scooped her up before she could cry out. Cole had leaped up two levels and caught her in mid-air. He twisted and threw himself back against the stacked bales behind him and they both came to a sudden stop. Her body slammed against his chest, and her head just happened to come to rest on his shoulder.

For a few heartbeats, neither of them spoke or moved. The only sound was the chug-chug of the hay elevator. She raised her head and met his eyes, which were just above her own. Instead of the usual cold gray, his were dark and intense. Without moving his head, he slowly lowered her legs until she was standing, but still trapped tightly in the circle of his arms. The suffocating heat of the loft now felt cool against her skin compared to the fire burning between them. Every nerve ending was on high alert.

His mouth was right there. Right. There. She could feel his breath moving across her cheeks, and she closed her eyes at the delicious sensation of it. She opened them again when she heard a low moan from deep in his throat. Whatever was happening, Cole was feeling it, too. He took a breath and blinked, his eyes flicking away from hers briefly. His hold loosened ever so slightly, and she felt a sharp pang of disappointment.

She could stop him. She could reach up and kiss him and stop him from letting her go. His lips were still just inches away. He shook his head slowly, as if he'd read her mind. His voice was raspy and labored when he broke the feverish silence.

"You and me are a bad idea, Hollywood."

She nodded and whispered the words back at him.

"Bad idea."

He released her and stepped back, putting more space between them. His voice was stronger this time.

"A very bad idea."

She suspected he was trying as hard as she was to convince himself of the truth of those words. His hand lifted toward her face but he stopped before he touched her. It didn't matter. She felt the zip of energy between his fingertips and her skin. Her lips parted as she closed her eyes and sighed. This bad idea was starting to feel really good.

Cole cursed under his breath and jumped down to the loft floor as if she'd hit him with a taser, leaving her standing alone. Their eyes were still locked tightly on each other, but the forced distance helped clear her head. Bales of hay tumbled off the elevator behind him and created a haphazard pile at the doorway. Someone was calling Cole's name. It was Arlen, asking what the hell was going on up there.

The corner of Cole's mouth slowly slid into a crooked grin. There was a light in his eyes she'd never seen there before. She returned the grin without really knowing why. They were each acknowledging *something*, while avoiding defining exactly what that something was. She only knew she wanted to experience it again, and she suspected he did, too, despite the risks involved.

"SO LET ME get this straight. You couldn't sleep last night because you *didn't* kiss the hot farmer from across the road?"

Bree leaned her head back against the rocker on the cottage porch and sighed. When Amanda said it that way, it did seem silly. But the reality was, even Maggie's presence couldn't help her sleep last night. Every time she closed her eyes she felt Cole's arms around her in the heavy heat of the loft; saw his mouth above hers, knowing he wanted to kiss her. She found herself smiling.

"I don't think I ever said he was hot."

Her cousin's laughter rang through the phone.

"Oh, honey, you don't have to. I can hear it in your voice. He is one hot hunk of farmer, and you want to jump his bones. Why else would you text me this early and ask if I was available to talk?"

"I didn't wake you, did I?"

"Hardly. Baby Madeleine starts kicking like

a fiend every time I lie down. If Blake tells me one more time that she's just dancing, I'm going to throttle him. *He* can carry the next baby."

Bree looked out over the fields as the sun rose above the horizon in a blaze of red. "So is your husband still being overprotective of his baby mama?"

"Yes, but stop trying to change the subject. I want to hear about the hot farmer. Spill it, cuz."

She started rocking and stared at the big white farmhouse across the road. "There's nothing to hear. He's consistently kind to Nell, but insults *me* every chance he gets. He obviously thinks I'm some kind of Hollywood prima donna who isn't worth his time..."

"He didn't insult you yesterday. He almost kissed you, and you *wanted* him to. When's the last time that happened? So why not just kiss the man?"

Why, indeed? She'd wanted Cole's kiss more than anything she'd wanted in a very long time. Their two bodies had been perfect together, and the energy they'd generated was nearly combustible. She remembered the conflicted look on his face when he stepped back from her. The words he said. *Bad idea.* Was he right?

"Amanda, I'm not staying here forever. Cole and I have nothing in common other than a few seconds of weird chemistry. Besides, he has issues." In the bar, she'd seen the darkness and pain in his eyes. The man carried a boatload of baggage.

Her cousin just laughed. "Hell, that makes you a perfect couple, since you have issues, too."

"Ouch. Has anyone told you that pregnancy has made you mean?"

"More than once, actually." Bree could picture her petite cousin tossing her blond hair over her shoulder. "But I prefer to call it 'refreshing honesty.' Look, you spent years running after some sort of security in money and fame that didn't exist. You clawed after that beauty crown, then you clawed after that superstar husband. During the divorce, you clawed after that beachfront mansion you love so much, even though Damian begged you to let him have it. You're clinging to a life that wouldn't have saved your mother from dying, and certainly won't bring her back. Cancer killed your mom, and money had nothing to do with it."

Bree stopped rocking. For a few seconds she stopped breathing.

"Uh-oh, I did it again, didn't I? Went too far? It's the hormones, I swear…"

"No," Bree said. "Not too far. A little blunt, but nothing you've said is untrue. Instead of security, LA only brought me false friendships and someone who wants to kill me."

"Do you have *any* real friends there?"

She thought about it. There were women she'd had fun socializing with, that she'd once considered friends. But when her marriage imploded, so did those so-called friendships. People didn't hesitate to ask her to *plan* their upscale events, but that made her the hired help. She was no longer a peer and rarely on a guest list.

"Bree?"

"Sorry. It's just a little shocking to me that I can't answer that question."

"But you *are* making friends in North Carolina, aren't you? Nell and Tammy and the hot farmer?"

She laughed. "Yes, I suppose I am. And I think they're the types of friendships that might just last, although I don't think I'd group the hot farmer in that circle." She really needed to stop thinking of Cole as the hot farmer. It wasn't helping. "But yes, I like the people here, and I think they like me, too."

"Then what are you afraid of? If your heart tells you to kiss the hot farmer, then do it. Who knows what might happen? After all, look at me. One unexpected kiss at the kitchen sink, and here I am, knocked up and married with an adopted son and..." Bree heard some muffled conversation in the background. "And here comes my charming husband now. Yes,

I'm warm enough out here on the balcony. No, I don't need a blanket… Or a pillow… Or tea… I'm fine, Blake. Go get ready for your meeting and relax, for the love of God. The doctor said yesterday the baby's not coming for another ten days or so… I'm talking to Bree… Hang on. My hubby wants to say hi…"

Blake's deep voice came across the phone. "How are you, Bree? Do you need anything? Is everything okay down there?"

Blake Randall was a man who wanted to do everything for the people he cared about, and she considered herself fortunate that he cared about her.

"Everything's fine, Blake. Really."

"I'm sure you're anxious to get back to your real life."

She stood and walked to the porch railing, taking a deep breath and enjoying the perfume of summer blossoms. What exactly *was* her real life?

"Um…yeah, I guess."

"Andrew called you last night, right? Your agent is going to leak the phony story?"

Andrew and Caroline McCormack had called her after dinner, laying out their plan to flush out the stalker. Her vanishing act hadn't been enough to get him to make a mistake yet, and the new security cameras around her Malibu beach house hadn't captured anyone sneaking around. It was as if he knew she wasn't there. So they'd hatched a plan to bring him out in the open.

"Yes, she'll leak it, but with a little more enthusiasm than I'd like. She's thinking this is some kind of huge publicity boost for me, which is totally not the point." When Sheila Silverstein heard about the plan to leak a story to the media about Bree needing a "rest" at an undisclosed rehab center in Utah, she'd leaped at it. Instead of being concerned that people would get the wrong idea and think Bree had a substance abuse problem, Sheila was gleeful that the media would jump to exactly that conclusion. Apparently everyone loved a comeback story, and she was convinced a stint in make-believe rehab was just what Bree needed to capture the limelight again.

"Oh, darling," Sheila had told her last night, "it's perfect! You know, that dancing show has been calling—it would work out beautifully for you to go there straight out of rehab…"

"Sheila, I'm not *really* going to rehab, remember? This story is a decoy."

"Just let me take care of everything. I know just who to leak it to. Everyone will assume you're at the Seventh Heaven center. The story will be off and running!"

"Don't get carried away, Sheila. Just leak a

little whisper that I might be recovering from exhaustion somewhere in Utah then sit back and do nothing. Don't do any interviews. And do *not* book me on anything until this is over and we have a chance to talk." The idea of going on television again sent a chill down her spine.

"Bree? Are you there?" Blake's voice brought her back to the present.

"Sorry, Blake. I haven't had my coffee yet this morning, so I'm a little out of it. Thanks again for everything."

"Don't worry about it. You're family. Here's Amanda."

"Hey, girl. So, about this hot farmer…"

"Stop calling him that!"

"Look, you're restless and anxious and you need a diversion. Why not have a little fling with the guy next door?"

Somehow she couldn't imagine having something as trivial as a fling with Cole Caldwell. She could see it going deeper, and darker, very quickly. She wasn't sure she was ready for whatever secrets Cole was hiding in the shadowed corners of his life. She changed the subject to Amanda's adopted son, Zach, and his excitement over the new baby. They ended the call without any more references to hot farmers.

But that didn't stop her from thinking about one.

# CHAPTER EIGHT

EIGHT STEAMING BLUEBERRY pies covered Nell's kitchen counter later that day. Bree put the last of the mixing bowls in the rack to dry, and the kitchen was neat as a pin after being Blueberry Pie Central for three hours. Nell was confident the pies would sell out quickly at the produce stand.

"But first," she said with a sly smile, "let's walk two of these over to Cole's place. He has company today, and I know they love my pie."

Bree was annoyed at the thought of visiting Cole, suspecting Nell was matchmaking again, but she forgot about that when she realized what Nell had said.

"Company?"

Nell nodded. "I saw the Jeep over there this morning. Some of the gang from Fort Bragg are here."

"Men he served with?"

"And women sometimes, but usually it's the three amigos—Juan, Jerome and Chris. He served with Chris on his second deployment.

The others he met in the hospital and in therapy groups."

"Therapy? For PTSD?" She was oddly relieved to think that he was getting professional help for those shadows that lingered even behind his rare smiles.

"Cole got impatient with the sessions and quit. Told me that working on the land heals him, but I'm not so sure. Having the boys visit him helps, though. It's an unofficial support group, and they take care of each other."

Bree had an overwhelming desire to meet the men Cole thought of as his friends, hoping they'd offer some clues to the pain she saw deep in his eyes. She picked up a pie and turned, but Nell stopped her.

"Before we go over there, you should know that these boys have more than just PTSD. Some of them have been hurt bad, lost limbs, been burned. You need to be prepared…"

"Nell, when I was Miss California, I visited burn units and VA hospitals all the time. I'm not saying it's easy for me, but I won't do anything embarrassing, I promise."

"Okay then, let's go."

They walked out into the blazing heat of the day. Clouds scuttled along the horizon, and Bree wondered if they might see some cooling rain soon. Nell followed her gaze and shook her head.

"When this heat breaks, we're going to have some dandy storms. And just when that old cow is getting ready to calve." Every afternoon she and Nell would drive up into the cattle pasture in Nell's small truck to check on Cole's beef cows and their calves. A surly old cow named Trixie was huge with calf, and Nell thought she'd give birth in the next few days.

"Is the rain dangerous for the birth?"

"Not really. Animals have been born out in the elements since the beginning of time. It's just inconvenient. Oh, look, the boys are on the porch."

Bree glanced up and saw three men sitting in the shade. They were watching with interest as she and Nell walked up the driveway. Cole wasn't with them. She pushed her hair behind her ear and smoothed her white cotton blouse. When they approached the porch, the guy with shoulder-length blond hair let out a low whistle.

"Miss Nell, you always bring us the best treats, but this takes the cake. You brought us an angel! An honest-to-goodness angel."

The black man sitting at his side nodded. "That is one fine woman. Welcome to Casa Del Caldwell, Miss…?"

"This is Anna, boys," Nell replied. Bree's stride faltered. She kept forgetting about her alias. "And you all behave yourselves. She's my guest and a special friend of Cole's, and I expect you to treat her as such, you hear me?"

"Damn, Nell, she belongs to Cole?" The black man shook his head dramatically. "That boy's so lucky he could fall into a pile of manure and still come out smelling like a rose!"

All three men stood when she and Nell reached the top step of the porch. The tall blond took the pie from Bree's hands and opened the door for Nell to enter the house in front of him. He winked at Bree.

"Honey, you sit right here with the boys and don't you go anywhere. I'll be right back."

The man standing farthest away, who'd been silent so far, stepped forward. He was shorter than the others, but stocky and built like a tank. He extended his right hand to Bree.

Or what remained of his right hand. It was a scarred stump with only two misshapen fingers and a stub of a thumb. Burgundy scars twisted up his arm and covered half of his face. One ear was missing completely, and one eye was clearly blind, with the pupil a hazy white circle. His nose had been reconstructed and was serviceable, but flattened. His top lip wasn't much more than a thin red line of scar tissue on the right side, but it was curled into a smile.

"Welcome, Miss Anna. My name's Juan Ramirez." His good eye was focused on her face, and she knew he was waiting to see how she would react. She sent up a silent prayer of thanks for the time she'd spent in those burn wards. She met his gaze with a smile, took his hand gently and shook it.

"Nice to meet you, Juan."

"My friends just call me Ramirez, ma'am."

"Okay, then. Ramirez it is." Even beneath the thickened scars on his face, she could see him blushing.

She turned to the broad-shouldered black man at her side and extended her hand. She didn't see any visible wounds until she felt her fingers grasping something solid. She was gripping a prosthetic hand. Beneath his long cargo shorts, his left foot was replaced with a high-tech metal prosthetic. Now it was her turn to blush.

"Sorry—would you rather we shook left hands instead?"

He shook his head, looking both amused and kind-hearted. "No, ma'am. As long as you don't mind?"

"Not at all." She swallowed and made sure to meet his eyes with a calm smile.

"My name's Jerome Willis, ma'am."

"It's wonderful to meet you, Jerome."

The tall blond returned from inside the house with Nell. Four longneck beer bottles dangled from the fingers of his left hand, and he extended his right. His sparkling blue eyes matched the sky perfectly, and his smile hinted strongly of mischief.

"Christopher Baldwin, ma'am. Glad to see Cole's taste in women is as good as his taste in friends."

Jerome and Ramirez laughed at that, rolling their eyes. Chris was clearly the class clown. He handed off the beers to his friends. She couldn't see any visible wounds, and he made her blush bright red when he read her mind and started patting his hands up and down his body.

"No missing appendages. My perfect body is perfectly intact, except for a metal plate in my skull and the scrambled brain inside of it. But don't you worry, darlin', I'm not gonna go postal on you today."

"Chris…" Nell scolded.

He laughed and held his hands up. "I'm kidding! The meds are doing their job and it's all good, Nell."

Bree turned to follow Nell down the porch steps, but Nell shook her head.

"Stay here with the boys, honey. Our work's done for the day, and you deserve a little fun."

"I think that's a great idea. Right, boys?" Chris winked. "Cole's girlfriend should definitely stay and have fun with us." There was no threat in his loaded words.

Nell laughed and waved goodbye as she headed off down the long driveway.

"Whoa!" Bree objected. "I am *not* Cole's girlfriend! We hardly know each other…"

"You mean you and me might have a chance?" Ramirez asked the question with a twinkle in his eye.

She returned his grin. "Well, you can try, Handsome, but I get awfully jealous and I'm sure there are girls all over you when you go out on the town."

He nodded as the other men laughed. "I've got moves, baby. I've got moves."

"I figured as much. I'd hate to go to jail for beating all those other women away from you. But I'm honestly not in the market, boys. Sorry."

Jerome handed her a beer. She wasn't much of a beer drinker, especially from the bottle. But she took a deep draught and raised the bottle in a silent toast, which they answered with looks of admiration. She glanced around the yard.

"Where's your host?"

Chris shrugged. "He's working, of course. He said something about moving a tree that fell on the edge of one of his fields. He said he didn't need our help, so we let him go."

They settled into easy conversation, punctuated with Chris's irreverent jokes at everyone's expense, including his own. When she didn't balk at his bawdier stories, and shared a few of her own, the three men relaxed and treated her as one of the guys. She knew it was partially because they still thought she might be Cole's girlfriend, but they also seemed to appreciate her humor and her acceptance of their visible and invisible scars.

As the conversation wore on, more bottles of beer made their way onto the porch. In a tangent she suspected was fairly common, the men started boasting of their battle scars and teasing each other, laughing and cursing with enthusiasm. Bree knew it was their way of trying to deal with their injuries.

"Ramirez, you lost an *ear*, man. I lost my leg! My leg!"

Jerome reached down and unfastened a buckle, and suddenly his prosthetic leg was in his hand. He shook it to emphasize its metal presence. Curious, Bree reached out, and he gave it to her nonchalantly. "I can't even compare myself to that idiot blade runner anymore, man, because he went crazy and killed his woman! And crazy is Chris's thing, not mine!"

"Damn straight on that, bro." Chris looked indignant. "Don't you go stealing my crazy gig!"

Ramirez gave them a disgusted wave of his hand. "Shut up, the both of you. I'm *scarred*, you idiots. Chris, you look like a freakin' Adonis, and Jerome, you can cover up the fake limbs with long pants and long sleeves. What am I supposed to do? Wear a blanket over my head?"

Bree emptied the beer she was holding and leaned back against the porch post, swinging her legs as she sat on the railing. The drink was refreshing, and she was having a shockingly good time. She tried to imagine her costars from *Hot Hollywood Housewives* sitting on a steamy Southern porch sharing cold beer with these earthy, damaged men, and she knew it never would have happened.

"So tell us, angel," Chris said with a wink. "What scars are *you* hiding?"

She blinked and sat up straighter. This was a testosterone-fueled contest for laughs, and they respected her enough to let her join in. She wasn't going to bring them down by talking about her stalker, or offend them by bemoaning her divorce from a wealthy superstar. So, with a completely innocent face, she braced Jerome's fake leg upside down on her thigh, folded her hands over the foot, and rested her chin there.

"Boys, I have you *all* beat in the suffering department. After all, I'm the one who has to be Cole's girlfriend!"

The last two words were fairly shouted, and the men howled in laughter. It was a tall tale, but since it was what they believed, the fact that she could joke about it left them all in hysterics. Chris was on his feet, applauding. Ramirez stood and bowed in defeat before sitting again. Jerome was wiping tears from his eyes.

Bree laughed, trying to ignore the rush of energy she felt when she said those words. Before she could consider what that meant, she heard a familiar voice.

"Girlfriend, huh? That's news to me, Hollywood."

She jumped to her feet and turned to face Cole as he pushed off the corner of the porch where he'd been leaning for who knows how long. He was staring hard at her, his lips thin and tight. A muscle in his cheek ticked dangerously. It was the same expression he wore in The Hide-Away a week ago.

"I wasn't seriously saying I was…" She couldn't bring herself to say the word *girlfriend* out loud again.

Chris moved closer to Bree, which didn't appear to help Cole's mood any.

"Hey, man, we thought you'd deserted us. Anna's been playing hostess in your absence."

Cole slowly turned his attention to Chris then nodded at Jerome and Ramirez where they sat. His foul mood quickly dampened everyone's smiles. He strode forward and grabbed Bree's forearm, propelling her away from his friends.

She barely had time to toss Jerome's prosthetic back to him.

"I need to talk to my new *girlfriend.*" He snarled the words as he yanked the screen door open.

"Easy, Cole." Chris rested his hand on Cole's shoulder. "We didn't make any moves on your girl, and she's cool by us."

Jerome and Ramirez nodded in agreement.

"Very cool."

"The coolest."

Cole just shrugged. "Make all the moves you want, boys. She's not *my* girl."

Bree found herself being pushed into Cole's house. The furnishings were sparse and the walls were plain. Just like the outside, the interior looked lived-in, but without signs of actual life. Her fleeting observation was forgotten when he spun her around to face him.

"What the hell do you think you were doing out there?"

She yanked her arm free and stood tall, looking him right in the eye. She knew the guy had issues, but she was not about to let him push her around every time they met. "Nell and I brought over some pies for you and your friends. They asked me to stay, so I did. I joined them in drinking a beer or two, and we had some laughs. Since you're supposed to actually *like* these guys, I don't understand what you're so angry about."

*"Really?"* He ran his fingers through his hair in agitation. "I hear you say you're my girlfriend, and see you using Jerome's prosthetic as a chin rest, and you think that's okay? These guys deserve to be taken seriously, damn it. They're not some freak show for your amusement."

She threw her hands in the air.

"You see, that's the problem with eavesdropping—you don't get the whole story. I was making a *joke*, Cole. Nell told them I was your friend, and they assumed the rest." She shook her head in disgust. "Honestly, do you really think I'd decide we're in a relationship just because you had me in your arms for a nanosecond yesterday and didn't do anything about it?"

His mouth opened, but she didn't give him a chance to interrupt.

"As far as taking your friends seriously, I've been around injured vets before. I let them take the lead in the conversation. I wasn't laughing *at* them, you idiot, I was laughing *with* them."

He looked confused and then his expression started to soften, which just made her more angry. That he was now having second thoughts didn't change the fact that he always jumped to the worst conclusions where she was concerned.

"Just how shallow and stupid do you think I

am?" She stepped forward, and he moved back as if pushed by the waves of anger rolling off her. "Do you think I asked Jerome to hand me his leg because I was tired and thought it looked like a comfortable headrest? Do you think I would do anything to make Ramirez self-conscious about his injuries?" She fought back the tears of indignation gathering in her eyes. "You know what? Don't bother answering that. You don't know me at all. And you never will." She brushed past him and he let her go without saying a word.

She paused just a moment at the door to brush the dampness from her cheeks before she faced the three men on the porch. They leaped to their feet when she stepped outside. She gave them her best pageant smile, but her face flushed as she realized they probably heard every word of the argument through the screen door.

Chris spoke first. "He's been in a mood all day. Don't let his snarl get to you. His bark is a lot worse than his bite."

She stared back at the door in silence then nodded.

"Right. I should go. It was fun, boys. You take care of yourselves, okay?"

She was surprised when Ramirez pulled her into a hug. "Hang in there, Anna. Cole's a hell of a good guy."

Jerome was next, his prosthetic firmly back

in place. "Now I know why's he's been so edgy. He hasn't had a lady friend in way too long. He doesn't know what to do with his feelings sometimes. We all have that problem when it comes to real emotions. They can be terrifying. That's why we crack jokes."

Chris wrapped his arms around her and held her close. It wasn't a romantic hug. It was more like friendly reassurance. His voice broke just a little when he spoke. "I'm really glad he's fallen for someone…"

She started to object, but he talked over her.

"Don't deny it. I can see it in his eyes. Even if he hasn't told you yet, even if he doesn't know it himself, he cares about you. He was jealous, Anna. You were yukking it up with his crazy friends, and he didn't like it one bit." Over his shoulder, Bree could see Jerome and Ramirez nodding in agreement. "We'll all catch hell for our language and stuff in front of his lady, but we can take it. Just don't give up on him. He's the best of us."

Their display of affection and concern, along with their fierce loyalty to their friend, rendered her speechless. Her composure slipped for a moment, then she took a breath and brightened her smile again. She didn't have the heart to tell them they were wrong. Wrong about Cole's feelings. Wrong about him being jealous over anything to do with her. She gave them each a peck on the cheek and turned away.

As she walked down the driveway with her back to them, her tears flowed freely. She wouldn't even consider getting involved with someone who so clearly had no respect for her. He was constantly pushing her away with his anger and insults. Did he do it as some twisted form of self-defense? Maybe.

But that didn't make it hurt any less.

"You are the stupidest guy I've ever met. You know that, right?"

Chris leaned back in his chair and propped his feet on the porch railing. He didn't look at Cole when he spoke, but there was no doubt who he was talking to, since Ramirez and Jerome were nodding along in agreement. The guys had carefully avoided bringing Bree up since her hasty exit. They'd shared a meal of grilled burgers and corn on the cob, talking about sports and politics. Now they were back on the porch, watching as evening settled across the countryside. Having had their fill of beer, they'd moved on to some fine Southern whiskey. As usual, his guests would be spending the night on the farm. There was always room in his home for these special friends. The same friends who were now staring at him in disappointment.

"Shut up, Chris. You know nothing about her." He drained his glass and reached for the bottle to refill it. Bree's words were still rattling around his head, along with the hurt he'd seen in her eyes. It had just been such a shock to watch her being all buddy-buddy with the guys on the porch, laughing and calling herself his girlfriend. Those words struck him straight in the heart, and he'd panicked.

"I'm pretty sure that's what she accused *you* of, man," Chris said. "Not knowing her. Why would you not want to know everything about a woman like Anna?"

He gave a short laugh and drained his glass. "You think you know so much, Chris. That's not even her real name. She's just playacting out here as Daisy Duke. She's a Hollywood diva, and she'll be heading back to Malibu any day now to drape herself in diamonds and hang out with her ritzy friends."

He felt a stab of regret for spilling her secrets, but then again, he'd trust these men with his own life, much less Bree's. So he told them the story of her arrival, and her claims of being chased by a stalker. And then, because they were fellow soldiers, he told them about his weird experience at the bar a week ago, when he went to get her and had some kind of flashback, dragging her forcefully out of The Hide-Away.

The men silently sipped their drinks as he talked about how hard she'd been working at Nell's place, and how she even helped put up hay yesterday. But he didn't tell them about holding her in his arms in the suffocating heat of the loft. He didn't tell them about staring down into her emerald eyes and feeling himself losing control. He didn't tell them how much he'd wanted to kiss her. Or how perfect she felt pressed up against him, completely vulnerable and oh, so tempting. How he'd somehow managed to step away from her. Or how she'd haunted his sleep last night, leaving him agitated and exhausted today.

The porch was oddly silent. He and his friends had been through a lot together, had confessed many sins and shared combat experiences that would make a civilian toss their cookies in revulsion. But right now they looked as if they *pitied* him, and that was something he'd never seen in their eyes before.

"What?" He barked the word at them, trying to deflect the awkward moment.

Jerome spoke first. "Oh, man, you're in deep, and you don't even know it yet. I had that same expression when Pamela steamrolled into my life. I hated her long before I ever realized I loved her."

Pamela had been Jerome's rehab nurse, and

from day one she'd bullied and badgered him to snap out of his depression and get to work regaining his mobility. He'd complained bitterly at her and about her nonstop, right up until the day he knelt down on his good leg and asked her to marry him.

Ramirez nodded. "You're right, Jerome. He's got that same tortured expression you wore for weeks on end."

"Shut up." Cole ground the words out. They were being ridiculous. Sure, he was physically attracted to Bree, and he enjoyed their verbal sparring, but to think there might be something *real* there, when he wasn't even sure *she* was real? Crazy. He stared out into the gathering darkness.

Chris's voice was low and quiet. "Didn't some actress just get murdered by a stalker? What was her name?"

"Nikki Fitzgerald," Ramirez said. "It was all over the news. This sicko had been sending her love letters and flowers and junk like that; then he broke into her house and raped her before killing her and then himself. Anna...or Bree... is smart to lay low if she's got a creep like *that* chasing her. They're no joke."

Jerome nodded. "I've got a buddy who works security in LA. He told me stalkers are their biggest nightmare, because they're so persistent and completely unpredictable."

Cole was silent. So that was the story with Nikki Fitzgerald. That was what Bree was trying to tell him when he was skeptical about her. God *damn* it. His hand gripped the glass of whiskey so tightly he was surprised it didn't shatter. Some freak was out there hunting for Bree. And he'd accused her of lying about it to get attention. He was such an idiot.

"You keep telling us what a diva she is," Chris said, "but I sure didn't see it. She's the real deal, Cole. Why are you so determined to shove her into that Hollywood box you've put her into? There's more to her than that. You're just afraid to lift the lid."

Chris was right about one thing. Brianna Mathews scared the hell out of him. Chris laid his hand on Cole's shoulder.

"She said you didn't know her, but it's obvious even to me she wants you to. Maybe it's time you tried."

He didn't answer. The four men sat there in the dark, drinking whiskey and sharing an occasional quiet comment for another hour before Cole stood abruptly, sending his chair skittering backward.

"You know where your rooms are, boys." He

started down the steps, ignoring the laughter behind him. It wasn't the cottage he went to, even though he could see the living room light glowing softly. He knew Maggie was there with Bree. Instead he knocked on Nell's door. She didn't seem surprised to see him there at ten o'clock at night, weaving just a bit from his intake of alcohol. His feet shuffled for a minute, then he finally forced the words out.

"I want to know more about Bree."

She nodded and stepped back. "Come on in. I'll make you some coffee."

An hour later they were sitting at the kitchen table, staring into empty cups. His mind was swirling with all of the things Nell told him. Some had made him laugh, like her stories about Bree in the kitchen, trying to learn how to make a pecan braid. Some things weren't funny at all, like the way she'd blamed her mother's death on her father's blue-collar income. But they painted a far more complete picture of Bree than he'd been willing to see before.

He'd been a jackass with her unnecessarily. It wasn't her fault that he was so messed up and afraid of letting anyone get close. He stood slowly and gave Nell a grim look.

"I owe her an apology, don't I?"

She shrugged. "You'd know that better than I."

He nodded and turned away. He was all the way to the door when Nell spoke.

"You know, Cole, that woman is the one for you."

"What?"

He turned to face her, and Nell's eyes bored into him.

"She's the one, Cole. She's *your* one."

"Did you drink some of Randy Wardon's moonshine when I wasn't looking?" His hands gestured wildly to match the suddenly wild pounding of his heart. "Because that stuff can cause hallucinations, which is clearly what's happening right now. You need to stop this matchmaking game, Nell, because Hollywood and I are not a couple and never will be."

She just chuckled, shaking her head.

"Oh, I know you, boy. You're going to deny it and fight it and fight her and do your best to blow it all up. But you mark my words, Colton Caldwell. She's your one. When it's all said and done, she's the one who can save you. If you let her."

He stared at her, stupefied. "I value our friendship more than you'll ever know. But you couldn't be more wrong about this, and if you keep pushing the subject, you and I are going to have words."

"Fine. I won't mention it again." Her voice was

serious, but her eyes were sparkling with amusement. "But that won't make it any less true."

Something shuddered way down deep inside his chest. His mouth opened, but no words came out. What could he say to make Nell understand that no one could save him, especially not that stubborn redhead in the cottage next door? He turned away, slamming the door behind him.

# CHAPTER NINE

BREE WAS STILL angry the next morning. She'd
barely slept. She'd kicked off her covers and
pulled them back up then kicked them off again.
Maggie finally gave up and moved to the floor
with a huff of irritation. Shortly after that, Bree
gave up, too, and poured herself a cup of coffee in the dark hour before dawn. She curled up
with her book but it didn't help. Reading about
Sir Haverly's throbbing manhood was more agi-
tating than romantic. She threw the book aside
and walked outside at dawn, watching as Maggie jogged back to Cole's house.

The Jeep was still there, so the guys had
stayed overnight. Bree liked Cole's friends. They
were funny and charming and kind. When Cole
showed up and ruined everything, they'd trod
the fine line of defending their friend while still
comforting her.

After that moment in the loft, she thought
maybe something had shifted between them. If
nothing else, perhaps a truce of sorts. But when
Cole told her he thought they were a bad idea, he

wasn't kidding. In fact, he seemed determined to make that true by pushing her away at every opportunity. Yesterday he'd treated her with contempt. Not only that, but he did it *publicly*, in front of his own friends. If nothing else, that had proven how little he thought of her and her feelings. She'd be a fool to give him another chance to crush her like that. She turned away from his lifeless home and vowed to put him out of her mind.

By midmorning, it was raining. Nell had been fretting about how dry everything was, so Bree knew it was welcome. Nell was off to someone's birthday dinner that afternoon, so she was on her own. She puttered around the cottage all day while the rain fell, baking an apple pie, then sliding a roast into the oven.

After dinner she settled in to try to finish the silly romance novel once and for all. It rarely took her this long to read a book, but with all the work she'd been doing at Nell's, most nights found her falling asleep on the sofa after reading just a few pages. Maggie's arrival was the only thing that roused her enough to make it into bed every evening. Sure enough, when her phone started ringing at nine o'clock, it woke her from a sound sleep on the sofa. The book slid from her stomach to the floor as she reached for the phone.

"Bree? Honey, can you come over? I can't find that danged Trixie anywhere, and I'm afraid she's off having that calf on her own." Nell sounded out of breath.

Bree sat up and started to pull on the tall rubber work boots Nell had loaned her, holding the phone between her cheek and shoulder. "Where are you, Nell? Did you call Cole?"

"He's not answering. I don't see his truck or the Jeep at the house." Nell was puffing now. "I'm up in the meadow. I walked up here when I got home to check on the herd after all the rain, and I can't find her anywhere. Drive the truck up, will you?"

"Of course," Bree said. "I'm on my way."

It took her a few minutes to drive Nell's truck through the gates and get to the top of the ridge. She spotted Nell waving wildly from the corner of the pasture. She brought the truck to a stop at the top of a knoll, with the headlights shining down on a muddy area where a lone cow was lying. Nell worked her way back down the rain-slicked slope to kneel at the Hereford's broad white head. Bree jumped out of the truck and followed. Trixie's eyes were closed and her ribs heaved with the strain.

"Is she in labor?"

Nell nodded solemnly. "Looks like she's been at it for a while now, and nothing's happening.

A leg might be turned back, or maybe the calf is breech. Doc Pritchard is out of town. We're going to have to do this ourselves."

"Do *what*, exactly?"

"Help her deliver this baby. I'm not strong enough to do it, honey, but you can."

She stared at Nell in stunned silence then repeated herself.

"Do *what*, exactly?"

Nell nodded to the cow's back half. "You'll have to reach in and see what's going on. You might have to help straighten out the little guy or gal so Trixie can deliver it." Nell must have read the naked panic on Bree's face. "If we don't do something, they'll both die. The calf may be dead already."

"No." Bree stepped away, shaking her head vehemently. This was far more than she'd bargained for. "I am *not* going to lie down in this mud and stick my hand up this cow's butt and into her...her..."

"Into her uterus, Bree. That's what you need to do."

Bree flung her arms wide and shouted. "I'm from Malibu, for God's sake. I can't..."

Trixie let out a low, trembling groan of pain and fear, stopping Bree's diatribe midsentence. She and Nell stared at each other then at the labored breathing of the cow. Nell was right. They were going to watch Trixie die here in a rain-soaked gully if they didn't do something. Bree took a deep breath and muttered a curse aimed at Cole. Nell just sighed.

"I think he and the boys went to visit a young man they've been helping. We're on our own here, Bree."

After swallowing another lump of panic, Bree sounded far steadier than she felt.

"Tell me what to do."

And that was how she came to be lying on her side in three inches of mud, her jacket off, one sleeve rolled up, with her scrubbed arm inside a cow. She shivered as rain started to fall again. Perfect. She dug her toes into the mud and gently pushed her hand farther inside, trying to ignore the occasional contractions that squeezed her arm like a vise.

"Here's a foot." Her fingers felt the slick little hoof and leg. It wasn't moving.

"Only one?"

"Yes."

"Okay, keep going. If the other leg is turned back, we'll have to push the calf back into the uterus and bring the leg up so she can deliver."

Bree grimaced. By "we," Nell meant that *she'd* have to do it.

"I don't feel any movement."

"Calves can asphyxiate if they're in the birth

canal too long. It's probably dead, but we can still save Trixie." Nell was scratching the cow's ears gently, cooing words of encouragement.

Bree groaned and pushed on. Her hand reached the wide head of the calf. She pushed past it and could feel the calf's right leg was turned back. Okay. Now she needed to slowly push the calf backward as Nell had instructed. She had to be careful not to let the baby's hooves cut the uterus, or Trixie could die from infection. She put gentle pressure on the body of the calf then gave a yelp of surprise.

"It *licked* me! I felt it lick me, Nell! It's alive!" Goose bumps raced across her body, and they had nothing to do with the steady rain now falling. Her hair was plastered to her face and one half of her body was submerged in mud, but she was grinning like an idiot. The calf was *alive*. She took a deep breath and willed her hand to move slowly and carefully. Eventually she had both legs extended up into the birth canal, with the calf's chin resting on them. Trixie gave a giant push, and a sprawling, wet bundle of calf and amniotic fluid came bursting forth. Bree quickly sat up and scooped the calf into her lap and out of the water. She and Nell, and even Trixie, all held their collective breath until they heard the nasally first inhalation from the reddish-brown calf with a white face. It tried to lift its boxy head on a still-too-weak neck, and big brown eyes fluttered open. Right there, Bree fell in love.

Nell laughed. "It's a girl! A little heifer. Cole will be pleased."

"Yeah, well, Cole isn't here. This is our baby." She had an inexplicable desire to just run home with this funny-looking creature and raise it herself. But Trixie had other ideas. She let out a long mournful call and her head dropped to the ground. Nell grew serious again.

"Bring the baby around front, Bree. Mama's too tired to get up, and she needs to see she has a reason to keep trying."

"I can't lift her."

"Grab her front legs and drag her, honey. They're pretty flexible for the first hour or so. You won't hurt her."

Bree pulled herself from under the calf and did as Nell instructed. The muddy ground made it easier to drag the calf. As soon as Trixie was able to put her nose on her baby girl, a chuckling sound rumbled deep in the cow's chest. Her long, pink tongue cleaned off the little one, who was now holding her head up and already trying to move her knobby legs. Bree was enthralled. Nell stood next to her for a few minutes then nudged her.

"We need to get them down to the barn where

they'll be dry for the night, so mama can recover. If we both try, I think we can lift the heifer into the back of the truck. If you hold her there, Trixie will follow us. I'll have to take it slow. There should be a blanket behind the seat. Go get it and wrap yourself up before you get chilled to the bone in this rain."

Bree looked down at herself and grinned. She was covered in mud and bovine body fluids. And she'd never felt so strong and happy. She'd just brought life into the world.

Nell read her mind. "If Malibu could see you now."

"I've never looked worse or felt better. Let's get them into the barn where I can see my new little godchild in the light." It took some work, but they were able to lift the heifer into the back of the truck. Trixie pushed herself up to her feet and let out a sad call. Bree sat on the lowered tailgate with her legs dangling off the back and the calf halfway across her lap. Trixie dropped her muzzle onto the calf and looked up at Bree as if to say she understood what they were doing. Bree rapped her knuckles on the side of the truck, signaling Nell to start the slow descent to the barn. The rain had stopped again, but it didn't really matter. She was soaked to the bone. And she couldn't wipe the enormous smile off her face.

COLE HAD SLEPT very little last night, and it had been a painfully long day. He and the guys had driven to the mountains in the western part of the state, leaving early that morning. They'd left his truck in Laurinburg and gone the rest of the way in the Jeep. Chris, Jerome and Ramirez dropped him off at his truck an hour ago so they could drive directly back to Fayetteville without him. Maggie made the long trip, and she was sound asleep on the seat by his side.

The purpose of the three-hour drive to the tiny town of Pull Tail Gap was to check up on a young soldier that Cole had met in the VA hospital months ago. Travis Walker had enlisted straight out of high school, following his best friend into the army. The two boys had grown up together, and went off to Afghanistan ready for battle. Good guys against bad guys. White hats against black hats. Just like in the video games and movies, they were going over to kick some ass then come home as heroes.

But that wasn't what happened. Travis's unit saw a lot of action, and took a lot of casualties, including his best friend. He came home a tense, angry young man.

Cole saw himself in Travis's bottled-up emotions and inability to connect with people. While Cole didn't figure he needed therapy sessions for himself anymore, he encouraged Travis to join a group with Chris and Ramirez, and he seemed to be responding well. They all thought the kid was making progress.

But Travis suddenly announced he was ready to go home a month ago, leaving the clinic and his support group. Their phone conversations and emails had gone from long and detailed to short and infrequent. He could feel Travis starting to withdraw, and it bothered Cole enough that he'd talked his buddies into making the drive.

He started to relax as he drove back through Russell. Everything in town, including The Hide-Away, was closed up tight, as it should be after sundown on a Sunday night. It had been raining here, and the roads were shiny, reflecting the buildings and trees in the glow of the scattered streetlights.

Pull Tail Gap was even smaller than Russell, but maybe it was where Travis needed to be; the same way that Cole belonged here. The kid had been happy today. Happier than Cole had ever seen him, actually. Not perfect—there were still dark, sad shadows behind his eyes when he thought no one was looking. But still, he was better than expected.

Travis's father was convinced his son was completely back to normal. Cole wasn't ready to go that far yet, but he had to admit the kid seemed to be pretty damn good. He was glad he'd talked the guys into the trip. It was one less thing to worry about.

He glanced down at his phone on the seat and shook his head. They'd gotten lost this morning, and the map app had thoroughly chewed up his battery power. It wasn't like he was expecting any calls anyway. He made the final turn toward home, and Maggie sat up as if she knew they were almost there.

"Let me guess," he said to his now-alert dog, "you can't wait to go visit your new part-time mistress tonight, right?" Maggie's tail flicked in happiness. He still couldn't figure out why the dog was determined to stay with Bree every night. Nell said Maggie made Bree feel safe, and that was enough reason for him to let the visits continue. Somebody wanted to hurt her, and on the odd chance they happened to find her here, they'd never get past his army-trained dog.

He was getting ready to turn into his place when he caught the flash of lights in the distance. Truck headlights were working their way slowly down the hill toward Nell's barn from the cattle pasture. It was after ten o'clock at night. Something was wrong.

*Really* wrong.

He stepped on the gas and cranked the steering wheel. His truck roared up the drive past

Nell's house. He slid the vehicle to a stop, leaped out and jumped the gate, running up the hill with Maggie bounding at his side.

Nell was behind the wheel of her truck, and she gave him a cheery smile and wave that settled his pounding heart. She gestured to the back of the truck with her thumb, so he waited for her to pass while he caught his breath. Trixie was following behind, the cow's attention fixed on the truck bed. He looked over and his knees went weak at the sight of Bree holding tight to a tiny, wet Hereford calf in her lap.

The glow of the taillights bathed them in crimson warmth. Bree's wet hair hung down the sides of her face, caked with mud. She had a splotch of dirt on her cheek and more on her chin. A blanket was draped over her shoulders; her clothes were dripping wet and filthy. And she was smiling. In fact, her smile lit up her face. She looked…joyful. And relaxed. Maybe that was it. She was always so uptight, but there was no edge to her right now. Her wide eyes dropped to the calf in her lap.

"It's a girl, Cole. It's a perfect girl." It took him a moment to realize she was talking about the four-legged creature, and not herself. Because right then, *she* looked like a perfect girl to him. He forced himself to look at the red-and-white calf. He was walking behind the slow-moving truck now, alongside Trixie. They were almost to the barn.

"A perfect girl." He agreed with her.

Her expression darkened and her smile faded. She'd just remembered she was supposed to be mad at him.

"We called you. Where were you?"

His face flushed with guilt. "I was out of town. My phone died. Sorry."

"We *needed* you, Cole." He took a sharp breath. People shouldn't need him. People had needed him in Afghanistan, and some of them were dead. Before he went any farther down that dark hole, Bree pulled him back.

"Hey…" He looked up and saw the regret in her eyes. Just like that night at the bar, she'd managed to peer inside his soul and see his pain. It was spooky as hell. "I'm sorry. It turned out okay. Nell and I handled it."

The truck stopped behind the barn. He stepped forward and lifted the calf into his arms. It weighed a solid eighty pounds or more, and he marveled that the two women were able to get her into the truck. Trixie ambled into the barn behind him. Nell had gone on ahead and turned on the lights. There was a large stall already bedded deep with straw. It was only a few minutes before the calf pushed herself to her feet and moved on wobbly legs to begin nursing. He heard Bree's sigh and turned to see her standing next to him, her arms folded on top of the gate.

"Look at that." Bree smiled as she watched the calf. "I brought life into the world tonight. I put my arm inside a cow and pulled out a real live calf. What a rush."

"You did *what*?" He couldn't possibly have heard that right.

She lifted her muddy chin proudly. "Her leg was turned, so I had to go in and push her back and fix the leg and then she came out, right into my lap. Then we had to drag the baby around so mama could see that she had a reason to live. Someone needed her. It was amazing."

His heart stuttered to a stop then restarted again. Trixie had to live because someone needed her. *We needed you, Cole.* He stepped back as if Bree had slapped him. She was too wrapped up in her joy to notice.

"Nell, we did it. They could have died, but you told me what to do, and I lay there in the mud and I freakin' did it!" She flashed him another dazzling smile. "When my arm was in there, the baby licked me. We thought she was dead, but then I felt that little sandpaper tongue on my arm. She hadn't been born yet and she licked me!" Bree's eyes were wide and bright in her dirt-stained face. He stepped closer. He was staring at her mouth, and she knew it. She stopped talking.

Nell cleared her throat. Bree flinched, and he knew she'd momentarily forgotten about the woman's presence, too.

"Bree, honey, you were a trouper tonight, but you're soaking wet and so am I." Nell nodded toward Cole. "I think you better get her back to the cottage, Mr. Caldwell. It's the least you can do after she saved Trixie and this good-looking heifer. I'm headed inside for a long, hot bath."

Cole surprised Nell almost as much as himself when he stepped up and enveloped her in a hug. It wasn't his usual style, but this wasn't a usual night.

"You're the best, Nell. Thank you." Bree turned away from them to watch Trixie and the calf. He dropped his voice so only Nell could hear. "I'm sorry I wasn't here. My phone…" She stopped him by setting her hand on his chest.

"Don't," she whispered. "Your Hollywood bombshell did okay tonight. She was scared out of her mind, but she did it anyway. That's the definition of bravery, isn't it?"

He couldn't answer, still stuck on the idea that Bree was somehow *his* Hollywood bombshell.

"Take her back to the cottage, honey, and make sure she gets warmed up so she doesn't get sick."

He nodded. "Go on inside, Nell. I'll close up the barn and take care of Hollywood."

Nell and Bree hugged tightly and laughed about their adventurous evening, ignoring the mud and goop that was beginning to dry to a crust on their clothes. He sent Bree to his truck with Maggie while he tossed fresh hay into the stall for Trixie and turned off the barn lights. It only took a few minutes, but when he got to the truck, Bree was already nodding off. Her adrenaline rush was fading, and she was starting to crash.

"Wake up, sleeping beauty. No rest for you until you chisel that gunk off your body." He backed the truck out onto the road. "I can't believe I'm even letting you in my truck the way you smell."

"Bite me, Plowboy." Her words didn't hold their usual edge. "I wouldn't be caked in this gunk if you'd been around. But honestly? I wouldn't trade tonight for anything. What a rush."

He parked the truck next to the cottage. Bree reached for the door handle and mumbled a soft "Good night." She looked over in surprise when he turned off the engine.

"I promised Miss Nell I'd make sure you were okay. That means walking you inside and making sure you don't collapse onto her sofa wearing those disgusting clothes."

She was apparently too tired to argue, because she just walked ahead of him into the cottage with a lazy shrug. She kept right on walking, straight into the bathroom. That left him and Maggie standing in the middle of the tiny living room, staring at each other.

"I don't know about you, dog, but I need a drink."

# CHAPTER TEN

THE REFRIGERATOR HELD two bottles of white wine. There was gin in the freezer. Neither appealed to him, so he started rummaging through the cupboards. He found what he wanted under the sink, of all places. Way in the back was a bottle of cognac, topped with a brilliant red and green Christmas bow. The cottage's last tenant was a shy young schoolteacher. Apparently one of the parents in her class didn't know she was a teetotaler, and had given her the expensive bottle of brandy for Christmas. She'd pushed the offending gift *way* out of sight and left it there when she moved.

He pulled juice glasses from the cupboard and poured two fingers in each. He emptied one and sighed at the fine burn then refilled the glass. He could hear the shower running and tried hard not to think about Bree stepping into the old claw-foot tub, drawing the plastic curtain around her and letting the hot water pour over her alabaster skin.

He moved out of the kitchen and looked desperately for something to distract him from his misbehaving thoughts. He couldn't stop thinking about her in the back of Nell's truck, covered in God knows what, laughing like she owned the world. That laugh of hers, so relaxed and natural, had done something to him. Something he could actually feel in his chest. He sat on the sofa with a loud groan. Maggie stretched out by the door and watched him with justifiable concern. This wasn't good. It wasn't good at all.

He ran his hand down his face. His foot bumped against something and he glanced down. A paperback book was lying open, pages down, on the floor, and he knew she'd dropped it there in her hurry to get to help Nell. He picked up the book and smiled. The cover art was a dramatic image of a red-haired beauty in the arms of a dark-haired knight. Good grief, was this what she liked to read? He flipped through the pages and shook his head. Chests were heaving on every other page.

He raised his head to find Bree standing in the archway leading to the hall, dressed in black leggings that stopped just below her knees. A large T-shirt advertising The Hide-Away fell to midthigh. Her hair was towel-damp and disheveled, falling in soft waves around her face. Her eyes were wide, and her hand rested on her chest as if she'd been surprised.

"I... I didn't expect you to still be here."

Why *was* he still here? Why wasn't he hustling his butt back home, where it was safe? "I, um, wanted to be sure you were okay. Are you hurting anywhere? Do you need anything?"

Her head tipped to the side. "So now you're suddenly concerned about me? Really? Because yesterday..."

It was time for her to get her pound of flesh over his lousy treatment of her at his place. Fair enough. He nodded his head toward the kitchen counter.

"There's a glass of cognac there for you. It will warm you up a little."

She glanced at it then back at him.

"Are you suggesting I'm cold?"

"I'm *suggesting* you were wallowing in mud a little while ago. I'm sure the shower helped, but...just drink the brandy, alright?" He ground the last words through his teeth. Damned if this woman didn't push every button he had and a few he didn't even know about.

She walked to the kitchen counter and took a sip from the glass, closing her eyes as the liquid slid across her tongue. He took a step toward her and stopped. Being any closer to her would be dangerous. But there was something he had to say.

"What you did tonight...it was really something, Bree. That heifer is worth a lot of money, but it's not just that. I wouldn't have wanted to lose her or Trixie. Losing animals is part of farming, but it's a part I have a particular dislike of." He'd seen enough dead bodies to last him a lifetime. She was staring at him now, her eyes intense but with a bit less fire. He knew he had to say the two words he spoke even more rarely than apologies.

"Thank you."

She blinked but didn't bend. She wasn't done with him yet.

"Yeah, well, you weren't here so we did what we had to do."

He nodded his head in agreement.

"I wasn't here when you needed me. If you hang around awhile, you'll learn I'm good at that. But I am sorry." He ran his fingers through his hair in frustration. She wasn't going to make this easy for him. "Look, I know I haven't treated you very well."

She took another sip of brandy. "Cole, I can handle the animosity, or whatever it is, when it's just you and me. I can take all your bull and give it right back to you. It's fine. It's our thing." He noticed her hand trembling just a little as she set her glass down. "But yesterday you embarrassed me in front of your friends."

He didn't mind making her angry. In fact, he

usually enjoyed it. But this was different. He'd hurt her feelings. She lifted her chin and tried to look invincible, but he could see the sting of pain in her eyes.

He took another step forward. "I acted like a jerk yesterday. I think you know that's generally my fall-back position." That got a hint of a smile out of her, and he had an inspiration. "Bree, you said I didn't know you. But you're wrong."

She snorted in surprise and disbelief, but he plowed ahead.

"I *know* you. I know your ex-husband betrayed you on television. I know you fought him tooth and nail to keep that fancy mansion on the beach. I know you think the lack of money is what killed your mom when she got sick." Her lips parted in surprise, and he took yet another step, unable to stop himself. "You picked yourself up and started your own business. And even in the awful situation of having some nutcase stalking you, you've been able to laugh and make friends while hiding out in a place that's totally out of your comfort zone."

He was only three feet away from her now, and he watched her eyes soften then harden again. Damned if she wasn't a tough nut to crack. He'd clearly proven how much he knew about her, and she still wouldn't give in. She glanced away then looked back to him. Her eyes glistened with moisture, and his stomach tightened.

She lifted her shoulder in a weak shrug.

"All you've proven is that you talked to Nell or looked me up on the internet. It doesn't mean you *know* me."

He closed his eyes, his hands flexing tightly at his sides. A montage of Bree moments started spinning through his mind. Scene after scene whirled across his closed eyelids like a movie. The day she strutted into the bar. Dancing with her. Watching her work on the farm. Pulling her up onto his tractor. The hayloft. Holding a newborn calf across her muddy lap in the back of a pickup truck. His heart started to thud in his chest, and a smile pulled at his lips. He opened his eyes and stepped closer. Bree leaned back and braced her hands on the counter behind her, her eyes going wide.

"Oh, I know you, Brianna Mathews. I know you handle your whiskey better than you handle your temper. I know you came into this town thinking you were better than anyone in it…" She opened her mouth to protest but he held up his hand. "But as soon as you realized total strangers were willing to help you and be your friends, you opened up to them. You returned their friendship. That tells me two things. You've known kindness in your life, but you weren't prepared for it, so you probably haven't experienced it in a long time." Her pretty mouth was still open, but no longer in anger. She was just staring at him, and the shimmer of tears in her eyes made them sparkle like emeralds over a flame.

"You defended me at the bar last weekend, even though we'd barely spoken a civil word to each other at that point. I don't know why you did that…" He stepped forward. "But I know I liked it. I know you're fearless, even when you're scared. Maybe *especially* then. I know you're not afraid to work hard and sweat hard and get dirty, and I'm pretty sure that surprises you almost as much as it surprises me."

One last step and he was right there in front of her. She lifted her hands and set them lightly on his chest, making him burn. She didn't push him away, but she didn't pull him in, either. She just stared up at him with those eyes that haunted his nights, and he saw the corners of her mouth slide softly into the beginning of a smile. He leaned forward and rested his hands on the counter on either side of her.

"I know you're not afraid to make friends with the three foul-mouthed clowns who claim to be my friends." Her lips quirked into a definite smile. "And you won them over so fast their heads are still spinning. They jumped on my case like a trio of mad hens after I chased you off, and I know *that's* never happened before. I know you lay in the cold mud an hour ago and helped my cow give birth. Even though you were furious with me, you still did that. And I know that saving that heifer gave you a rush like nothing you've ever felt, because it was *real*. And I suspect you haven't done real in a while."

She shook her head, and the motion caused some of that moisture in her eyes to spill over. He quickly caught the tears with his thumbs and wiped them away.

His hands remained on either side of her face, holding her there. She didn't pull away. He felt a surge of adrenaline shoot through his veins. Danger be damned, because he wasn't pulling away, either. His next words came out in a hoarse whisper.

"I know that when you landed in my arms in the hayloft, and you pressed your body up against mine..." He moved in and pushed his hips into hers, letting her feel his hardness. "I know you felt the same thing I did, all this heat. I was smart enough to turn away then." He lowered his head until their noses were brushing against each other. She still hadn't blinked. "But I'm not feeling very smart right now..."

Those last words were spoken against her lips.

His hands cupped her face softly and she sighed, her breath blowing across his skin. This was still a bad idea. But when her hands twisted into his T-shirt, he was lost.

He wanted to take this slow, to be careful. Really, he did. But that plan detonated on contact. Her lips were soft and pliant when their mouths met, and she parted them with a soft moan that went straight to his core.

Men had been plunging their tongues into women's mouths for centuries. Staking their claim. Grabbing the first taste of a woman. And yes, hinting at that other penetration they had in mind. Kissing like this, tongue against tongue, was natural. Primal even.

But Cole knew that *never* in the long history of kissing had there ever been a kiss like this. Things quickly spun out of control, their heads turning and their mouths moving against each other aggressively. She tasted like cognac and toothpaste, and hell if it didn't hit his nervous system like crack cocaine. His hands started to slide up and down her body, fingers grabbing at every curve. She was trembling in his arms like a tuning fork, like she was ready to come just from this. Just from kissing like this.

It wouldn't be Bree's style to just passively let him kiss her. She gave as good as she got, tugging, pushing, sucking, biting. She was staking her own claim, holding his head in place while she devoured him. Twice their teeth clashed together, and neither of them flinched.

This was Bree, and he damned-well *knew* her. He never wanted to let her go. Fear washed over him like a bucket of ice water at that realization. Going further was a mistake. She'd only end up hurting him. And worse, he'd hurt her. His hands flexed against the cheeks of her ass one last time, pulling her against his rock-hard pelvis as if in defiance of where his brain was headed. Regretfully, he finally released her and stepped back.

There was a tiny cut at the corner of her mouth, probably from being pinched between his teeth and hers. Thousands of years of men and women laying claim on each other. Primal. Natural. And scary as hell.

He took another step back. She raised her hands then dropped them, as if she knew she couldn't stop him. Then she did something that just about destroyed him. She smiled, slow and knowing. The smile was sultry and sensuous, made more so by her kiss-swollen lips. Her eyes were languid and her posture more so as she leaned back against the counter. She knew what that kiss had done to him. She was inside his head, and that was a place he didn't ever want her to see.

He took another hurried step backward. "Nothing's changed, Bree. We're a bad idea. Nothing's changed." His voice sounded high-pitched and defensive to his own ears, as if he was trying to convince himself more than her.

She arched a brow, challenging his statement. *Everything* had changed with that kiss, and he, for one, might never be the same again. He spun and marched to the door. Every good soldier knew when to retreat. Her voice stopped him in his tracks.

"Don't run away, Cole. You can decide to leave, and that's fine. But don't run." He glanced over his shoulder at her in confusion. She shrugged. "My mom used to tell me that all the time. First when I was competing in the pageants and then when she was sick. She told me I should never let anyone see my fear. 'Don't let 'em see you sweat, Bree.' That's what she'd tell me."

Her smile faded. It certainly explained a lot about her approach to life and her inability to turn down a challenge.

"She told me that it was fine to *decide* to walk away if that's what I wanted, but that I should never let anyone think I was retreating."

He swallowed hard. How had she known that

retreating was exactly what he'd been trying to do?

"Even when she got sick, she refused to show fear. She told me the cancer might end up victorious, but that she'd never bow down to it. And she didn't..." Bree frowned then looked at him for a moment as if she'd almost forgotten who she was talking to. Another smile slid across her face. "So walk away if that's what you want. But don't run from me. From this." She gestured between them, trying to capture the odd energy there. He barely won his struggle to stay at the door instead of crossing the room to scoop her into his arms again.

They stared at each other long and silent. If he stayed, he knew where they'd end up. It would surely be memorable. But would it be worth the doubtless pain afterward? He shook his head. She deserved better than him.

"I'm sorry, Bree, but we both know I'm doing the right thing. I'm not running..." Not anymore, anyway. "But I am walking away. One of us has to."

He stepped out onto her porch and slowly closed the door behind him. He looked down and realized that Maggie was still inside with Bree. Rotten traitor of a dog. He rubbed his hand across the back of his neck and sighed.

That woman.

That kiss.

No way in hell was he going to be able to sleep tonight.

Or maybe ever again.

"SO TELL ME again how you reached into a cow's back end and pulled out a live calf."

"Really, Amanda? I just told you I kissed the hot farmer, and you want to talk about the cow?" Bree leaned on the gate inside Nell's barn and watched in adoration as Trixie's baby slept in the deep straw she'd just bedded their stall with. Mama was standing watch close by. She snapped a quick picture with her phone.

"Oh, honey, you locking lips with Hot Farmer was a foregone conclusion. I saw that one coming a week ago. But you acting as midwife to a cow? I did not see *that* at all." There was a pause, then she heard Amanda squeal, knowing she'd just received the photo she'd texted to her. "Oh, my God, she's so precious! Maybe I should fly you back up here to Gallant Lake so you can help my pregnancy along."

"How is your little one doing?"

Amanda sighed. "Bree, I don't think this baby will ever arrive. In fact, I told the doctor that yesterday, and he just laughed at me. He told me he'd never known one yet that didn't show up sooner or later." Bree wanted to laugh but wisely controlled the urge as Amanda continued mournfully. "I waddle when I walk, and if my husband tells me one more time how beautiful I am, I'm going to throw a lamp at his head. I don't want to be pregnant anymore. I'm over it."

"How much longer does the doctor say you have?"

"Probably another week or so. I'm not even dilated yet. Do you think you'll be able to come up here by then?"

Bree turned away from her pride and joy sleeping in the straw and walked to the doorway on the shaded side of the barn to try to catch a breeze.

"Caroline sent me an email this morning saying someone was calling around and asking some pretty specific questions about me in the town where the Seventh Heaven rehab is located, so the plan might be working. Are you seriously not going to ask me about the kiss?"

Amanda laughed. "I figured if you wanted to talk about it, you would. And clearly you want to. So, please, do go on. Was Hot Farmer a hot kisser? Or was he a disappointing dud?"

Bree's fingers moved to her mouth. She'd hardly slept last night. Every time she closed her eyes, she felt his lips on hers.

"He was not a dud."

"That's a good thing. So you kissed him back?"

Oh, yeah. She'd kissed him back. So hard their teeth clashed and cut her lip. It was perfect.

"I'll take that silence as a yes. Did anything happen after this smoking-hot kiss?"

"He left."

"He left? Why did you let him do that?"

Cole kept insisting they were a bad idea. Last week she would have agreed whole-heartedly. But after that kiss, she really didn't know. There certainly couldn't be anything long-term between them, but would a little summer fling really hurt anyone? She closed her eyes as her head fell back against the barn door. Of course it would hurt. They'd both be singed around the edges. Which didn't make it any less tempting.

"Hel-lo? Earth to Brianna?"

She moved back inside the barn. "I don't want to start something that I can't possibly finish. Pretty soon I'll be out of these cornfields and back in Malibu where I belong. Starting anything with Hot Farmer doesn't make sense."

"When does having sex with someone new ever really make sense, Bree? But sometimes you have to take a chance, like Blake and me. It's not that complicated."

"Says the woman living in a castle with her newly adopted eleven-year-old son. The same woman who's eight months pregnant after getting married six months ago after almost dying.

Yeah, there was nothing at all complicated about you deciding to have sex with Blake."

Amanda laughed so hard she snorted, which made her laugh even harder. "Well, when you put it *that* way…" Her voice grew somber. "But honestly, none of that *felt* complicated once we realized we loved each other. It felt like all the missing pieces were falling into place in our lives, locking us together in the best possible way."

Bree took that in for a moment then shrugged. "The difference is there's no chance of Hot Farmer and me falling in love. Those complications would litter the ground in our wake if we ever started a relationship. Cole's right. We're a bad idea."

"Hmm. I'm not convinced. You deserve some happiness. And that might just be in the form of a hot, sweaty, sexy farmer who's not a dud in the kissing department."

After the call ended, Bree went up into the loft to throw down more hay for Trixie and her calf. Nell was keeping them inside one more day after the difficult birth. Nell had already christened the calf "Malibu."

That evening, she and Nell played dress-up with the few clothes Bree brought with her from Gallant Lake. Nell was going on a shopping trip with her girlfriends. It was only a two-hour drive to Raleigh, but the ladies were planning on staying overnight so they could go out for a nice dinner and hit the outlet mall before heading home.

Nell walked into the living room of the cottage wearing a soft, swishy skirt with a lacy top, and twirled in the middle of the room. She'd probably faint if she knew how expensive the ensemble was.

Bree smiled. "You look terrific, Nell. Very cosmopolitan."

The older woman blushed. "Well, that's a word that's seldom been used in my direction. But I must admit, I feel pretty in this skirt. Wait until the gals see me in this getup!"

"You'll knock their socks off at dinner, Nell. And my green cotton dress will be comfortable for shopping on the second day."

Nell tilted her head and gave Bree a serious look. "Are you sure you're okay watching things here while I'm gone?"

"Of course. It's only one night. If anything serious happens, I can call Ty or Cole."

"Would you really call Cole?" Nell's eyes were sharp. "You seemed a little cool to him last night." Bree did her best to keep her face neutral. Nell had no idea how much things had warmed up between Cole and her at the cottage.

"We…uh…declared a truce."

They stepped onto the porch with two glasses

of wine. Bree looked over her shoulder at the ever-darkening horizon. "It looks like we could have more rain."

Nell stopped and looked up at the sky. "If we have a thunderstorm while I'm gone, I need you to do something, and you probably won't like it."

"I know, I know. Make sure the horses and pigs are inside, close the barn doors, try to shoo the chickens under cover, bring Shep in the house…"

Nell was shaking her head. "No. I mean, yes, do those things before you head home, so you don't have to come back in the rain to do it. But I need you to go to Cole's if there's a bad storm."

Bree laughed. "Nell, I'm not afraid of storms. I don't need to run to Cole for comfort!"

"It's not you who needs comforting."

Her laughter faded. Surely Cole wasn't afraid of thunderstorms. He was a grown man. He was a soldier. A soldier… Her eyes closed in understanding. He'd been in battle. And battles were loud. Guns. Mortars. Missiles. Land mines.

She met Nell's worried eyes. "He gets flashbacks during storms."

"Pretty bad ones." Nell nodded. "I was driving home a few months ago and stopped by to deliver some goodies from the church bake sale. A sharp spring storm was rolling in. He was white as a ghost. I thought he was ill, but it only took one clap of thunder for me to realize he was having a panic attack."

Bree felt tears welling in her eyes at the thought of Cole, with all his pride, being found in such a fragile state. That must have just about killed him.

"So now, if I know a storm is coming, I'll go to him, or he'll come to my place, and we'll play cards and talk and do anything we can think of to keep him distracted from what's happening outdoors. During the last storm, he was so anxious that I put him to work reorganizing the jars of canned produce in my pantry. I said I needed them to be alphabetical, and he spent an hour in there trying to figure out what was in each jar and putting them in order. When he came to dinner a week later and saw them all back where they'd been originally, he realized I'd made up the task just to keep his mind occupied." Nell winked at Bree. "That's one of the few times I've actually gotten a kiss from Cole."

Bree didn't say anything about having already earned a kiss from him.

"So you want me to go to his house and what…reorganize his sock drawer?"

Nell just shrugged as she turned away, ever the matchmaker.

"Oh, I'm sure you'll think of something."

The sock drawer sounded like the perfect solution. She and Cole could organize socks together if it stormed.

# CHAPTER ELEVEN

"OKAY, NORA," BREE SAID, stretching like a cat on the cottage's worn sofa as she held the phone to her ear. "When are you headed to Gallant Lake again?" Her cousin was flying from Atlanta to spend time with Amanda after the baby arrived. Bree and her cousins were as close as sisters. As the oldest, widow Nora was the clucking mother hen of them all.

"I'll probably go up a couple weeks after the baby is born, but Amanda will be fine," Nora said. "Women have babies all the time. I'm more concerned about you. I saw the rehab story on GMA this morning, and they made it sound like you'd had some kind of mental breakdown."

"Damn that agent of mine! I told Sheila to drop some *subtle hints* that I was being treated for exhaustion in Utah. She wasn't supposed to make me into headline news. What if someone in Russell sees all of that and recognizes me?" Bree stood and started to pace. The idea of having to leave here was chilling.

"You said you've changed your looks, right?

Just keep a low profile, and let the publicity flush out your stalker so you can go home. You must be dying to get back to the beach house. And speaking of the beach house, you'll never guess who called me after the story aired this morning."

"Who?"

"Your ex-husband."

"Damian?" Bree froze. The last thing she needed right now was her ex-husband interfering in her life. "What is he calling *you* for? You didn't tell him where I was, did you?"

"Of course I didn't tell him where you were. He said he couldn't reach you and was worried, but I didn't buy it. He asked me to remind you that if you're feeling stressed, he'd be happy to take the house off your hands if it would help."

That figured. The only communication she and Damian had had since the divorce revolved around the house. He was furious she'd won it from him, and was constantly trying to renegotiate the agreement that he'd pay the mortgage and taxes, in hopes of forcing her out. Those expenses were substantial for the lavish home that had been featured in Architectural Digest just months before their divorce. He must really be getting desperate if he was resorting to calling her family about it.

"As if you'd ever give up that gorgeous house,"

Nora continued. "It must be torture for you to be away from Malibu. I can't imagine you, of all people, being trapped in corn country."

A steady rain started to fall in the darkening evening, but luckily there were no signs of severe weather.

"The next time Damian calls, tell him to go to hell, Nora. I've got to go close up the windows. It's starting to rain. Call me if you hear anything from Amanda."

"Will you be okay there by yourself?"

"Oh, sure. Nell's animals are safely in the barn, except the cattle, of course. I love the sound of rain on the tin roof of the cottage. The smell of the fields after a good rain is incredible. And you should hear the bugs and frogs singing once the rain stops."

"Who are you, and what have you done with my cousin? She's a tall redhead, wears designer clothes and thinks dirt is vulgar? Ring any bells?"

"Very funny. She's still here. But I have to say it's been quite the experience for me so far. You wouldn't believe some of the things I've done in the past two weeks."

"Yeah, well, when you come up to Gallant Lake to see Amanda's baby, I expect to hear every detail. Take care and stay safe out there, farm girl."

Bree closed the windows and picked up her book, which was nearing its conclusion. The brave knight was rushing to rescue his love from their enemies. Would he reach her in time…?

A flash of light woke Bree, but it was the roar of thunder that propelled her to her feet. It was dark, and she hadn't heard the storm approaching. Wind gusted against the walls of the cottage, and another flash of lightning flickered outside the windows.

*Cole!*

She'd promised Nell she wouldn't let him be alone if it stormed. The clap of thunder sounded like cannon fire, even to her. Her heart jumped, and she grabbed a jacket and bolted out the door. The storm was bearing down as she ran toward his house, with nearly continuous lightning dancing across the sky. The heavy rain hadn't started yet, but the sky lit up with a brilliant blue light as she dashed from his driveway to the front porch.

He yanked the door open after her second knock.

"What?" he barked at her, blocking the doorway. What was she supposed to say? *Hi, I'm here to babysit you…* She suddenly felt ridiculous. What if Nell was just looking for some way to bring her and Cole together by making up a story about Cole being afraid of storms? Her face flushed in embarrassment.

"Umm... I thought...do you...want company?" She shrugged innocently, as if it was the most normal thing in the world for her to drop by his house at ten o'clock at night. Sheets of rain started sweeping across the yard behind her. She worked up the courage to meet his eyes and took in a sharp breath. Nell hadn't exaggerated. He looked raw.

His face was ashen, and his body more rigid than she'd ever seen, which was saying something. There were tight lines of tension around his eyes. His mouth was drawn thin. Another flash of lightning brightened the sky, and his entire body flinched. That was when she felt her heart break for him. She reached for his arm, but he jerked away from her, closing his eyes as the thunder rumbled loudly.

"Please, Cole. I didn't want to be alone during the storm. Let me in."

He glared at her for what seemed like an eternity then stepped back.

"Suit yourself."

She walked past him and breathed a sigh of relief. She was in. Now what?

He slammed the door closed and started pacing the floor of the living room. Most of the lights were blazing, highlighting the gleaming hardwood floors and sweeping staircase in the main hallway. She moved down the hall, figuring she'd find the kitchen back there. Sure enough, a cheery yellow country kitchen stretched across the back of the house.

"I could really use a beer. How about you?" she asked with false bravado. He watched her silently, clenching and unclenching his hands. She opened the refrigerator and pulled out two bottles. She tucked the top of each bottle under the hem of her tank top and twisted off the caps. His eyes were on her every move. Okay. She was taking his mind off the storm. That was good. She flashed him a smile before putting a bottle to her lips.

"Come on, admit it, I look good drinking beer out of the bottle. Who knew?" He took the bottle she offered him, but he didn't drink from it or return her smile.

"Nell told you to come." It was a statement, not a question.

"Yes."

A rumble of thunder rattled the windows. A muscle twitched in his cheek. It took all her strength not to reach out to him.

"What did she tell you?" He was staring at the beer in his hand.

"Not much. She said storms remind you of… being overseas."

"So you're not afraid of thunder?"

"No, but I'd rather be with you than alone."

"Why, because you and I are so close?" He took a deep swig of the cold beer, emptying half the bottle.

She laughed, determined to lighten the tension. "Okay, I confess. I really came to see Maggie." She dropped to her knees next to the dog, who promptly rested her head in Bree's lap.

Cole's face softened fractionally and he set his beer on the side table. "You're a great pair. One lies and the other swears to it."

The atmosphere in the room relaxed, but not for long. A brilliant yellow light filled the windows, and the resulting thunder sounded like someone had set off dynamite in the front yard. Bree let out a yelp of surprise and jumped to her feet, losing her balance. Cole cursed and reached out to catch her. His hand tightened on her arm at the crash of the thunder. He shook his head slowly and set a hand on her other arm. The thunder rolled on forever into the distance, rattling the windows.

Without thinking, she reached out and ran her fingers across the tattoos on his left arm, following the rough ridges of his scars as she brushed over his T-shirt and up to where the tat peeked out at the base of his neck. Then her hand traveled up to rest on the side of his face. Instead of pulling away, he closed his eyes and leaned into it, like a child desperate for comfort. She stepped closer and whispered his name.

When his eyes opened, there was nothing childlike about the look she saw there. His grip tightened on her arms, as if he was afraid she'd slip away. After another blazing flash of lightning, he spun and pushed her against the wall. She wondered if he could hear the pounding of her heart over the sound of the rain against the windows. When the thunder roared, he dropped his mouth onto hers.

His body flattened hers against the wall. Their teeth clashed together and his tongue pressed inside before she started standing her ground. She twisted her fingers into his short hair and tugged. He grunted and set one hand beneath the cheeks of her bottom, lifting her feet off the floor. She wrapped her legs around his hips and held his bottom lip in her teeth. She felt as though her body was burning from the inside out.

His fingers dug into the soft skin of her thighs, yanking her legs higher as he pushed her against the wall.

"Bree..." He grazed his teeth across her chin and down her neck. She felt him take a little bite of the skin at the top of her shoulder. Her head

fell back as his mouth ran lower, trailing kisses
and nibbles over her breasts.

"Cole...oh my God..."

She didn't know how they got upstairs, but
apparently he carried her, kissing her the entire
way. He paused at the foot of a large bed.

"If you want me to stop, tell me now."

"Don't stop...please..."

She was airborne, and gave a squeal of surprise before hitting the bed he'd thrown her onto.
They stared at each other. She didn't want either
one of them to overthink this, so she sat up and
grabbed the bottom of her shirt, yanking it over
her head. A hiss came from his lips. He moved
to the side of the bed, his eyes never leaving
hers. He pulled off his own shirt and unbuttoned
his jeans. Bree shifted her hips and pulled her
shorts down, discarding them along with her
underwear. She'd never felt so brazen and bold.
She reached for her lacy bra, but he stopped her.

"Don't." She had a hard time inhaling.

He climbed onto the bed and ran his hands
slowly up her legs, across her thighs, over her
waist and up to her breasts. He was naked now,
and she felt him hard against her. She whispered
his name. She was vaguely aware that a storm
was still raging outside, but it was no match for
the passion between the two of them. He twisted
his hand into the side of her bra and yanked. It

fell apart under his assault, pulling across her skin. She took a sharp breath and closed her eyes. She'd never in her life wanted anything as much as she wanted this.

"It's been a long time…" Cole breathed the words across her ear as he tore open a wrapper and rolled on a condom. "This first time might just be for me, Bree. I won't be able to wait for you, but I'll make it up to you before the night's over… I promise…"

"Yes…okay…fine…" Her words came out in gasps. She just wanted him inside her. Right now.

And then she had him. No preamble. No gentleness. He filled her, and her blood burned brighter than the lightning flickering in the windows. He was urgent, but not rough. Demanding without causing pain. His eyes were closed, and there was an edge of desperation to his moves. The thought danced across her mind that he was using her. That he didn't know or care who she was. She was a means to an end. A distraction from his nightmares.

And she didn't care, because it was perfect.

She tossed her head back and forth on the sheets and heard herself saying shocking things. Dirty things. Demanding things. He was grunting his answers to her, his breath hot on her neck. Everywhere their bodies touched was slick with perspiration. No. It was sweat. Good old-fashioned sweat. She dug her nails into his back and felt him flex his hard muscles against her fingers. She was ready for him to take what he needed. This was a gift she was giving freely.

Then he stopped moving. Her eyes flew open and she let out a whimper of protest. Cole was holding himself up, his arms braced on either side of her. He stared down, and she watched as his face softened. He lowered his head until they were eye to eye. His words nearly caused her to detonate on the spot.

"Come with me, Bree. I won't go without you. Come with me…"

He knew who he was with. He knew it was her. And it mattered to him. Their bodies fell into a slow, seductive rhythm, and their whispers were less vulgar, more intimate.

"Do you like this, baby?"

"Oh, yes…please…"

"Am I making you happy, Brianna?"

"You have no idea…"

"Are you ready to fly, sweetheart?"

"Yes! Yes… Oh…" She could barely grind out the words as she felt her body catapulting into ecstasy. She cried out his name and, just as he promised, she was flying. His hands grasped her hips tightly and he took what he needed before falling on top of her, breathing heavily.

When she finally came back to her senses, Bree could hardly believe it. She'd just had wild, rough, crazy sex with a man who spent most of his time infuriating her. And she wanted to do it again. Laughter bubbled up in her chest, causing him to lift his head and stare at her in consternation.

"You find this funny, Hollywood?"

"I find this many things, Plowboy. I just can't articulate them all. I'm overwhelmed. Completely overwhelmed."

OVERWHELMED.

Yeah, Cole thought, that about summed it up. He rolled off her and drew her close to his side, keeping his arm wrapped tightly around her.

"Ow…" she murmured as he squeezed her.

"Really? After what we just did, a *hug* is making you say 'ow'?"

She laughed. It was a deep, throaty, whiskey laugh, and his pulse leaped at the sound of it. Then he thought about what he'd just said. He relaxed his grip just a bit, not willing to let her go, but never wanting to cause her pain.

"What we did…did I hurt you?" He lifted his head to look at her. He recalled digging his fingers into her soft flesh and demanding her compliance. He'd probably left bruises. She raised her green eyes to meet his gaze then gave him a typical Bree smirk.

"I think we both got exactly what we wanted, don't you? By the way, how's your back?"

He rubbed his back against the mattress. Yeah, he was pretty sure she drew blood with those fingernails. "Feels damned good to me."

She gave that deep laugh again and he let it wash over him for just a moment. But there were things they needed to discuss. He needed to control expectations. He didn't want any woman clinging to him, thinking he was—shudder—boyfriend material.

"Bree…about what just happened…" He cleared his throat, trying to say the right thing and not hurt her feelings. "It was probably a…"

"I swear to God if you say the word *mistake*, I will make sure your balls never leave this room. I will remove them from your body by hand."

And then he was laughing. Out loud. *Again.* What was this woman doing to him? She raised her head, surprised.

"You have the best laugh. You really need to do it more often. If I knew all it took was the threat of castration…"

"Stop it, for God's sake!" He was still chuckling. "Enough! I wasn't going to come anywhere close to calling tonight a mistake, so stow your fingernails, Hollywood." He took a deep breath.

What *was* he going to say? Oh, yeah. Expectations. "You were amazing. I just don't want you to think that…you know…that things will change when tomorrow rolls around."

"Are you telling me that when the sun comes up, you're still going to be a jackass?"

He laughed again. "I can pretty much guarantee it, honey. Did you think you'd cured me?"

She gave him an exaggerated shrug of her shoulder. "A girl can always dream."

This woman just slayed him. He couldn't resist any longer and rolled over so that she was on her back and he was propped up above her on one elbow. He leaned down and kissed her smiling lips lightly.

"If anyone could do it, you could." He grew serious. "But I don't want to hurt you, Bree. Don't expect…"

She put her fingers over his lips and sighed. "Do you always talk this much after sex? I get it. Incurable jackass. And I'm still the same spoiled Malibu diva I was before. I'll be back in LA soon enough. I'm a big girl, and I get it. So relax, okay?"

He nodded and kissed her fingertips without saying anything. It made no sense how much he hated to think of her leaving. She slid her hand to the side of his head, tenderly working her fingers into his hair. Her serious expression faded back to a mischievous smile.

"Since we both agree we'll go back to our evil ways in the morning, I think we should take advantage of the remaining hours of darkness, don't you?" The thunderstorm was fading into the distance. The storm inside him was just getting started.

He had a fleeting worry that more of Bree Mathews might be more than he could handle emotionally. But there was no way he was turning her down.

His hands shifted her body underneath him, and his mouth fell on hers, claiming her again. He lifted his head and gave her what felt like a face-splitting grin. His smile muscles were seriously out of shape. "It's a deal. For the rest of the night, nothing else matters but what we do right here in this bed. And oh, baby, what we're going to do…"

They spent the next few hours exploring each other. Kissing, stroking, nibbling, giggling, loving, sighing, cursing, laughing, and both, at one point or another, crying. Cole kissed tears from Bree's cheeks as he brought her to sweet oblivion again and again. He nearly lost his mind with the loving of her. No…with the love-*making*. He was so grateful for the simple act of being able to feel, not only with his lips and his fingers, but also with his heart. His own tears spilled over when she finally fell into exhausted sleep in his arms, and he was thankful for the darkness. He was lost in her. He was lost *to* her. He never wanted to see the sun come up again.

# CHAPTER TWELVE

THE RED LED numbers on the alarm clock were blurry at first, but Bree forced her eyes to focus and saw that it was just before five in the morning. She was in Cole Caldwell's bed. And she was alone. The coolness of his pillow told her he'd been gone a while. Her body ached in the sweetest way. She smiled into the dark, empty room. Who knew sex could be that good? No, it wasn't just sex…well, some of it was. But mostly it was lovemaking of the highest degree. Intimate and hot and dirty and beautiful. And in between, they'd talked at length about random things like favorite foods and movies. It felt so natural to be in his arms. She stretched and stood. It was still dark outside, which meant they had time to share before turning into pumpkins in the light of the day.

His T-shirt was hanging on the footboard post, and she slipped it over her head, inhaling his earthy scent. It barely covered her bottom, but she was hoping she wasn't going very far. Or keeping it on for very long. As tired as she was, she wanted more of him.

She found him on the balcony above the front porch, stretched out on a wicker chaise, staring toward the horizon, which was just beginning to blush pink. He wore only cargo shorts, unzipped and hanging low on his hips. Maggie was lying on the floor nearby, and her tail moved in a tiny wag when she spotted Bree in the doorway. Without moving his head, Cole spoke.

"You should be sleeping."

"So should you." She pushed the screen door open and walked over to him. His jaw tightened when he saw what she was wearing. The heat from his gaze started with her bare legs and rose all the way up to her face. She gave him a crooked smile. "This flowered chaise lounge doesn't really look like something you'd buy."

He grunted in typical Cole style. "It was a gift from Nell. I spent a lot of nights out here on an old fold-up vinyl chair, and she thought this would be more comfortable." He shifted to the side. "Are you going to stand there and critique my decorating skills, or are you going to set yourself down and join me?"

"Such a romantic." She sat carefully to keep the T-shirt anchored at her thighs, then leaned back and nestled her head on his tattooed shoulder.

"Why do you sleep outside?"

"I just do." His tone was sharp. He worked his fingers up and down her back, and his next words were softer. "It's a combat thing. Shelter isn't necessarily good. You don't hear things indoors. Your options are limited. You can end up trapped. I tried to sleep outdoors whenever I could when I was over there, and I still have times when I feel safer outside."

"Safer from me?"

"If that was the plan, it clearly didn't work, did it?" He gave her a quick squeeze.

She liked this version of Cole. Honest. Open. Just a little bit playful. Would this man really disappear when the night faded into morning? She rubbed her cheek against his skin and felt the bumps of his scars.

"You got the tattoo to hide the scarring?"

"Yeah."

"And the scars are from…?"

Silence. His fingers were still moving across her skin. Back and forth like a metronome. She was just about to apologize for asking when he finally started to speak.

"Our vehicle was hit by a roadside bomb in Afghanistan. It flipped and caught fire. Those armored vehicles are built for protection, not for easy exits. The doors are small, and once a fire starts inside, there are only seconds to escape. I was near a hatch, so I was able to get out. I was burned when I reached back in to help..."

She was at a loss as to what to say. "Did you get them out?"

His fingers continued their path across her back, over and over.

"Not all of them. And the ones who did..."

His voice trailed off, and she knew he was back there in his mind, seeing flames. Hearing God knows what. She waited, knowing there was nothing she could say to help him.

"It was an ambush. They were waiting to shoot at us after the bomb went off. So the ones I pulled out...were shot at anyway. I got these burns for nothing."

"No one else survived?"

"Two besides me. And Maggie. Three died, including Scott, her handler."

"But you saved two, Cole. And you're alive. I'm glad you're alive."

His hand stopped moving. He started to say something then stopped. It was time for her to change the subject.

"The sun will be up soon."

"Yup."

His fingers began moving again, now randomly tracing circles across her back.

"What happens then?" She lifted her chin and

rested it on his chest, looking at his very serious face.

He stared back at her, and she could see him struggling. She waited.

"Tonight was insanely good, Bree. But it was also just plain insane. You and I are not a good idea."

"So this was just a moment out of time? Do we *have* to go back to our antagonizing ways and pretend it never happened?"

"A moment out of time." He sighed. "Everything in me is telling me to say yes, let's pretend it never happened. I know that's the smart thing to do." His hand slid down her back to cover her behind. His fingers moved, and she felt the T-shirt being pulled higher. "But my body's not done with you yet, Brianna. If you keep showing up at my door, I'm gonna keep pulling you inside. I'll bury myself in you every night if you'll let me, because I'm a man, and I'm not a total idiot."

He kissed her forehead gently.

"But it won't change anything in the long run. I'm bad for you. I'm bad for everyone. That story I told doesn't begin to cover how or why I'm so screwed up. That day wasn't the worst of what I've seen. It was just the last in a long list of terrible things. I have a hot temper and it has a hair trigger. I have some really dark days when

I can't be around people. I have pain that even you can't take away. I'll say things and I'll do things that will hurt you. Not physically, but I will hurt you. And I don't know if I'll be able to cope with that when it happens."

His hand was resting on her bare bottom now, and he gave a gentle squeeze.

"You should be walking away from me right now, Bree. I don't want you to, but you should be walking away."

They stared at each other silently. She didn't doubt the truth of what he said. He could hurt her. He might even break her heart beyond repair. But she saw in his eyes what he couldn't say. He needed her. And she wasn't going anywhere.

She raised her hand and rested it on his cheek. He leaned into it just as he had last night. Was she strong enough to tame the beast inside him? She shifted and moved her body to straddle his. His eyes narrowed, but he smiled.

"Whatcha' doin', Hollywood?"

"The sun's technically not up yet, Plowboy. And I'm not done with you…" She lowered her lips onto his and felt his hands lifting his shirt higher around her waist while they kissed. He raised his hips so she could lower his shorts then mumbled something and gripped her hips to stop her.

"Condom…"

"I haven't been with anyone since Damian, and I'm still on birth control." She kissed his lips lightly. "You know, just in case."

"Just in case, huh?" He returned her kiss. "I haven't been very active myself, and always careful. You're the only one who can make me lose my common sense."

As she lowered her body onto his, his lips parted and he groaned. She had the power to do this to him, and it was a wonderful thing. He shifted so he was sitting more upright, and they were face-to-face when they started moving together, skin to delicious skin. Her muscles were protesting, but that was soon forgotten in the heat of the moment, and it wasn't long before he had her flying again, crying out his name and collapsing with her arms around his neck. He held her there as they both tried to regain control of their breathing and heart rates. She closed her eyes to the sound of his voice whispering her name, and the touch of his fingers in her hair.

The sun was very definitely up when she woke again, lying in Cole's empty bed. She had a hazy memory of him carrying her inside. She stretched and smiled, looking at the clock. It was after eight. She felt like someone had taken a delightful but persistent sledgehammer to her body from head to toe. She stood and slid his T-shirt back on, deciding it may have just become her favorite attire. But she did pull her panties on this time before heading downstairs.

The house was empty. No Cole. No Maggie. She looked across the road to Nell's place and smiled. His black truck was there, and the horses were out in the paddock. He'd gone to do her chores. She gave herself a quick, contented hug and headed into the kitchen. She'd repay him with breakfast. His kitchen was well stocked, and it wasn't long before she had bacon frying, coffee brewing and French toast on the griddle. Through the window over the sink, she saw his truck pull around to the back of the house. She was singing "This Girl Is on Fire" to herself and really started to belt it out when she got to the chorus. She heard the screen door slam and grinned. What would Cole think about finding her dancing around his kitchen in his T-shirt?

But it wasn't his voice that rang out from the living room. "Yo, Cole! I need a hand with some new equipment at the bar. Can you give me an hour or so this morn…"

Ty slid to a halt at the entrance to the kitchen. Bree froze with the spatula in her hand, feeling her face go twenty shades of crimson.

"Holy shit." Ty blinked then blinked again and glanced away when she reached down to tug the

T-shirt over her bare thighs. He grinned as he stared at the floor. "Good morning, Brianna."

Before she could form coherent words, Cole came into the kitchen through the back door. He glanced from her to his brother and smirked. "You might want to try knocking, Ty." He slid his arm around her waist, pulling her close. "Smells great in here. Got enough for my brother?"

She sputtered, and he clarified his question. "Got enough breakfast, that is. That's the only thing I'm sharing." He looked at Ty, who was staring stupidly at the two of them, as if he'd never seen Cole with a woman in his home before. She felt a flush of pride as she realized he probably hadn't. At least not in a long time.

"We have plenty of food, but I'm not exactly dressed for company." She handed the spatula to Cole. "Can you take over while I run upstairs?"

"Upstairs?" Ty repeated. She blushed again, and Cole laughed out loud. Ty stepped back at the sound and stared at his brother as if he was a science experiment of some kind. Cole shrugged at him.

"What? You thought I'd shag her on the living room floor instead of my much more comfortable bed?" She smacked him in the stomach and he laughed again. Ty seemed frozen in shock at this point.

"Turn around, Ty, so Hollywood can go fetch her clothes with at least a little dignity."

Was it really necessary to emphasize yet again that she'd slept in his room last night? She shook her head. There was something appealingly caveman about his boasting.

"Turn around? Oh, yeah, of course. Sorry, Bree." Ty turned to face the wall opposite the stairs.

She ran past him and up to Cole's room to dress. He'd destroyed her bra last night, so she'd have to go without. She grabbed a cotton shirt from Cole's closet and pulled it on over her tank top, tying it at her waist above her denim shorts. It gave her a little more camouflage on top so she wouldn't be flashing her boobs at his brother. Her cheeks warmed. Cole still seemed to be in a playful mood. Maybe the sunshine wouldn't ruin them after all. She hummed to herself as she headed downstairs.

Then again, she should have known it wouldn't last. His eyes were stormy gray when they met hers as she joined them at the well-worn kitchen table. She smiled at him, but he just shook his head and went back to attacking his breakfast. Ty washed down a forkful of French toast with coffee before looking at her sheepishly and mouthing, *Sorry*.

Bree started her breakfast in silence, hoping

the awkward moment would pass. But finally, she couldn't take the drastic switch in mood any longer.

"Okay, what did I miss?" She asked the question brightly, hoping to lighten the tension.

It was Ty who answered. "I was just telling Cole about your generous gift to the bar and asked him for help hooking up the new sound system." So he was angry because she'd hooked Ty up with a karaoke system? She'd forgotten all about giving that phone number to Tammy last week to pass along to Ty.

"It seemed the least I could do to repay your kindness, Ty. Helping with the car. Tammy and Emily being so great with getting me new clothes and a new look. Tammy mentioned you were saving up for one, so I made a few calls, that's all. Do you like your breakfast, Cole?"

He raised his head and she was stung to see that flat look in his eyes. "It's fine."

Ty chuckled affectionately as he grabbed the last slice of bacon. "Cole, don't be an idiot. It's delicious and you know it. The sound system isn't some charity donation. Bree just set us up with a supplier who sold it for less than wholesale as a favor to her. Why are you so ticked off about it?"

"Yeah, Cole. Why *are* you so ticked off?" She arched a brow in his direction. He glared back at her.

"It feels like charity. The rich starlet comes to the poor little country town and starts throwing money around to win friends…"

"Wow." Before Ty could say more, Bree leaped to her feet, sending her chair scraping across the wooden floor.

"Is that really what you think? That I'm *buying* friendship? A few dollars for Ty and his family? Farm chores to win over Nell? And what about you? All I had to do was spread my legs and we were friends for a few hours, right?"

Ty had a violent coughing fit.

"Because if I didn't give myself away, no one around here would want to be with me, right?"

"Damn it, that's not what I…"

She left the room before he could finish. This felt sickeningly familiar. Leave it to Cole Caldwell to take an act of kindness and make it sound cheap and fake. She was almost out the back door when a strong arm wrapped around her waist. Her anger still burned bright, and she tried to pry his arm away by sinking her nails into his flesh.

"Stop." His breath moved across her ear. "Just *stop*. Listen to me, okay?"

She gave up her attempts to escape but stood stiffly with her back to him.

"Look, I told you my anger is on a hair trigger. I told you that, didn't I?" She nodded, her shoulders easing against her will as he pressed a kiss to the base of her neck. "When Ty said you got the bar a $20,000 sound system, I...reacted badly. I'm sorry." She felt him smile against her skin. "Hell, I haven't said those words in months, and you've got me saying them every damn day. I don't know if it's because you make me screw up more, or if you just make me care when my screwups hurt you." Another kiss. "Don't leave this house angry, Bree. Not after last night. Don't leave angry."

Her head dropped down, only to see Maggie sitting at her side, looking up with dark, worried eyes. "I'm sorry for what I said about spreading my legs..."

He chuckled into her neck and she relaxed against his solid chest. The fight was over. "Yeah, that was a little tough to hear in front of my brother, but I guess I deserved it."

She turned and looked up at him, relieved to see a softer light in his eyes. "Is Ty still here? He must think we're crazy."

Cole shook his head. His hands rested lightly on her hips. "He's headed back to town. Ty *knows* I'm crazy, and he's now having serious doubts about your judgment. He didn't seem all that surprised to find us together, though. And he certainly wasn't surprised to see us going at each other's throats. I told him I'd meet him at the bar later and help with the new system." He kissed her lips softly. "Breakfast was great."

She leaned into his kiss, but he brought her out of her warm thoughts with a sharp smack on her behind.

"Now get up to Nell's. I cleaned stalls for you, but I have my own place to run." She grinned and turned away. Her hand was on the back door when he spoke again.

"Brianna." She looked over her shoulder, and the heat in his expression made her heart jump. "I've got to drive over to Bladenboro this afternoon to look at a cattle hauler, but I'll be back tonight. I want to see you."

She watched the emotions move across his face. Desire. Affection. Fear. She knew she was mirroring the same. This was uncharted territory for both of them. She lifted her chin and shrugged, acting far braver than she felt.

"You know where I live, Plowboy. If you forget, just follow your dog. She knows the way."

"Do you have any clue what you're doing?" Ty handed Cole a drill while Cole balanced a speaker against the wall with his shoulder. Cole grunted.

"With this speaker? Yeah, I think I've got it covered. It will definitely be attached to the wall when I'm done."

"I wasn't talking about the speaker, and you know it. What's the deal with you and Bree?"

"She showed up during the storm last night, and things...just happened." He leaned into the drill and sank the last screw into the wall. "I gave her full disclosure on the odds that I'll make a mess of things, like I did this morning. She's still in." He shrugged at Ty's dubious expression. "Maybe she's as screwed up as I am."

Cole stepped off the ladder.

"I'm worried about Bree being hurt," Ty said. "But I'm more worried about you. You're my brother. She's going to be back in California as soon as they catch whoever's stalking her. Have you really thought this through?"

Cole frowned. He didn't like to think about Bree leaving Russell. It just didn't compute for him. But she was a product of Tinseltown. She'd been married to a movie star, and she'd probably end up married to another one. He was nothing more than a diversion while she hid out in his humble little part of the world. But maybe that was what made this thing between them work.

"Ty, having an end date is what we both need. I've been out of circulation for a long time, and so has she. Might be good to have a fling with someone who doesn't expect long-term in any way, shape or form. We scratch each other's itches, so to speak, and we already know how it's going to end, so there won't be any drama when it's over."

Ty handed him a cold beer from behind the bar. "Scratch your itch, huh? And am I right in guessing she takes care of your itch very nicely?"

Cole smiled and shook his head. "Between you and me? Best. Sex. Ever. Hotter than hell. But it's more than that...it feels different with her..." He realized he'd said far more than he'd intended. "Ty..."

His big brother gave him a smile. "Look, if anyone deserves a few nights of hot, sweaty sex with a gorgeous woman, it's you. Just be careful. With *her* heart, and with *yours*. I saw that adoring look in your eyes when you walked into the kitchen this morning."

Cole slid onto a bar stool. "You've been hanging out with Tammy and Emily too much. You're starting to sound like a girl. Bree and I talked it out, and we've established reasonable expectations."

"Little brother, she made you *laugh*. Out *loud*."

Yeah, there was that. He shook his head. He wasn't ready to examine that too closely.

"We're just two adults having a mutually beneficial, and very temporary, sexual relationship. Nothing more." If he kept saying it out loud, he might just start to believe it.

Ty stared at him then grinned. "Okay. Whatever you say."

The front door opened and Tammy walked into the bar with Emily following. Before the door closed, Emily bolted straight to the dance hall, eager to inspect the new karaoke machine.

Ty called after her. "I still have to finish programming it, Em." Emily nodded as she examined the control board.

Tammy rolled her eyes and sat next to Cole, accepting the cold soda Ty offered her. "It's all she's talked about since you told her it arrived. She's already making a list of the songs she wants you to order. Oh, and by the way, she announced that she expects her sixteenth birthday party to be held here at the bar. During the afternoon and alcohol-free, of course."

Cole frowned. "Isn't her birthday two months away?"

"Yup. That's how excited she is about karaoke, Uncle Cole." Her smile faded. "Umm…did you happen to watch the news this morning?"

Ty choked back a laugh but went silent when Cole leveled a glare at him and shook his head.

"The morning shows were all talking about Bree," Tammy said. "There's some story about her having a breakdown and running off to a rehab center in Utah."

Bree had told him about the fake story somewhere around 2 am. Those whispered conversations in the dark felt just as intimate as the sex, if that was possible. The false rumor would hopefully force her stalker to make a mistake. She hadn't mentioned anything about it becoming national news, though.

"They were showing a lot of pictures of her on television, Cole. I'm guessing tonight's entertainment shows will all be doing the same. It's a lot of publicity for someone trying to stay anonymous. Even people who never saw the reality show are now seeing her face."

"Not that many people here in Russell have seen her…" he started, but Ty interrupted.

"Except for that Saturday night right here in the bar."

Tammy nodded, looking guilty. "We were so caught up in changing Bree's looks that we let our enthusiasm run away with our good sense. It's hard to disguise that gorgeous face."

Cole thought about how that gorgeous face looked last night, under him in bed. And later, on top of him on the chaise. Laughing in the back of Nell's truck. Fierce with anger whenever they quarreled. The silence was broken when Emily started singing a Carrie Underwood hit on the karaoke system. Leave it to a teenager to figure out the technology faster than her dad. The sudden noise was enough to kick his mind back in gear. If anyone in Russell started asking questions about Bree, her safety could be at risk.

"Other than that night, hardly anyone has seen her, and they've all met her as Anna. Arlen and his dad saw her when we were putting up hay…"

Ty interrupted. "I'll talk to Arlen. He and George can be trusted."

"I know. But what about the crowd in here? All the guys she danced with…"

"It's not the guys you have to worry about, Cole." Tammy gave him a thin smile. "It's women that watch entertainment news. Like Amber and her posse. Amber said Bree looked familiar, and that worries me."

Cole's pulse slowed and his body settled into battle readiness. This was a situation. And he knew how to handle situations. His response team was already gathered in this room. They just needed a plan.

"We need to keep Bree out of sight and off the radar."

"Should she move out of the cottage? Maybe in with Nell?"

Cole hesitated just long enough for his brother to start chuckling again.

"Baby, if she moves anywhere, it won't be Nell's place." Ty winked at his wife's confusion. "Guess who was cooking breakfast at my brother's place this morning, wearing nothing but his T-shirt and a satisfied smile?"

Tammy's jaw dropped.

"Cole, you didn't!"

"Hey!" He threw his hands up in defense while sneaking another glare at his big-mouthed brother. "We're both adults, Tammy."

His sister-in-law looked as if she didn't know how she felt about this development, and he couldn't blame her. He wasn't sure how he felt about it, either.

"She cooked you breakfast?"

"Apparently they worked up an appetite." Ty looked proud of himself until Tammy and Cole rounded on him. He busied himself wiping down the bar.

Cole thought for a minute. "Look, we basically live on a dead-end road. Other than the produce stand, there isn't any traffic, so we can keep her out of sight. Tammy, do you think there's any way Amber would listen to you and keep her mouth shut if you explained the situation?"

"Maybe, but I doubt it. We're not exactly close, and I wasn't all that pleasant to her in the bar. But..." She looked at him, tipping her head to the side with a smile. "She might listen to you."

"No. No way." He didn't want anything to do with his former fiance.

"She's a shrew, but she's not completely evil,

Cole. She had feelings for you at one time. She accepted your marriage proposal, after all."

"And then ran out and cheated on me. Not a real good sign of true love."

"Perhaps. But she still dumped you, not the other way around. You're not the bad guy in this scenario. She might feel guilty enough to help you."

He shook his head, but not quite as vehemently as before. Tammy had a point; it just wasn't one he wanted to agree with. "I'd head straight home now, but I've got an appointment in Bladenboro…"

Tammy stood. "Don't worry about it. Emily and I will go to Nell's this afternoon and stay with her. Em can run the stand so Bree stays out of sight."

Cole didn't answer. He didn't even notice when Tammy and Emily left a few minutes later. He'd not only let a woman break through his defenses and make him feel things. He'd also allowed himself to get pulled into her orbit and invested in her safety. That wasn't supposed to happen, and he felt more vulnerable than he had in a long time.

## CHAPTER THIRTEEN

BREE WAS HAPPY to see Tammy and Emily pull up that afternoon. It had been a long, quiet day with far too much time to think. Too much time to wonder if the night of unexpected intimacy and passion was the best thing to ever happen to her or the biggest mistake of her life.

Tammy insisted Bree stay on the porch with her so she could duck inside if someone pulled up while they were relaxing there. Emily happily went to work reorganizing Nell's produce stand, cleaning displays and touching up the signs with a permanent marker.

Tammy broke into Bree's thoughts. "Are you sure you're okay with the media going nuts about your story? I mean, they're making you sound like an addict or something. Doesn't that make you crazy?"

Bree just shook her head. "The media always makes me crazy, but we *want* the publicity this time. And frankly, I couldn't care less what the media thinks of me. I just hate that this mess has managed to follow me to my hideaway."

She looked at Tammy and grinned. "No pun intended, of course."

Tammy reached for the iced tea, but the pitcher was empty. "I'll refill this, but maybe we should start dinner? We could have it ready for Nell when she gets home."

When Nell arrived that evening, she was carrying an armful of shopping bags and wearing a wide, relaxed smile.

"My goodness, look at all these pretty ladies in my kitchen! What's the occasion?"

"Tammy and Emily were afraid I was going to be upset about seeing my face plastered all over the news tonight. They keep forgetting that the only bad publicity is no publicity." She forced a laugh, but the truth was she'd been feeling more and more apprehensive about the story airing. A year ago she would have been eager for *any* kind of publicity, but now she wanted the press to leave her alone. She was just so weary of it all. "They'll make a big deal about it until the next scandal comes along. It's such a circus." There was a beat of silence in the kitchen. "Come on, let's go see how bad it is."

She turned on the television and clicked through the channels until she heard a familiar tune. It was the theme from *Spotlight Tonight*, one of several "news" programs that survived by spreading celebrity gossip and sensational stories about the entertainment business. Bree used to watch it religiously to see what was happening in her world. That felt like a lifetime ago.

"Bree, they're showing the story!" Emily grabbed her arm in excitement.

A photo montage was running behind the solemn-faced anchor, who was talking about Bree's sad fall from glory. She was the former Miss California who married one of the sexiest actors in Hollywood, lived a life of excessive luxury then was publicly betrayed by her husband. Now she'd apparently suffered an emotional breakdown and vanished. Two "friends" appeared on screen to say how worried they were about her. Both women had stopped returning her calls shortly after her divorce. Yeah, right, they missed her.

There were whispers about the Seventh Heaven drug treatment center in Utah. The center denied Brianna Mathews was a patient with them. The anchor winked at the camera, saying "We all know what *that* means, don't we?" The story ended with a video of paparazzi surrounding the gates of Seventh Heaven, hoping for a glimpse of poor, tragic Brianna Mathews. A chill settled over her. They looked like vultures.

The show's host was back on screen now. "Brianna's agent hinted that a comeback was being planned, and we hear she might be dancing next season on a popular show. Also, she has a cook-book coming out for the holidays. We reached out to her ex-husband, Damian Maxwell, but his representatives said he had no comment. Of course, Damian is filming the action-hero movie that's supposed to be his *own* comeback, and they're predicting a blockbuster hit..."

Bree straightened her back and lifted her chin, harnessing her sudden panic with a deep, slow intake of air. She'd become national news. Her face was on every network. The paparazzi would be offering boatloads of money for further clues to her exact location. They were focused on the Utah angle for now, but how long would she be safe here?

"Bree, darlin', it's okay," Nell said softly.

"No. It's not..." She started pacing the floor. "I shouldn't stay here, Nell. But I can't go home. Hell, I don't even know where home *is* any-more."

The beach house in Malibu no longer felt like home. Not only was she not safe there, but she didn't know who she *was* there. She dropped her head in frustration and was surprised to see her hands were steady, although she felt like she was shaking so hard she could barely stand.

Nell's arm slid around her shoulder. "Oh, honey, haven't you figured it out yet? Child, you're already home."

BREE COULDN'T STOP replaying Nell's words in her mind when she got back to the cottage.

*Child, you're already home.*

Those four words resonated in ways she couldn't define. While California no longer felt like home, she hadn't considered that she may have found a home right here in this tiny North Carolina town. Her new friends. The Hide-Away. The farms that stretched on for miles. The hard and rewarding work. The sexy, temperamental farmer across the road. Could she make a home here? She snorted. What would she do? Run a farm? Plan five-star events in Russell?

She ruffled through the final pages of the paperback she'd just finished, with the hero and heroine riding off victoriously into the sunset. She was relieved to hear Maggie's soft whine outside the front door, if only for the distraction from her spinning mind. She opened it and jumped back.

Despite her sassy words to Cole that morning, she didn't expect to see him taking up the entire doorway, his hands braced above the frame as Maggie trotted inside. He stared at her so intensely she was tempted to look down to see if her clothing had burst into flames. His mouth was a grim straight line, but when their eyes met, his gaze softened and warmed.

"Hollywood."

He didn't move. He was waiting for an invitation. He'd manhandled her last night—hell, they'd manhandled each other—but he wasn't assuming anything tonight.

"Plowboy."

She leaned against the door frame and lifted her chin saucily. The corner of his mouth twitched and threatened a smile until he glanced over her shoulder.

"Why is my dog on your sofa?"

"It's comfortable. A lady likes to feel pampered now and then."

"Is that right?"

She gulped as his eyes raked up and down her body before meeting her gaze. His hand cupped her cheek and he brushed his thumb across her lower lip. She was suddenly filled with emotion to the point of nearly choking. His proximity was sending her heart into double-time. This was just supposed to be a little fling, but that wasn't how it felt right now.

"Are *you* looking for a little pampering, Hollywood?"

She swatted a mosquito on her neck. "Right now I'm looking to stop an invasion of insects. Come inside." She forced herself to turn away, suddenly afraid of betraying the emotions she still hadn't identified. As the door closed, Maggie jumped off the sofa and settled on the rug, not wanting to push her luck in front of her master. Cole stared at Bree, and a frown flickered across his face.

"Did you see the news?"

"Typical Hollywood nonsense," she said with a shrug. "I'm worried the paparazzi bloodhounds will find me here, but for now they all seem to be in Utah." She remembered his angry words right after she arrived, so concerned she'd embarrass his friends and family. "Cole, at the first hint of trouble, I'll leave. I won't let anything happen…"

He shook his head sharply. "Don't. I know why you're saying that, but don't. I was wrong to accuse you of being here for any reason other than the one you gave me." He pulled her close and smiled slowly. "Now about that pampering…"

Something fluttered inside her when she looked into his eyes. Something warm and sure and strong. Something that scared her half to death.

*Child, you're already home.*

No.

She had a *life* in California. It was fine to daydream about retiring to the country, but in reality it made no sense. She had catering clients in LA. She had a book coming out in a few months, which meant a publicity tour. She had a twenty-million-dollar mansion on the beach.

People would say she was crazy for walking away from that. She *would* be crazy! Besides, no one had even *asked* her to walk away from it.

Cole repeatedly said they were a bad idea. He was worried he'd hurt her. But he had no idea how much pain he could actually cause, because she was falling for him, and falling fast. She pulled back, then smiled brightly to soften the surprise in his eyes.

"Pampering? Let's start with a nice glass of cognac, okay? Are you hungry? Want some cheese and crackers? Let me just put something together…" She walked to the kitchen while she babbled. He was clearly doing his best not to laugh at her.

"Why, that would be lovely, Miss Mathews. Brandy sounds delightful. And cheese. I can *always* use more cheese. Do you need any help finding the good china?"

"No, no. Just stay there. I'm fine." She scrambled into the kitchen, her face flushed. What the hell was wrong with her? She glanced up and saw him watching her, his arms folded, a curious grin on his face. She couldn't remember the last time she'd had a panic attack, but she was having one now, and she didn't know why. *Focus, Bree!* The bottle of Courvoisier was still sitting on the counter, so she only had to find two juice glasses. That mission accomplished, she brought a brick of cheddar out of the refrigerator and started searching the drawers for a knife. The silence allowed her to think too much, so she started babbling again.

"So did you buy the cattle hauler?"

"Yup. It'll be delivered next week."

"That's nice. What color is it?"

"You want to know what *color* my cattle hauler is?" He stepped up to the counter directly across from her. "Why are you freaking out? Is it the news story? Is it us?"

"Us?" Her voice sounded high-pitched in her own ears. "What do you mean? I'm just being a g-good hostess…" She stuttered to a stop when she looked up at his knowing eyes. A nervous giggle bubbled up and she couldn't contain it. "Oh, my God, you're right. I'm *totally* freaking out." She shook her head. "I guess it's everything. My brain's in overdrive."

*And I might be falling in love with you…*

"It's after dark, Hollywood. That's our moment in time, remember? Our safe place." His voice did something to her skin, causing it to tingle all over. And his eyes. Those slate-gray eyes were *her* safe place. What the hell was she doing in the kitchen when Cole Caldwell was standing right there in her living room? She pushed the kitchen drawer closed, pulling her hand out at the same time. That was when she felt it. The chilling slice of a knife blade so razor-sharp that it didn't even hurt as it cut across her palm.

She braced for the pain that was sure to follow, letting out a hiss of breath.

COLE KNEW BREE was having a panic attack of some sort. She'd bolted into the tiny kitchen, babbling about cheese and crackers. Was she having second thoughts? If she was smart, she'd send him packing. If *he* was smart, he'd walk back home and leave her alone. But he couldn't make himself do that. He wanted just one more night with her. As if one would ever be enough.

She drew a sharp breath as she closed the drawer, her eyes wide with surprise, confusion and…pain. His skin instantly went clammy from her expression alone, because it reminded him of someone else's face just two years ago. Lieutenant Walt Simpson had that same expression on a mountainside northwest of Kabul when a sniper's bullet sliced through him. The shooter was so far away that the sound didn't even register until it was too late. One minute they were trading jokes and insults while eating a cold MRE dinner, and the next, Simpson looked at him with wide eyes and paling skin. Cole saw the stain of blood spreading on his friend's chest just before Simpson slumped to the side and died with that surprised look on his face.

He closed his eyes and tried to focus on pulling air into his lungs. He wasn't in Afghanistan. He was in Nell's cottage, and this wasn't Lt. Simpson. It was Bree. His eyes snapped open.

She was looking down at her hand, frowning as a thin white line across her palm became a wider red line. She was bleeding. *Damn it.* She glanced back up at him and her brows knit together.

"Cole, are you okay?"

He stepped back and shook his head to clear it. She was the one bleeding and she was worried about *him*. A wash of shame moved over him. He could not have another flashback episode in front of her like he had at The Hide-Away, or in his house last night. She was going to think he was crazy. He moved quickly around the counter and slid one arm around her waist, reaching for her hand with the other. His voice was far calmer than his heart.

"Hold it up, baby, and put it under running water. That's it." He pivoted her to face the sink and turned on the cold water. She let out a short cry of pain that nearly brought him to his knees. He ground his teeth together. He was a soldier, this was a situation and he could handle it. He heard himself murmuring words of comfort as he opened the cupboard near the sink where Nell stored a first-aid kit.

Somehow he managed to hold himself together and inspect the wound before dressing it carefully with gauze. It was a clean cut, and not as deep as he'd feared. Whatever he was saying seemed to work, because Bree was leaning into him. But he'd never be able to recall the words. He was lost in a battle between the part of his mind that wanted to *run*, and the part of his mind that wanted to *stay* with this woman as long as possible.

"Cole?" Why did her voice sound so far away? "Cole? Where are you right now?"

His eyes snapped up to meet hers. "What? What do you mean?"

"You went somewhere else in your head for a few minutes." She was facing him, her hands resting lightly on his chest as she leaned back against the counter. "I could see it. Feel it. Was it the blood? Is it like thunder to you?"

He didn't know how to explain that it was her eyes, going wide in pain and surprise, that took him away. How could he tell her about watching a twenty-two-year-old lieutenant die silently on a sunny day in the midst of a discussion about food rations? He didn't want her to know about those things. It was bad enough that *he* knew. His skin felt tight and hot, and he started to move away, but she was too quick. Her hands wound into his hair and she pulled herself up to plant her lips on his, and just like that, everything felt good and right and safe again. He was on a freaking roller coaster ride of emotion.

"Bree…" He started to speak against her lips, but she pressed into him and he forgot what he intended to say. He just wrapped his arms around her and pulled her in tight, allowing her to explore his mouth while his hands explored her body.

This, he thought. This was what he needed. This was a lifeline thrown into the wind to save him. He let her distract him with more kisses. He needed her here. Just for a little while.

He lifted her up and set her on the kitchen counter, standing between her legs. They smiled stupidly at each other for a long moment, then he pulled her to him and started carrying her toward the bedroom.

"No cheese and crackers?" She asked the question with a sarcastic tilt of her brow.

"I don't need food right now. But I do need you." Stunned that he'd said those words out loud, he quickly amended them. "I need to be in bed with you."

Her eyes went soft and dark. "Is this part of my pampering?"

"Sure, Hollywood. Anything you want." He clicked off the hallway light with his elbow and pushed the bedroom door closed behind them with his foot. "Anything you want. I'll give it to you all night long."

She sighed against his neck and nodded, knowing no words would be needed for a while.

# CHAPTER FOURTEEN

BREE WAS SOUND asleep when a hand came in loud and shocking contact with her derriere. She sat up with a jolt, rubbing her butt cheek and glowering in the dark. Wait. It was still night. Why was she awake? Oh, yeah, someone spanked her bottom and woke her. It could only be one person, and he was about to pay for it.

"Cole, what the hell? It's the middle of the night!"

His voice next to her ear made her flinch. In the darkness, she didn't realize how close he was. "It's almost dawn, Hollywood. Get dressed. We're going to greet the sun in one of my favorite places."

"Unless that place has a cappuccino machine, I'm not interested. Wake me when the sun is up for real." She started to lie back down, but a strong arm wrapped around her shoulders and pulled her upright. An arm that had clothing on it. Her eyes were adjusting to the lack of light, and she realized he was already dressed. He pulled her to her feet.

"Get dressed, Bree. We're going for a little ride."

In less than fifteen minutes, they were stretched out in the back of Cole's pickup, wrapped in a blanket and sipping on hot coffee from the thermos he'd filled. He'd driven up behind Nell's house to a stand of trees at the top of the hill. He'd swung the truck around and backed up so that they faced the eastern horizon, where a thin slice of pink was beginning to show. To the left was the small gully where Trixie had given birth to Malibu. The cattle were grazing and casting curious glances at the big truck parked in their midst.

"So this is a favorite spot, huh?" She was sitting between his denim-clad legs, leaning back against his chest. His arms wrapped loosely around her, and his fingers intertwined with hers. She felt him nodding against her head.

"One of them. The best morning spot, for sure. Wait until you see all the farms spread out in front of us as the sun rises. It's really something."

"Where are your other favorite spots?"

"Other than inside you?" The words were murmured low into her ear, and she closed her eyes and sighed before answering.

"Yeah, besides that."

"There's a little swimming hole back behind my place that's a good thinking spot in the evening."

"The one you talked about on the tractor? Where you have bonfires?"

"Nah, the bonfire place is farther up the road, where there's room for a crowd. This is a private spot. The river has a pretty good current, so my great-granddaddy dug out a swimming hole for his boys where the water would be more still. There's a big old tree there with a rope on it. Ty and I grew up swimming in that hole, and I still drive back there at night and just think."

"You have a lot of thinking spots, Cole. What are you thinking so much about?"

"Things you don't want in your head, Bree. Things I don't like to talk about, but that I need to think about, to try to exorcize them from my brain."

"You know they have counseling for those kinds of thoughts, right?" Nell had told her he didn't believe in therapy, but surely a professional could help him.

"I'm not a big believer in that stuff. Chris dragged me to his therapy group, but I couldn't take more than a couple sessions. They want to make you relive everything, in detail, in front of a group of guys who all have their own horrible memories. Instead of unloading, it feels like

I'm just piling my shit on top of theirs, and vice versa. I have enough nightmares of my own. I don't need theirs."

"You have nightmares?"

He nodded. "I told you I'm a mess. Some days are fine, but there are days when I'm just barely hanging on. Far worse than what you saw during the storm or at the bar…"

Looking to lighten the mood, she wiggled back against him and peered up at his face. "I kinda liked you during the storm, Plowboy."

He kissed her lightly. "I'm sure you did, Hollywood. But you're missing the show."

She turned back to the east and smiled as the sky slowly turned from black to dark blue to pinky-peach. The soft light shifted across the farms below them, making the haze on the fields glow like fire. But she was distracted at the thought of him not reaching out for help to deal with his issues. In Hollywood, everyone went to counseling for something. She couldn't comprehend why he didn't want professional help.

"So if a group wasn't for you, how about private sessions? Have you tried that?"

"You're not going to let this go, are you?" She didn't answer right away, so he filled the silence, just as she'd hoped. "I've looked into all that stuff. Chris and Ty want me to go to the Flat Rock Retreat, which is an inpatient program over in the mountains that specializes in PTSD. But I can't just walk away from the farm for two months and go to some fancy place. It's not covered by the VA and it ain't cheap. I'll deal with this on my own. Lots of guys do. In fact, I was visiting a kid who agrees with me that day you helped Trixie give birth."

"Really?" So that was where he was. "How's he doing?"

He shrugged. "He's good. He's working on his father's farm. Travis and I believe working on the land and just putting all that crap behind us is the best way to go, and it seems to be doing the trick for both of us." He dropped a kiss on the top of her head. "And that's enough on that topic. Now it's your turn. Are you really okay with all this media business?"

She considered a moment.

"It was hard to see all those clips about my marriage, the reality show meltdown, the divorce. It wasn't pretty."

"Do you want to talk about it?" He pulled her in close. She didn't want to, but it wouldn't be fair to refuse after she'd pushed *him* so hard. So she leaned against him as his fingers traced circles on her arms and she told him all about the romance made for Hollywood—a beauty queen and a popular actor who'd just been voted the year's sexiest man.

Their wedding had been paid for by an entertainment magazine in exchange for exclusive rights to the photos. It was a surreal experience, saying her marriage vows on the lawn of the Beverly Hills Hotel while helicopters full of paparazzi hovered overhead. The mix of opulence and chaos was a foretelling of what their life together would be like. Money flowed like champagne, and it gave her a feeling of security that she hadn't experienced since her mother died. Nothing bad could happen as long as she had enough money and influence to deal with it.

"Then Damian's show was canceled, and things went to hell. He started drinking and I suspected he was using cocaine. Damian had this reputation as Mr. Happy-Go-Lucky, but he got angry a lot those days." Cole's arms tightened around her. "Every time he went to an audition and didn't get the part, he'd come home and…vent."

"Tell me exactly what that means." Cole's voice was low and tense.

"It's not as bad as you're thinking. Just a lot of yelling and breaking things. He finally checked in to rehab after things got a little too crazy one night."

"Define crazy."

"He was high, and I was furious. We had a

horrible screaming argument. You know I have a hot temper, and I was in his face…"

"Don't blame yourself for someone else's actions, Bree. What happened?"

"He shoved me up against the railing on our third-story balcony and it started to give way. We both felt it, and for just a second, he pushed harder before yanking me back to safety. It scared both of us, and he went off to rehab. He begged me to wait for him, and I did. Not as much for him but because I liked our lifestyle, and I didn't want to lose it. I loved our home in Malibu, the parties and all of it. That sounds shallow, but that's who I am. Or was. I don't know…"

After a brief pause to control her spinning thoughts, she quietly finished the rest of the story. She and Damian joined *Hot Hollywood Housewives* to jump-start his career. In the third season, with no good roles being offered, Damian started to unravel. Her husband became a cliché, inhaling white powder off cocktail tables through rolled hundred-dollar bills on camera. And he was cheating on her with one of the other wives. The show set it up so she'd walk in on them having a romantic dinner while on camera.

"I flipped over a restaurant table, and the rest is history. I quit the show and hired a divorce lawyer. All I wanted was the beach house, and the judge gave it to me. Poor Damian's still try-ing to get it back. First he appealed the judg-ment, and now he wants to buy it from me." She looked up and found Cole gazing at her. He seemed deep in thought. "And then the stalker showed up, and that safe life I'd wanted so much started to feel really scary."

"Do you think the stalker could be Damian?"

"No. His career is finally heating up again, so what's the point? The movie he's filming is supposed to be a hit, and I'm glad for him. Our marriage was a farce and he was a train wreck, but I never hated the guy."

The horizon turned orange and pink and sil-ver. Birds were beginning to sing a lovely morn-ing chorus in the trees around them.

"It's so beautiful here."

COLE LOOKED DOWN at Bree gazing out over the Carolina farmland he loved so much, and shook his head in wonder. Her hair was pulled back into a simple ponytail, and her freckled skin re-flected the colors of the sunrise, all pink and peach.

"It *is* beautiful," he agreed.

He wasn't prepared for what he felt when they were together. It was more than the terrific sex. Everything was just so damned easy with her. Sure, they liked to bait each other verbally, but that was just their way of handling the passion that was always bubbling beneath the surface.

She was still staring at the horizon when she spoke again.

"Where do we go from here?"

"Well, I'm thinking breakfast sounds like a good idea. If Nell heard us drive by earlier, she's probably got something ready for us."

"You know I'm not talking about that, Cole. What are we going to do about...us?"

His heart drummed solidly against his ribs. It was a fair question, but he had no idea what the answer was. He couldn't expect her to walk away from her West Coast life and stay here. And he had no interest in joining her in Hollyweird. Sure, this felt perfect, wrapped around each other and sated from a night of great sex, but that could only carry them so far. His life was here, and hers was there.

"Nothing's changed, Bree." He forced the words out. "We're still a bad idea. We only work after dark and between the sheets." She stiffened in his arms, but he didn't stop. "Plus, I'm dealing with a lot of crap right now and it's not fair to drag you into that."

"You mean the way you dragged me up here so we could watch the sun come up together? Yeah, that's really twisted, Plowboy."

He couldn't help but smile at her ever-present

sass, but he didn't let her distract him. "Look, I may not want therapy, but I know I have stuff to work through. I need to figure out how to get back to living a normal life again, and I don't think you and I are anywhere near 'normal,' sweetheart."

"There may not be a way to go back to the normal you knew before. But you can create a new normal, Cole. You can move forward by inventing a new path."

A new path. Could that path possibly include a pretty redhead with a sharp tongue and a sharper mind? He quickly dismissed the thought as setting himself up for heartache. She was going to be heading back to Hollywood soon. But she was here now. Before he could talk himself out of it, he heard himself speaking.

"Why don't you stay at my place for a few days? It's farther from the road, and you can sit on the back porch and be out of sight of anyone driving by. You'll be safer there."

"And I assume you think your big bed would be perfect for those after-dark activities we're so good at?"

"I don't assume anything. If you want to use a guest room…"

She tipped her head back and met his eyes.

"I want to be with you, Cole."

Damn, if those words didn't make his heart

flutter like a girlie little butterfly. This woman was so bad for him in so many ways. He forced his voice not to waver.

"Look, whatever this is that's going on between us, let's keep it real. We know it's temporary, so let's not pretend it's more than it is. Let's promise to be honest with each other about how we feel and what we want. Okay?"

She stared at him for a beat then nodded. "Okay. And as part of that promise to be perfectly honest?" She waited until he shifted behind her in impatience. "The sun is up and it's time for breakfast, Plowboy."

He looked up and blinked at the bright sun now more than halfway above the horizon. A new day had begun. And tonight he'd be going to bed with this woman in his arms. They'd agreed that whatever this was between them was for after dark, and they knew it was short-term. What could be more perfect?

So why did something feel just a bit off?

# CHAPTER FIFTEEN

THE NEXT FEW days passed for Bree in a quiet, happy haze of work and sex, with a little sleep here and there as needed. Cole worked the farm every day. Bree would have a hearty dinner prepared when he got back to the house, and they'd talk as they ate, laughing and arguing. Cole would help with dishes, then they'd curl up together on the sofa, on the back porch swing, or, more often than not, head straight to his bed.

It felt comfortable and natural. She tried hard not to question that. She was living in the moment and refusing to think about the future. To do so was to allow shadows into their happy, if temporary, partnership.

With every day that went by, though, that sense of satisfaction was growing into something stronger and deeper, and she was pretty sure Cole felt it, too. She sat on the back porch one particularly steamy afternoon and watched him driving the tractor through the fields, towing some contraption that had long arms spread out on either side, spraying something on the fast-growing soybean plants. A pitcher of sweet tea was on the table next to her, and she held it up the next time he glanced her way. He nodded and pulled the towering tractor behind the house, unhitching the sprayer at the edge of the field.

He pulled off his ever-present ball cap and tugged his shirt over his head, using it to wipe the sweat from his face. She really liked that move. His body was hard and his farmer's tan, ending where his T-shirt sleeves began, just made him look sexier in her eyes.

"You gonna stare at me all day or are you gonna bring me some tea, Hollywood?"

She didn't move, other than rolling her eyes sarcastically. Just because their relationship was feeling comfortable didn't mean they'd ever be Ozzie and Harriet.

"Come get it yourself, Plowboy. You could use a moment out of the sun."

He silenced the tractor and jumped to the ground, tossing his sweaty shirt over the porch railing. She squealed when he leaned over to kiss her, lifting her up and against his sticky skin, but she quickly wrapped her arms around his neck and kissed him back. Even his sweat smelled good. He set her back in the chair with a crooked grin then quickly drained a glass of tea, which she then refilled.

"You're spoiling me, woman. You'd make one hell of a farmer's wife."

Her eyes went wide and his glass stopped halfway to his mouth, as if he'd just realized what he said. He frowned.

"Of course, there aren't many farmers to marry in Malibu, are there?"

And there it was. The five hundred-pound gorilla they'd both been ignoring for days. They'd had a lot of fun playing house, but there was an end coming. She had a home in California, and she couldn't stay here forever. Caroline had called just last night to say someone in Utah had been spotted on security cameras sneaking around the rehab center, but the police had missed him. Once he was caught, she could return to her oceanfront world. Her frown matched Cole's.

The future was knocking on the door, trying to pull them out of the fantasy. Her fingers tightened on the glass of tea she held. She came here to hide from danger, but there was a very real possibility she'd leaped from the frying pan directly into the flames. Because losing this… this…*thing* that was happening between her and Cole? That might just be the most dangerous threat of all.

She knew now that she was falling in love with him.

Had fallen.

She was in love. With a farmer from North Carolina.

Cole looked as troubled as she felt. He emptied the second glass of tea and set it down loudly on the table, muttering something about heading to the fields. The tractor rumbled back to life, and he was gone without another word.

SHE DIDN'T THINK Cole had been angry after that awkward moment on the back porch, but by dinnertime, she wondered if she'd missed something. He was never late for dinner, but she'd been keeping a casserole warm for an hour now and the sun was settling on the horizon. She walked outside to look for his tractor and was surprised to see it parked next to the barn. But his truck was gone. She'd been so lost in her own swirling thoughts that she hadn't heard him leave. Or maybe he'd come back while she was upstairs showering. She frowned. He rarely passed up an opportunity to join her in there.

Maybe he drove off to get cattle feed. Except the feed mill shut down hours ago. She walked through the house and looked across the road to Nell's. He wasn't there. And Maggie was gone. Maybe Ty needed help with something. That must be it. Cole had gotten busy with some project at the bar and lost track of time.

She called The Hide-Away and Ty answered with an enthusiastic greeting. It sounded like there was a busy weekend crowd there.

"Ty? It's Bree." She spoke loudly so he'd hear her. Her voice bounced around the living room and she suddenly felt embarrassed. It really wasn't her place to keep track of Cole's whereabouts. But she'd felt a strange sense of foreboding from the moment she saw that his truck was gone. "Tell Cole his dinner's getting cold. If he's staying there for a while, I'll eat alone."

"I haven't seen him, Bree. Is everything okay? You guys have a fight or something?"

She shook her head, even though he couldn't see her over the phone. "No, nothing like that. I just didn't realize he'd driven off right at dinnertime, and I assumed he was at the bar. He must have lost track of time. Have a good night, Ty."

She sat at the table and stared at her still-empty plate. She couldn't shake the feeling that something was wrong. Had his words about her being a farm wife scared him that badly? They'd promised to be open and honest with each other, but he'd clearly been spooked. But then again, she hadn't told him she'd fallen in love, because she didn't know what he'd do with that. She didn't know what *she* was going to do with it, either.

She was so lost in thought that the ringing

phone made her jump. She ran to grab it from the kitchen counter, hoping to see his name on the screen, but it was Nell.

"Bree, is Cole with you?"

"No. He took the truck and went somewhere. Maybe he went to look at some equipment or something. What's wrong?"

"I just got a call from Chris."

"Cole's friend?" A chill settled into her chest.

"He's worried about Cole. That friend of theirs, Travis, the boy who lives in the mountains?"

"What about him?"

She heard Nell's voice crack. Bree closed her eyes and grabbed the edge of the counter to steady herself. She didn't want to hear what was coming next, because she knew in her heart that it was bad. Really bad. "Nell, tell me."

"The poor boy killed himself yesterday, honey. With a shotgun. His parents called Chris and asked him to be a pallbearer. They told him they'd already spoken to Cole. Now he's not answering anyone's calls. Not from Chris or Jerome or even from me. Chris is worried, Bree. He's afraid that Cole might…"

She thought about the website she'd looked at yesterday on Cole's laptop about counseling for veterans. As many as twenty veterans committed suicide every *day*. Would Travis's death be enough to push Cole to do the unthinkable? She started shaking so badly she could barely hold the phone.

"Nell, he's not at the bar. I already called there. Where would he go? Is there someone around here he'd turn to?"

And why hadn't that someone been *her*?

"If it wasn't you, me or Ty, then I don't know. I have to ask you a hard question, Bree. Is his shotgun still by the back door?"

Cole told her he kept it there for protection. She turned slowly, already knowing what she was going to see. The double-barreled shotgun was no longer leaning against the door jamb.

"It's gone."

The silence seemed to go on forever while Bree remained frozen in place, staring at the door, willing his truck to pull up outside. Willing him to walk in with a logical explanation.

"I'm going to drive into town and track down Ty and Tammy," Nell said. "They might know some places to look. It's getting dark, and we shouldn't wait another minute."

"I'll come with you…"

"No. He might come home, and you should be there." Nell noticed her lack of response. "Bree, honey? Are you hearing me?"

Her "yes" came out as a whisper. Night was falling outside, and in her heart, as well.

"Don't panic, darlin'. He's probably just sitting somewhere thinking. Or drinking. Or both. Maybe he's driving around to blow off steam. There must be someplace he goes when he needs to think."

Nell ended the call and Bree set her phone down with a shudder. Where the hell was he?

*There's a little swimming hole back behind my place...*

Bree straightened, the sudden rush of adrenaline nearly knocking her off her feet. He was at the swimming hole! She knew it just as sure as she knew how to breathe.

She didn't care that she was wearing a yellow cotton sundress. She didn't care that she only had canvas skimmers on her feet. She ran out the back door and past the barns behind the house. She ran through the dark fields, thankful for all those days spent running on the beach back in California. She was also thankful to see the moon rising, giving her at least some light. Her strides were strong and sure, with the exception of a few missteps in the soft soil. She was halfway to the river before she realized her phone was still sitting back at the house. It didn't matter. She just needed to find him.

Cole had a shotgun with him. The thought gave her a fresh surge of speed, and before long she was thrashing through the dark undergrowth, having no idea where the path was. She ignored the sting of branches whipping against her exposed arms and legs. For a moment she thought she might be lost, but she burst through the last of it, stumbling into a clearing and nearly colliding with the side of Cole's black truck. Maggie was inside and looked relieved to see reinforcements arrive. She barked as Bree tried to open the door, but it was locked. The windows weren't open far enough for her to reach inside. Cole's cell phone sat on the dashboard. With a curse, Bree turned away. The moonlight cast a silvery glow on the ground.

He was sitting on a log, staring into the water. He did nothing to acknowledge her presence, even though he must have heard her thrashing through the bushes. The shotgun was resting in his lap, and one hand was loosely wrapped around the grip. He didn't speak until she moved closer.

"Don't."

The single word was sharp and hard, like the expression on his face.

"Don't what, Cole? Don't try to help you? Don't be here? Don't care?" She stepped in front of him and dropped to her knees to meet his haunted eyes. "I'm sorry, but I can't obey that order. I heard about Travis…" She flinched at the pain that shot across his face. "I'm so sorry, but you know it wasn't your fault."

"He told me he was walking away from the group sessions like I did." He sounded defeated. "He thanked me and said it was the best thing he'd ever done. He said he was fine. And now he's gone. Just like the others..."

She rested her hands on his knees. He still wouldn't look at her; instead, he stared out at the water. "Like what others, Cole?"

"All the ones who've died. Not just the ones who never came home, but the ones who came home as different people. The ones who got tired of the fight and found a way out of the pain." He finally looked in her direction, but his eyes were dull and unfocused. "Sean Jenson. Marty Cortez. Vickie Walker. Tim..."

"Who are those people, Cole? Tell me about them." She needed to keep him talking, to make him reengage with the world. To come back to her. His expression didn't change.

"Comrades from Fort Bragg or ones I met at Walter Reed. Marty drank himself to death. Sean wrapped his car around a tree a mile from his house on a sunny day. Vickie swallowed a bottle of pills. Tim took a shotgun, just like Travis."

Bree could hear her own heart pounding in her ears. The death and destruction he described was almost too much to bear, and she was just listening to words. Cole and his comrades had lived it. They'd all lost friends who'd seemed okay but weren't.

She felt brutally inadequate. She had no idea what to do or say to make that kind of horror bearable. She only knew she had to snap him out of it, bring him back to the world where he and she had laughed and loved. Her smile trembled as much as her heart did.

"Come back to the house with me, Cole. Everyone's worried. All the people who care about you. Those names you shared…"

His face contorted in anger. "They aren't *names*, they're *people*! People like Travis who aren't here anymore. That's the point of all this, Hollywood. They figured out how to get themselves to a better place. A place with no more pain…"

"No, they didn't. They took an escape route, yes. And perhaps understandably so. But to a better place? Maybe for them, but what about the destruction they left behind in *this* place? Did any of them have spouses? Children?" He didn't move, but his eyes flicked away from her in acknowledgment. "What about *them*, Cole? What does *their* place look like? Their parent is gone. Their lover is gone. Their child is gone.

That's a forever pain, Cole. *Forever.* That's the destruction those people left in their wake."

"You can't possibly understand." His lips curled into a snarl.

Good. His anger was something she could hold on to. It was an emotion, and it was better than the frightening numbness she saw when she first stumbled into the glade. If she could keep him angry, she could keep him talking so they could figure a way through this.

"You're damned straight I don't understand. Because it's bullshit!" His nostrils flared, but she pushed ahead. "Do you really think those friends of yours had no chance for happiness in this world? Do you really think they were doomed to be miserable all of their days? Do you think *you're* doomed, Cole?" He opened his mouth to speak but she rolled right over him. "It's not your fault that Travis lied to you and said he was okay when he wasn't. You once told me not to blame myself for someone else's actions. Don't those words apply to you, too?"

He dropped his head, and she thought for a moment that she was getting through to him. She wanted to reach for the gun, but she was afraid it might go off. Instead she stood, hoping to distract him. She turned to face the inky water and walked up the bank to the large oak tree standing there. When she turned back, Cole's eyes were following her.

His voice was strained when he spoke, as if he was in a battle of wills with himself. "I should have known what Travis was planning. But I'm lousy at helping people. I thought Vickie was doing great. She had parents who loved her and supported her. I even asked her out for drinks one night, thinking we had a lot in common. She turned me down with a kiss on the cheek, and the next week she was dead. Sean's wife was expecting their third child, and he had everything to live for." Cole took a ragged breath. "I remember clapping him on the back and feeling so damned happy for him. That was a week before he slammed into that tree. And Tim? Well, Tim was engaged to his high school sweetheart. He was telling everyone how great he was feeling, reaching out to thank people who'd helped him. Then one night, he did just what Travis did. He took a shotgun…"

Cole's next move startled her. She thought maybe he was going to drop the shotgun, but to her horror, he braced the stock on the ground between his legs and faced the gun straight up. His fingers were nowhere near the trigger, but tears sprang to her eyes when he dropped his forehead onto the barrel. Maggie was barking wildly in the truck. "How could they do it, Bree? I just don't get it."

A moan escaped her lips, and her stomach roiled in protest. She backed up and the old rope that was hanging from the tree brushed across her shoulder. She grabbed it for support as her legs nearly gave way in fear. He was no longer aware of her presence. His eyes were closed as he continued to rest on the shotgun. He looked weary and broken. He was hurting. He was afraid. But he did *not* want to pull that trigger. She just had to help him realize it.

She lifted her chin and forced her voice to remain steady. There wasn't much else to do but call his bluff and pray he'd come to his senses.

"You know what? Fine. If that's really what you want, Cole, then *fine*. But god-damn it, if you're going to pull that trigger, you're going to do it in front of me. I'll be the last thing you see before you go off to your happier place."

He raised his head and looked at her, his brows gathered in confusion. "What? I'm not going to pull…"

"Please don't do this, Cole. We have something here between us, and you can't do this. Not now."

"You shouldn't want anything between us. I'll just bring my garbage into your life and destroy it. I'm no good for you. I told you that before. Hasn't tonight proved it?"

"I don't believe that. I know you care about me. Please…" Her fear was making it difficult to breathe, much less think of a more persuasive argument that didn't involve begging.

He shook his head sharply. "I'm no good for anyone. You can't rely on me. You *shouldn't*. Look at me. God help me, look how weak I am. You can't put your trust in me…" He dropped his head again, but the shotgun was now tilted off to the side. Her heart squeezed tight in panic. Her hands wrapped around the rope and she had a crazy idea.

"You're wrong, Cole. I'm going to jump into this water right now, and you're going to have to stop me or save me. One or the other. I trust you to do one or the other."

She tried not to think about the dark, murky water below. Cole raised his head slowly.

"You can't swim."

"No shit, Sherlock."

Was it her imagination, or did she see a glitter of something other than anger in his eyes when he heard the sarcasm in her voice? She pulled back on the rope, as if getting ready to swing out into the darkness. She was really hoping he'd stop her before she ended up in the water.

"This is me, trusting you."

"Go ahead, Hollywood. But don't count on me to save your ass. That water is ten feet deep, so you'll have to figure out how to swim pretty fast."

"I'm serious. I'm jumping in." *Please get up and stop me...*

"Why would you do that?"

She stepped up onto a rock right at the edge of the steep bank, keeping the old rope in her hands as if she knew what she was doing. "I don't want you to hurt yourself, Cole. I need you to put that gun down and come help me."

She met his eyes and lifted her chin defiantly.

"Hurt myself? Bree, I'm not…" He looked down at the shotgun and back to her. "It's not even loaded…"

In the next breath, several things happened at once. The large rock she was balancing on rolled out from beneath her, bouncing into the water with a splash. Instinctively, her fingers tightened on the rope, which kept her from falling, but sent her swinging out over the dark pool. Which was where the rope broke, dropping her into the center of the deep water from six feet above. There wasn't time to make a sound before she went under. She could feel weeds or something slimy against her legs, but she never touched bottom. Her arms jerked out straight and she started to thrash, hoping she was heading toward the surface, but it was too dark to tell which way was up. It crossed her mind that she might just die here in the blackness. Then she felt an iron grip around her waist, tugging her hard against a solid body. Her mouth opened in surprise and she swallowed what felt like gallons of water.

She and Cole broke the surface together. Cole was towing her to the shore, but she was in complete panic mode, coughing up water and trying to pull away. She struck out at him and struggled to escape his grip.

"Let go of me, you son of a…! Let go of me!"

He ignored her and swam with confidence toward solid ground. She was still swinging at him when he turned and spoke slowly, as if talking to a wild animal. His hands held her firmly.

"Put your feet down, Bree. It's shallow now. You can walk from here…"

Still sputtering with anger that was more terror than anything else, she shoved herself away from him and immediately went underwater again. Was he trying to kill her?

He pulled her up and held her closer now. "Brianna, stop fighting me. You need to put your feet down. Stand up, Hollywood."

For some reason, her brain couldn't comprehend his instructions, and she started going under again. Cole swore and dragged her up onto the dirt, not stopping until only their lower legs were still in the water. She lay on her back next to him and closed her eyes, trying to settle the adrenaline that made her feel like her body was trying to break free of her skin. Facing death will do that to a woman. Cole's lips landed on her forehead and he stayed there, pressed against her. He was trembling. Perhaps overcome with the trauma of almost losing her? Her eyes snapped open.

Nope.

He was laughing. Not just a little chuckle, but a whole-body-shaking belly laugh. His eyes were closed tight, as if he was trying to stop but couldn't. At last he pushed himself up and looked down at her, shaking his head and grinning.

"We're a hell of a pair, aren't we?" Her heart swelled as she looked deep into his eyes, sparkling with life again. She lifted her hand to his cheek and he kissed her palm before leaning into it. "Honey, I was never going to shoot…"

She couldn't bear to hear him say it. "We *are* quite a pair, Plowboy." Maggie was barking hysterically in the truck, in an absolute frenzy.

Cole looked up and down the length of Bree's body. "Are you okay?"

When she nodded, he stood and pulled her to her feet. Her hair hung down in dank strands, her cotton dress was plastered to her body and revealed pretty much everything, and she'd lost a shoe. But he didn't seem to mind any of that when he tugged her into his arms and plunged his tongue into her mouth as if his life depended on it. She wrapped her arms around his waist and kissed him back. He was okay. They were okay. But Maggie was still *very* unhappy.

They pulled apart and went to the truck to release her. Fortunately, dogs didn't hold grudges, and she leaped around their feet enthusiastically once the door was opened. Cole walked toward the log again with Maggie prancing at his side. He bent to pick up the shotgun and glanced up to meet Bree's stricken face.

"I can't believe you thought I was going to do that. I would never…" He looked at the gun in his hands then back to her. "Damn it, I must have scared you to death. It was a stupid thing to do." He pulled back and sent the gun spiraling out over the river. It splashed into the darkness and vanished. She didn't let herself breathe again until he turned back to face her.

"It's not like I don't have other guns," he said, "but neither of us needs to be looking at that particular one again." He walked up the bank and stopped just inches from her, not touching her with anything but the warm and solemn caress of his eyes. "I'm sorry, Bree. You didn't deserve to be put through that."

Something finally connected in her brain.

"Did you say it wasn't loaded?" He'd never intended to harm himself. "Maybe you should have shared that fact a little earlier in our conversation."

She'd nearly drowned for nothing. Then she stared into his dark eyes and knew it wasn't really for nothing. He'd been in pain, and even if it wasn't exactly suicidal pain, it was bad enough. He'd suffered a shocking loss, and who knew what might have happened if she hadn't come after him. No, she didn't regret it. She'd saved him, even if it wasn't from imminent death.

The corner of his mouth quirked up as he watched her processing her thoughts.

"You're something else, Hollywood." She just nodded, suddenly exhausted from the emotional roller coaster of the past couple of hours.

"Brianna…" He put his hands on either side of her face and stared into her eyes. "What happened here…what I did…what you thought I might do…" He closed his eyes and inhaled deeply before opening them again. "I haven't been in that dark of a place in a long time, but I have been there before and I'll probably go there again. The nightmares. The losses. The memories. The anger… Just like Travis and the others, I can't unsee what I've seen. Sometimes it's too much. It's all just too damned much to take. You deserve better."

She pushed up onto her toes and kissed his lips softly. Her love for him nearly broke her heart in two.

"You don't have to bear that burden alone. I'm right here. You have friends. Family. You're not alone, Cole. But I do think you need to find a therapist you can work with. Promise me you'll think about it."

He nodded. "I'll talk to Chris about that inpatient place at Flat Rock. Maybe I do need some help."

She stared at him then gave him a grin. "I knew you needed help from the first day I met you hunkered over a glass of whiskey."

"Is that right?"

"Mmm-hmm. I just had no intention of being any part of it. Or you. But here we are."

## CHAPTER SIXTEEN

"HERE WE ARE," Cole agreed. He tried to rein in all the emotions careening back and forth inside his head as he stared down at the irritating, irresistible woman standing in front of him. How had they gotten to this place, where she was as much a part of him as breathing? He shook his head and looked over her shoulder at the black water.

Bree couldn't swim. She was especially terrified of water she couldn't see through. And while her unexpected plunge wasn't part of the plan, she'd been standing there daring him to stop her from jumping in. She'd trusted him to rescue her, even after he told her he wouldn't.

He hadn't ever intended to pull the trigger. That was why he'd dumped the shells out of the gun before he got out of the truck. He frowned. If he never intended to harm himself, then why did he take the time to unload the gun? Because he didn't trust himself, that was why.

He wanted to understand what Travis was feeling and thinking when he decided to end his life.

What demons had forced the kid to that point?
Were those same monsters inside his own nightmares? That was what he'd been wrestling with
when the rock flipped out from under Bree's
feet and she'd plunged into the water without a
word. Before the water had finished splashing
from her impact, he'd forgotten about demons
and leaped in after her.

He looked down at her beautiful face and
swallowed hard. She was patiently waiting for
him to sort things out in his head and decide
what their next move would be. Her eyes were
warm and filled with emotion. He couldn't de-
scribe it, but it was more than affection he saw
there. More than lust, although her hand was
now resting on his buttock, and she gave him a
playful squeeze as if she knew exactly what he
was thinking.

His arms slid around her. He didn't kiss her,
just pulled her in and held on tight. It occurred
to him that she was like an anchor. Not the kind
that got wrapped around bodies to drown them,
although he knew she was capable of pulling
him under. But right now? Right now she was
the kind of anchor that kept a fragile craft from
being swept to sea. The kind of anchor that dug
in and held, even in the roughest storms. The
kind of anchor that might just save a man's life.

The only thing powerful enough to make

him think of leaving this safe haven was the increasing hum of hungry insects overhead. He nudged Bree toward the truck reluctantly, and she climbed in with as much reluctance as he felt. He wrapped his arm around her shoulders and nestled her against his chest.

"You knew where to find me."

"It's one of your favorite places."

She shivered in his arms, and he wasn't sure if it was from adrenaline or cold. Just in case, he reached behind the seat and fished out an old blanket. He wrapped it around her and pulled her close, leaning back against the door. Bree curled her legs up onto the seat, and Maggie settled down on the far side, resting her head on Bree's feet. They all just needed a moment to decompress.

"Did you tell anyone where I was?"

She didn't lift her head, yawning as she answered.

"No, I just ran out the door as fast as I could, and I forgot my phone…."

He shifted and reached for his phone on the dash where he'd tossed it hours earlier. It would be irresponsible not to let someone know they were both alive and safe.

Ty answered before the first ring finished.

"Where the hell are you? Is Bree…"

"Bree's with me. We're fine."

"Jaysus, man, you had everyone in a freaking panic here. Your house has more people in it than it's probably ever had. Tammy, Emily and Nell have been crying their eyes out. Chris and Jerome just got here from Fayetteville. Arlen stopped over after I called him looking for you. We almost called the sheriff…"

"Ty, take a breath and listen to me, okay? We're both fine." He glanced down and realized Bree was sound asleep against him, worn-out from the emotional evening he'd put her through. Was staying here by the water a way to avoid dealing with the firestorm that was surely waiting for them? Yup. But it was also a way for him to have a few hours to get his head straight, and for Bree to recover. He'd certainly slept in less hospitable places than the cab of a truck. "We'll see you in the morning."

"In the *morning*?" His normally calm brother sounded like he was about to crack. "Are you kidding me? How am I supposed to keep everyone under control until the *morning*? Where *are* you?" Ty took a deep breath and lowered his voice. "Are you really okay?"

"It's been a hell of a day, Ty, but I'm really okay. We'll talk tomorrow. Tell Chris and Jerome to make themselves at home for the night. Hell, you can *all* stay there if you want. Give everyone my apologies or whatever."

"So Bree knew where to find you?"

"She did. And it's a damned good thing." He heard Ty's sharp intake of breath. "We'll be there for breakfast."

He swiped the phone to end the call. One more reach behind the seat produced an old jacket, and he shoved it between him and the door to act as a pillow. Bree's lips parted as she sighed and rearranged herself against him. He dropped a kiss on her head then leaned back to close his own eyes, welcoming the peace of an exhausted sleep.

Her mumbled cries woke him when morning was just a sliver of pink through the trees. She was dreaming, and his heart fell when he realized what she was dreaming about.

"Please, Cole… No…don't pull the trigger… please…"

His T-shirt was soaked with her tears. She was sobbing in her sleep, dreaming of him holding a shotgun to his head. Guilt swept over him for putting that horrible image in her mind. He stroked her back softly with his hand and whispered what meager comfort he could.

"Shhh, baby. It's just a dream. I'm okay. Shhhh…"

Her body stilled, then she took a deep breath and settled against him in a peaceful sleep once again. His fingers continued to trace up and down her back. She'd thought she was going to watch him shoot himself right in front of her.

She deserved better than a man like him. His arm tightened around her instinctively. That might be true, but he couldn't let her go yet. She was the anchor holding him to shore. There was another emotion swirling through him that he refused to acknowledge. It was an emotion he didn't dare confront, because it frightened him more than anything he'd ever experienced on this earth, and that was saying something. He rested his chin on her head and closed his eyes, refusing to acknowledge the warmth in his chest and the peace in his mind, all because of this woman.

They woke together when Maggie gave a soft whine, signaling her need to leave the truck. The sun was up, and Cole guessed it was near seven in the morning. Bree stretched and yawned. She looked at him, and his breath left him momentarily. Her multicolored hair was a wild tangle around her face, and her green eyes were dark and full of emotion. She tried to smile, but couldn't quite get there. Was she remembering her nightmare? Or thinking about the reality of what happened on the banks of the swimming hole?

They stared at each other in silence, then she leaned forward and kissed him softly on the lips.

She never blinked, and he finally had to close his eyes just to protect himself from the intensity of her gaze. She rubbed her hands against his chest before sliding them down his belly. In an instant, his body reacted and the kiss went from innocent to sensual. His fingers dug into her upper arms and his breath hitched.

But he pulled away, breaking the moment.

"There's nothing I'd rather do than make love to you on the seat of this truck, Brianna, but we have enough explaining to do as it is. We have to go face the music."

"You talked to Ty?"

He nodded. "Last night. Apparently I have a houseful of ticked-off family and friends that I... *we* need to deal with. Besides—" he stretched and reached across her to open the door for Maggie "—a cup of coffee sounds really good to me right now."

"We still need to talk."

"I think we have enough talking coming up in the next few hours to cover every detail and answer every question."

He knew they had to discuss what was going to come next for them as a couple. But not today. Today he just wanted to deal with calming everyone down, and then he was going to get rid of them all and take Bree to his bedroom, where he'd bury his worries by burying himself in her.

BREE WAS TUCKED tightly under Cole's arm while he drove across the fields. She was still wrapped in his blanket, since her sundress was a wrinkled, shrunken and nearly transparent mess after getting soaked last night. She reached up and wove her fingers through his where his hand rested on her shoulder, feeling the tension radiating from his body. His fingers tightened on hers as the house came into view, surrounded by vehicles.

Ty's truck was there along with Tammy's SUV. The Jeep was there, so Chris and Jerome had stayed the night. Arlen's blue truck was parked beside the barn, and he was walking toward the house. He stopped and turned when he heard them coming then called out something, probably announcing their arrival. As Cole pulled up behind the house, people started pouring out the back door.

She glanced up at Cole. "I guess heading on down to the road and driving away is out of the question?"

Cole grunted. "Don't think it didn't cross my mind. But we'll have to face them sooner or later." He turned and put his hands on either side of her face, staring hard into her eyes. "I need to know you're with me, Bree. I frightened you last night, and I'm sorry. Tell me you're not going to walk away. Not yet."

Her heart clenched at the last two words. *Not yet.* He still expected her to go eventually, and of course, he was right. She had to go back to Hollywood. Her life, such as it was, was waiting for her there.

But not yet.

"It'll take more than a dunk in dark water to chase me away."

His expression remained solemn as he leaned forward and kissed her lips softly.

"I don't want to chase you anywhere but into my bed, but first…"

They looked out the windshield at the people waiting for them to emerge. The only smiling face was Nell's. Everyone else looked tired and worried. Ty was the first to grab Cole and embrace him when they left the truck. Tears welled in her eyes as the two brothers stood silent for a long moment, eyes closed, just holding each other in a bear hug. Finally Ty clapped Cole on the back a couple of times and they stepped apart. Awkward handshakes and manly embraces were exchanged with Arlen, Chris and Jerome. The men all looked into Cole's eyes as if assessing his well-being.

"Girl, you look like you spent the night sleeping in a truck." Nell laughed as she reached up to tame Bree's wild hair.

Emily's eyes were wide. "Miss Bree, are you *naked*?"

The men had been in quiet conversation, but all talking stopped at the girl's question. Bree blushed. The blanket covered the short dress completely, so it probably did look like she was standing there in the farmyard with nothing on. She let the blanket slip off her shoulder, revealing the strap of her sundress.

"No, I'm not naked, Emily." She straightened and met the men's eyes. "And I didn't *get* naked, either, so just erase that thought from your heads."

Cole gave her that crooked grin that always made her pulse jump.

"Nope. I'm not gonna erase that thought, sweetheart." He looked sternly at the other guys. "But *you* are all going to do what the lady said, right?" They nodded in agreement.

The light moment seemed to alleviate some of the stressful undercurrent, and they headed inside the house, where Nell had her famous baked breakfast strata cooling on the counter. Bree excused herself briefly to run upstairs, shower and change into jeans and a T-shirt. When she returned, they filled their plates and sat at the table, talking about the weather and crops and baseball. It was an intentionally neutral conversation. This was their way of allowing Cole and Bree to feel welcomed and accepted without judgment. She loved them all for that.

The realization made her sit straighter. She *did* love them. She loved Nell, with her flour-dusted apron still on, and her sweet, knowing smile. She loved Tammy and Emily, wearing matching Miranda Lambert T-shirts. She loved Arlen. He and his dad were hardworking men who may not say a lot of flowery words, but they stood by their friends unflinchingly. She loved Chris and Jerome, eating with gusto and nudging each other in the good-natured camaraderie born on the battlefield. And Ty, at his brother's side, murmuring a soft word occasionally, shoulder to shoulder, making sure Cole knew he was there. Her feelings for these people overwhelmed her.

Cole looked up and met her eyes. For just a moment she could see herself sitting at this same table ten years from now, with the same friends, exchanging the same intimate glance with Cole. The vision startled her so much she dropped her fork. Everyone laughed, but Bree felt panic pulsing through her veins.

Her heart was growing roots here, and that wasn't smart. Her home was a Malibu beach house. Whether they caught the stalker or not, she needed to get back to that world before she lost herself in the Carolinas. Or was she *finding* herself at long last? Cole was still staring at her, as if he could read the panic in her eyes. He leaned forward, but before he could speak, Nell started gathering up plates and shooing the women into the kitchen. Ty grabbed Cole's arm and pulled him out to the side porch, followed by Chris, Jerome and Arlen.

Nell's hand rested on Bree's shoulder. "The boys need to talk, honey. He scared us all. And you, taking off without telling anyone where you were—what were you thinking, girl?"

Bree grabbed a dish towel and took a plate from Tammy at the sink. "I was only thinking of getting to Cole as fast as I could. I'm sorry I made you worry."

Her thoughts kept wandering back to Malibu and her so-called life there. If she vanished overnight, would *anyone* notice? Would she come home to a houseful of worried friends and family? She shook her head. She already knew the answer. She'd been gone for weeks and no one other than the paparazzi seemed to care. On impulse, she pulled Emily into a hug, and the girl responded by wrapping her arms around Bree's waist.

"I really do love you, Miss Bree." The words

made Bree close her eyes tightly, and she whispered her answer.

"Guess what, Emily? I really love you, too."

# CHAPTER SEVENTEEN

JEROME AND CHRIS sat in the wicker chairs on the porch, quietly waiting for The Conversation to begin. Arlen leaned up against the railing and lit a cigarette. Ty paced back and forth, running his fingers through his hair and muttering to himself. Cole braced himself for the rare appearance of his older brother's temper, because Ty was definitely getting ready to blow.

He slapped his hand hard against the porch column and spun to face Cole. "What the *hell* were you thinking? You take off and don't tell anyone a damned thing and leave us all scared shitless. We didn't know where you were, and we didn't know what you were going to do. Did you think about anyone other than yourself, you stupid, selfish jackass?"

Cole couldn't remember his brother ever stringing together that many curse words in one outburst. He didn't know if he should laugh or apologize. Before he could decide how to react, Ty poked him in the chest with his finger. "Talk to me right now, brother, and make it good."

Cole's temper flared, but cooled quickly when he looked into Ty's eyes. He saw the same fear Bree had shown last night. Guilt stabbed at him, and he dropped his head.

"I'm sorry, all right? I'm not going to keep repeating it, but you have to believe me. I'm sorry. I had a hard time of it. I took the news about Travis…" He sucked in a breath after speaking his friend's name. Travis was gone. The knowledge felt like a weight on his shoulders that couldn't be shifted. "I took the news badly. I sort of…lost it. I thought I needed to be alone, but that was a bad idea. I kept thinking about what happened. Why it happened."

"You took Pop's shotgun."

"I did."

"Where is it now?"

"At the bottom of the creek."

A heavy silence fell on the porch as they processed that information. Chris spoke first.

"You did more than scare *us*, didn't you, Cole? You scared yourself, too."

He wasn't a man who blushed, but he could feel redness heat his cheeks at the memory of resting his head on the shotgun barrel. It was a stupid, reckless thing to do, even if the gun *was* unloaded.

"She saved me." He didn't realize he'd said

the words out loud until he saw the worried look on Ty's face.

"She's *leaving*, Cole. They're closing in on the stalker. Caroline called Nell last night and said they hope to have an arrest soon. Bree will be going home…"

"No. I need her here."

Chris, Jerome and Arlen exchanged worried glances, but Ty's expression was pure frustration.

"Really, Cole? You *need* her. Really?" Ty's hands lifted in disbelief. "What you need is professional help. If nothing else, Travis just proved that going it alone is not an option."

"I'm not alone. She can save me. I just need her to stay." Even as he said the words, he knew how unrealistic they sounded. He ignored the niggling doubts, but Ty didn't.

"You *need* her." Ty shook his head. "Do you *need* her the same way you needed alcohol after your first tour? I seem to recall you telling me you 'needed' the escape the whiskey provided. We almost lost you to the booze back then, and you know it. Or maybe you need Bree the same way you needed to party every night with girls like Amber after you got back from your second tour? You knew damned well she was running around on you, and you still proposed, because you *needed* her."

He winced at the truth of those words. He didn't want to hear any more. He stepped forward, daring Ty to continue, but his brother didn't blink, even when their chests were nearly touching.

"I helped you pick out a diamond ring for Amber, because you *needed* her so much and I just wanted you to be okay. Or maybe you *need* Bree the same way you needed Maggie after your last tour. You told me everything would be fine if you could just find Scott's dog and bring her to the farm. I didn't question it. I tracked her down in Memphis and we paid that police department thousands of dollars to replace her with another bomb-sniffing dog, all because my baby brother *needed* her. She was finally going to be the thing to save you, and I thought it just might work. Except Maggie couldn't save you, could she? Because you locked her up in the truck, didn't you?"

Cole blinked away from Ty's silent accusation. They both knew it was true.

"And now you're telling me Brianna Mathews can save you at last. And I'm supposed to believe it. The girl's going home to Hollywood." He paused for emphasis. "*Home* to *Hollywood*. Think about that. Damn it, I think Bree is awesome, but if you think she can save you, well…

you're just flat-out wrong. You need more help than any of us can provide, including Bree, and you damned well know it."

Cole looked to Chris and Jerome, hoping for some support from the guys who served. But Chris was staring hard at his feet with a frown, and Jerome was shaking his head sadly. He stood and placed his good hand on Cole's shoulder.

"He's right, man," Jerome said. "You're not being fair to Bree. You can't expect her to do for you what you're not willing to do for yourself."

"That's rich, Jerome, considering you've told me a dozen times that Pamela saved *you*."

"She did. But not in the way you're thinking. My love for Pam forced me to be a better man, and part of that was getting the help I needed. She was my *reason* for finding my way, but she didn't do it *for* me. She couldn't. And neither can Bree. She'll try. But it'll break her." Jerome and Cole looked through the window to where the women stood in the kitchen, all talking at once. Bree laughed at something and pulled Emily into a hug. He barely heard Arlen's quiet words from the porch rail where he sat.

"Remember that day you came up into the hayloft and that redhead was all jacked up and mad at you? I'm surprised the barn didn't combust from the sparks between you two. I don't think that happens twice in a lifetime, man. Don't blow it. Listen to these guys."

Inside the house, Bree turned and met his eyes. She smiled reassuringly, apparently seeing his uncertainty. It was no surprise, since he'd long ago realized she could see into his soul. And just like that, he was no longer uncertain. He walked away from the men, tossing a last comment over his shoulder to his brother.

"Don't worry about me. I'll be fine."

Ty kicked a chair across the porch and spat out another string of curse words behind him. Bree met Cole halfway across the living room, wrapping her arms around his waist. He hadn't told her as much, but she had to know how much he needed her. He dropped his head to her shoulder and breathed in her scent as if it was pure oxygen. She shivered as he ran his nose up her neck to her ear.

"Make everyone go away," he whispered. She squeezed him tight for just a second and nodded. Stepping back, she looked to Nell.

"Cole and I both need to get some rest. Do you think...?"

Nell smiled. "Say no more." The older woman turned to Tammy and Emily and caught the attention of the men watching through the open door. "Breakfast is over, folks, and we've all seen that Cole and Bree are safe. So let's give them a chance to relax, shall we?"

Ty started to object, but Tammy shook her head sharply and he closed his mouth, satisfying himself with a final glare in Cole's direction before turning away. Jerome pulled Bree into a bear hug while Chris tugged Cole aside.

"I can't say much, Cole, because you know how far down *I've* been. Further than you, and longer. But I can tell you this much." His bright blue eyes met Cole's head-on. "I didn't get out of it alone, and neither will you. And I'm not talking about civilian help. I'm talking trained professionals." His eyes flicked to Bree and Jerome. "Remember how much you hated having greenies join our crew? Those new kids fresh from basic that didn't know what the hell they were doing? Great guys, eager and willing, but clueless, right?"

Cole nodded. He remembered the wide-eyed recruits that would arrive in Afghanistan.

Chris gave him a crooked grin. "What did you used to call it when they showed up?"

"I called it amateur hour."

Chris nodded. "Exactly. They meant well, but their lack of know-how put us all at risk. Look at her." Bree was smiling at something Jerome was saying. "She wants to help, but she's an amateur. You need more than an amateur right now, brother. You need trained professionals walking you through this battle."

Cole shook his head, wanting to deny his friend's words, but they both knew Chris was right.

Nell was the last to leave. She gave Cole a long, serious look.

"You've got a reason now to get through this. Use it."

Bree looked confused, but Cole knew exactly what Nell was trying to say. It was the same thing everyone else was trying to beat into his head. He just wasn't ready to accept it, not even from Nell. He tugged Bree close and held on to her, never breaking eye contact with his neighbor.

Nell laughed out loud and turned away.

"Oh, you are one stubborn Southern boy. But underneath all that stubbornness is a smart man. You'll figure it out sooner or later."

LATE THE NEXT MORNING, Bree sat on the front porch sipping her coffee, lost in thought. Maggie was stretched out on the floor at her side, snoring softly. Cole was working on irrigation lines in the field between the barns and the river.

She hadn't been surprised when he interrupted her shower yesterday after everyone finally left. The result had been two very clean people making love hard against the shower wall. And against the bathroom vanity. In the hallway. The living room. And finally, all night long in Cole's bed. He'd been almost desperate in his pursuit of her, as if he was trying to lose himself in her in more ways than one. There was a dark edge to his need, and it worried her. He was a man on the edge, and she didn't know what to do for him. Hot sex was great fun, but it wasn't the answer. What was it going to take for him to lay his demons to rest?

His brother and friends were convinced that Cole needed the residential program offered for veterans in the mountains of western North Carolina called Flat Rock Retreat, but they said he kept making excuses. Should she get out of the way so he could seek the professional help he needed? She suspected his almost desperate drive to have sex yesterday afternoon was the desire to avoid discussing that, or anything else serious.

Her phone chirped with an incoming message from her very pregnant cousin.

How's life with the hot farmer?

Bree sighed and started typing.

Complicated. How's the pregnancy?

The next words she saw made her frown then laugh.

Also complicated. False contractions. Screaming back pain. Fat ankles. Stuck in bed by overprotective husband. I was really hoping to live vicariously through your country love affair. Are you ready to go home, then?

Bree shook her head. Malibu no longer felt like home to her. Maybe that would change once she got there and sank her toes into the beach. But in her heart, she knew it wouldn't. Her lifelong pursuit of the trappings of wealth had been exposed as a fraud.

But was any security to be found in North Carolina, here on a farm with the damaged man she loved so much? Did he even *want* her to stay? Or did he need her to leave so he could focus on healing?

Hello?

The ping of Amanda's text made her jump.

I'm here. But how'd you like it if I was there?

In Gallant Lake? Seriously? Did they catch the stalker and not tell me?

Sometimes Bree almost forgot that there was someone out there threatening to kill her.

They're closing in on someone. And it sounds like you could use the company.

Oh, Bree, I would LOVE it! :) So the fling is over with Hot Farmer?

She leaned back and stared out across the fields. Whatever she and Cole had together was nothing as frivolous as a fling. If she really loved Cole, then she might just have to walk away from him, at least temporarily, so he could find healing. The thought made her feel both sad and hopeful.

Like I said—complicated. I'll tell you about it when I get to Gallant Lake. Hopefully before the baby arrives.

This baby is never going to arrive. Take your time. Nora told me about Damian calling her. What an idiot. He needs to give up about that house already!

Bree stared out across the fields, which were turning greener by the day as the soybean plants grew tall. Across the road, the cattle were grazing on the hill and a couple calves were jumping around in play. Malibu was probably one of them. A truck pulled up to Nell's produce stand, and a man in overalls emerged and stood talking to Nell. It was Arlen's father, George. Two horses stood in the shade of the barn, tails flashing as they swished at flies.

No, this wasn't her environment. But it could be, couldn't it? She started typing.

Maybe I should just sell it to him.

There was a long moment of silence, and Bree laughed when she saw a response appear.

W-H-A-T ? Does this have something to do with your "complicated" relationship with Hot Farmer? Are you going country on us?

Two squirrels raced up the tree in front of Cole's house, causing a bird to flutter out of the leaves in surprise. A small green lizard was sunning itself on the balcony railing, bobbing his head as if he was listening to hip-hop. A breeze rustled the tree branches and felt refreshing on her face. The scent of soil and new growth floated in the wind, and she felt truly content.

*Child, you're already home.*

With a phone and a computer, she could run her event planning business from anywhere.

Bree felt a sense of calm unlike anything she'd experienced.

I gotta run—Zach's got a game today. But this conversation isn't over, young lady. For now let me just say... YOU GO, GIRL!

Since she was using a burner phone, she didn't have her contact list handy. But her agent, Sheila, also represented Damian, so it only took one quick call to track down his number. Sheila must have given him a heads-up, because he answered the call from an unfamiliar number and spoke her name.

"Brianna? Babe, is that you?" She rolled her eyes. Every woman in his life was "babe."

"Hi, Damian. How are you?"

He sounded agitated. "Come on, babe, how do you think I am? Your face is all over the news, and my phone's been ringing off the hook. A reporter said you were in rehab, which I knew was bullshit. Your cousin wouldn't tell me anything, and now Sheila tells me you have a stalker. Why did I have to hear that from our agent and not you?"

How typical of Damian to focus on his own injured ego instead of her. He'd yet to ask if she was okay. Blinking against the sun, she dragged the chaise back to a shaded corner by the screen door and sat.

His voice quieted. "You should have told me about the stalker, Bree. I could have helped. I have security connections in Hollywood."

"I have my own security connections, Damian."

"I have to admit, babe, I thought Sheila was joking when she told me you were hiding on a farm somewhere. You must be going out of your mind."

"Actually not. I'm thinking of making a change."

"To move to a farm?" He gave a sharp laugh. "That's not the Brianna Mathews I knew!"

Bree watched a pair of hummingbirds zoom around the porch rail. He was right. She was no longer the Brianna Mathews he'd known.

"I've changed, Damian. It happens when people grow up."

"That's good. And you're not the only one who's grown up and changed." There was a moment of silence then a sigh. "*You* may not have gone to rehab for real, but I did. I was in for three months last winter, and I've been clean and sober ever since. You always told me I needed to get my act together, and I finally did."

"I'm glad to hear it, Damian. I'm happy for you." And she truly was. He'd been in a fast downward spiral when they'd split.

"Thanks, babe. It hasn't been easy. But I'm working hard at it."

"That's good, Damian. I'm happy to hear you sounding so…solid."

He laughed. "Do I sound good enough that you might consider my offer to buy back the beach house?"

"Actually, that's why I called. I'm giving you first dibs before it hits the market."

"For real? Wow, things really *have* changed for you. That's big of you to give me first dibs on the house I bought for you in the first place."

Bree examined her short nails and smiled. "My money from *Hot Hollywood Housewives* helped keep the lights on in that house while we were married and you were snorting white powder up your nose and whoring around instead of working, so skip the guilt trip, okay? You can buy it from me or watch me sell it to someone else."

Instead of arguing, he laughed. "Okay, okay. What's your price?"

"You know it's worth twenty-five, but you can have it for twenty."

"Twenty million? That's more than I paid the first time!"

"Yes, but it was an outdated relic back then. We remodeled, plus I've done even more work since you left, and the market's changed. I'm offering it at less than market value because I want the cash. I have plans." It was an idea that had come to her during the night, as Cole slept exhausted at her side. Something had to be done to help people like Cole and his friends. Selling the beach house would give her the funds for the particular something she had in mind.

"Plans, huh? Let me guess. You're going to build a big mansion on some old stretch of land and watch your ranch hands work…"

"Not even close. Do you want it or not?"

"Damn, you really would sell it out from underneath me, wouldn't you?" There was a pause, and she knew he was calculating finances in his head. "Fine. This movie is already getting a lot of buzz, and they've asked me to sign on for the sequel. I'll pay the twenty, but I want something in return. I need to rebuild my image, and I want your help."

She held her phone away from her and stared at it, certain she hadn't heard him right. "Your image? What are you talking about?"

"Look, if we could be seen together after the stalker is caught, make people think we've reconciled, and that you've forgiven my… indiscretions…"

Which would, of course, give him tons of publicity as the reformed bad boy of Hollywood just as he started his promotional tour. He was going to use her sudden flood of media attention as a way to redeem himself.

"Maybe you could come to the movie premiere as my date."

She laughed. "Your date at the premiere? Why?"

"Look, if we convince the world that we're in love…"

"In *love*? Damian…"

"Hear me out, Bree. Come to a couple premieres. This movie is going to be a hit, and your support will make me look like a good guy at last." He paused. "It would help us both. Don't you have a book coming out soon?"

"Yes, but what you're asking for…" Bree pressed her fingers against her forehead. This was turning into the strangest conversation.

"Give me *something*, Bree. We had some good times together, didn't we? Before I blew it all up?"

"We did have some good times…" It was true. In the first couple years of their marriage, life was one big, overblown party. As if sensing a softening of her position, Damian kept pressing.

"Remember how much fun we had in Paris on our honeymoon?" The world was her oyster back then, and everything she looked at, Damian bought for her. She felt she'd finally put her troubles behind her.

"I remember Paris."

"And do you remember the parties we had at the beach house? Remember when Mr. Five Oscars was singing on the balcony and his wife started pelting him with ice cubes?"

Bree laughed. "Of course. We were newlyweds, and I couldn't believe all those famous people were actually in our home. We had some great times."

"Look, babe, I know I made a mess of it back then. But I'm trying to be a better man now. If *you* forgive me, the public will forgive me. If you won't do the premieres, maybe just have dinner with me one night? Give me a kiss somewhere where the press will see it. Say you'll do that, and I'll buy the house this month."

She thought she heard a noise behind her, but she couldn't see anything through the screen door. Maybe Cole was back from mowing. Even if he wasn't, she should get lunch started. How would he react when she told him she was willing to stay here in North Carolina with him? "You want to kiss me in public? We'll talk about it." There was no way she was playing along with Damian's games. "Let's get together as soon as I'm back in LA." When the call was over, Bree laid her head back on the chaise and closed her eyes, smiling to herself.

Everything was starting to fall into place.

## CHAPTER EIGHTEEN

COLE STOOD BY the screen door, his hands clenched tightly at his sides. When he'd walked in, he'd planned on dragging Bree upstairs for more time in bed. Working in the hot sun hadn't been enough to banish the thoughts of Travis, of the riverbank, of everyone pushing at him. In her arms was the one place where he felt safe; where he didn't think about anything else but her. He needed Bree to drown out the voices for him. Making love with her was his temporary cure. When he heard her laughter on the porch, he figured she was talking to one of her cousins. But what she said as his hand reached for the door made his blood turn to ice.

She was talking to her ex-husband. The idiot who'd lied to her, cheated on her and laid his hands on her. The idiot she was now talking to in a soft, intimate voice. The conversation cut him to the quick.

"In *love*? Damian…"

And there was more. None of it sounded good to his ears, especially when she talked about being the guy's date at a premiere. She'd be back on the red carpet in front of the cameras, right where she wanted to be.

"I remember Paris...we had some really good times." She laughed as she said that. She *laughed*. With her ex-husband, the movie star.

"...kiss me in public?...Let's get together as soon as I'm back in LA."

She was making plans to leave him. A day after making love to him on nearly every surface in his house, she was sitting there on his porch, talking to her ex about going home.

She looked across his soybean fields, but she was probably imagining the blue Pacific Ocean stretching out in front of her. She was feeling the ocean breeze blowing through her long, red hair as she stood in her beachfront mansion, alongside her movie star husband. That was where she belonged. Not here. Who was he kidding, thinking she'd ever stay with him in Russell?

*Let's get together as soon as I'm back in LA.*

It wasn't just the words that burned. Her voice sounded excited, enthusiastic, eager to see the guy. She smiled to herself when the call ended and she lay back in the lounge, closing her eyes in obvious satisfaction. So clearly relieved at the thought of leaving his farm and returning to California.

He was such an idiot.

"I'M SUCH AN IDIOT."

Cole downed a shot of whiskey and slammed the glass down on the bar. Maggie sat up at the sound, leaning against his legs at the bottom of the bar stool. Ty shook his head when Cole nodded at the glass for another refill.

"You're done drowning your sorrows for today. I made a pot of coffee, and I've got a burger on the grill for you." Always the big brother, Ty was staring hard at him with worry. Cole had been at The Hide-Away a few hours now. He'd driven from the farm and away from Bree right after hearing the call with her ex-husband. He could still see her there, holding on to the porch pillar in his rearview mirror, shading her eyes from the sun and looking surprised at his hasty exit.

He was the one who'd been surprised. After a day and night of making love...although for Bree, it was apparently just having sex...she could sit there so cool and composed while planning a Hollywood reconciliation with Damian Maxwell. How could he have misjudged her so badly?

As if reading his thoughts, Ty asked, "Are you sure you heard her right, man? That doesn't sound like Bree..."

He'd replayed her conversation over and over in his mind.

"I know what I heard, Ty. She was talking about Paris, about being in love, about going to some premiere. She can't wait to get back to LA. I swear to God, she was talking about *kissing* the guy! Maybe the whole stalker story was just a way to get her husband back, and she's been lying to us all along."

"Cole, you told me what she did at the river to save you. That didn't sound like a woman who was faking her feelings. And when she called here just now looking for you, she didn't sound like a woman getting ready to dump your ass. She sounded worried."

Bree had called The Hide-Away to make sure Cole was safe. Ty told her he was helping with a construction project at the bar. She probably thought he'd driven away with another shotgun in his hand. He scowled. Was she just hanging around to keep him safe, like some kind of babysitter?

Ty took the coffeepot and started to fill two mugs. "I don't think sneaking off without telling you is Bree's style. You need to talk to her and see what she's thinking."

"Aren't you the same guy who said she was just like Amber?"

"What? I never said that!"

"You did. You said it yesterday on the porch."

Ty frowned then shook his head vehemently.

"No, no, no. I was talking about you cling-ing to things you *think* you need. You thought you needed Amber two years ago. Yesterday you needed Bree. They're not the same women by any stretch of the imagination. I was just making a point about your refusal to face your demons. You cling to people and booze and dogs as a way to distract yourself from the real issue." He slid a mug of coffee into Cole's hands. "The real issue is buried inside you, and you run from it by ei-ther grabbing on to something as tightly as you can or lashing out with irrational fury. You're head over heels or over and done. It's damned hard to keep up with."

Cole stared into his coffee in silence. It ticked him off that he couldn't figure out a way to deny what his brother said. He finally muttered a lame protest. "That's not true."

"No? Twenty-four hours ago you were ab-solutely certain that Bree was single-handedly going to save you, remember? You were ready to take on anyone who disagreed, even me. And today? Today she's a back-stabbing bitch you can't wait to get away from."

Cole tensed. "I didn't call her that."

Ty laughed bitterly. "Oh, so now you're *de-fending* her again? Damn it, even I can't keep up with you anymore."

A pounding pain started to build behind

Cole's left eye. Every thought seemed to contradict the last, and he was losing track faster than his brother was. He pinched the bridge of his nose and closed his eyes. He just needed...

And that was the problem, wasn't it? He needed Brianna Mathews, but she apparently didn't need him.

He pictured her standing at the edge of the creek, daring him to come save her. So brave and wild and beautiful in the moonlight. He didn't doubt that she cared about him, but he sure as hell wasn't going to be her charity case. Not when she was planning on returning to her ex-husband.

"So what are you going to do?" Ty leaned back against the cash register and folded his arms.

That was the million-dollar question, wasn't it? Cole rubbed the back of his neck and sighed.

"The first thing I'm going to do is go to Travis's funeral. Chris is coming to pick me up. We'll drive over to Pull Tail Gap tonight. Everything else can wait." Including Bree Mathews.

"You know, Cole, Pull Tail Gap is less than an hour from Flat Rock."

Yeah, he knew. That fact kept buzzing through his head like a nagging mosquito, poking and annoying him. After Travis's death and Bree's betrayal, it was probably the right place for him. But it was the wrong time. He couldn't leave the farm in midsummer. Maybe in November, after the soybean crop was in…

"There's never going to be a perfect time. You know that, right?" His brother had always been able to read Cole's mind. "Arlen and I can handle the farm and the cattle. Tammy doesn't have any summer classes, so she can run the bar during the day. You'll be back in time for harvest. Go get yourself straight, Cole, then come home and deal with Bree and get on with your life."

"After six weeks? She'll be long gone."

Ty lifted a shoulder. "I hate to sound like some sappy Facebook meme, but if Bree won't wait for you, then she wasn't meant to be yours in the first place. And you're no good for her or anyone else like this."

Cole drained his coffee and set the empty mug on the bar slowly, belying the tension buzzing beneath his skin.

"Maybe I'll go in November."

"So YOU'RE SELLING your beach house?" Nell refilled Bree's glass of sweet tea. "And starting a catering business here?"

Bree pulled her legs up and tucked her feet beneath her on Nell's porch swing, taking a sip of tea before answering.

"I'll design the menus and recipes, the decor, the location and stuff like that. It's what I've been doing in LA since the divorce, but it's weird planning events for people I used to socialize with. With Fort Bragg only an hour away, I'm sure I could pick up some business with the military. There must be plenty of weddings going on up there. It would be easy to do events in Charlotte or Raleigh from here, too. A lot of the work can be done online."

Nell nodded. "You won't do much business in Russell, but if you're willing to drive, you'll do well enough." She lifted a brow. "Of course, I'm assuming you're planning on living here?"

Bree looked across the road to Cole's farm. Cole hadn't exactly extended an invitation to stay forever. "That's the plan, but is the cottage available for a while, just in case?"

"Why sure, honey. But do you really think you'll need it?"

She felt the blush spread across her cheeks. "I hope not, but I'm not going to press my luck."

"And if you do end up in the cottage instead of with him? Is small-town life going to be enough for you after being a big star and all?"

Bree frowned, not liking the possibility that Cole wouldn't want her.

"Well, I don't know about staying in the cottage forever, but I'm sure I could find something I liked here. A nice little farm of my own." She smiled. "Maybe I'll give you some competition with the produce stand."

Nell laughed out loud. "You know, I bet you could do just that, honey. You're serious about this, aren't you? You don't care about that fancy life anymore?"

Bree stared at the well-worn floorboards of the porch in silence. There was a time when she'd believed money equaled security and protection from problems, but she'd been so wrong. Her lips curled into a smile at the irony.

"I used to care a whole lot, Nell, but not now." She emptied her glass. "Now the money is just a means to an end. I'm thinking of starting a foundation to help veterans. If I can figure out a way to use the money to provide help to guys like Cole, Chris, Jerome and Ramirez, then all the hell I went through climbing that stupid and useless social ladder will have been worth it."

She glanced back over at Cole's place and frowned. He still wasn't home from The Hide-Away. He'd left in a crazy hurry before lunch, and his attitude had been…off. After all, they'd basically spent twenty-four hours making love in nearly every room of the house, but instead of being relaxed and happy, he'd acted like a caged animal when she found him in the kitchen. He snarled a few words in answer to her questions then muttered something about needing to go.

And go he did, driving off the property in a roaring cloud of dust. When he didn't answer her calls or texts, she'd had a moment of panic and called Ty, who assured her that Cole was at The Hide-Away, busy with some project.

His moods swung so wildly that she had no idea how he'd react to her plans to stay. Before his agitated departure earlier, she'd have expected the plan to be welcomed with enthusiasm. But now there was a nagging fear knocking at her heart.

The roar of an engine caught her attention. A Jeep drove up Cole's driveway toward the house. She stood and watched a lone driver exit the vehicle. Chris was back, but why?

"Nell, I…"

"Say no more," Nell said. "Go see what's happenin', honey, and we'll talk tomorrow."

Before she could reply, a dusty black pickup followed the Jeep to the big house across the road. Cole was home. Instead of feeling happy as she trotted back to see him, she felt an odd sense of dread settle over her, and she couldn't shake it.

## CHAPTER NINETEEN

COLE WAS UPSTAIRS packing a duffel when he heard Bree arguing with Chris in the kitchen. He couldn't make out her words, but he sure knew the tone. It was her angry voice, sharp and sexy. He ignored that last thought and grabbed the garment bag in his closet that held his dress uniform. Proper attire for the funeral of a comrade. His chest tightened at the thought of laying Travis to rest. He was just a kid, and his life shouldn't have ended this way. Cole shook his head. He couldn't think about that now. He had to face Bree and her deceit first.

The voices grew more distinct as he headed down the stairs. Bree and Chris were at the front door now. They clearly hadn't noticed his presence, because their argument never skipped a beat.

"This isn't a good idea, Chris. I don't think Cole can handle this funeral. You didn't see how Travis's death affected him. You didn't see…"

"Cole's a big boy, and he can make his own choices. If he didn't want to go, I never would have questioned it. But he said he wants to go, so he's going. I would think that would be something you'd understand, since you're leaving, too."

"What?" Bree stepped back and looked surprised.

Cole had told Chris what he'd overheard that morning, and Chris squarely had his back.

"Yeah, I know all about your plans, so don't pretend to be all brokenhearted about Cole leaving."

Her confusion gave way to anger again. "I don't know what the hell you're talking about. This isn't about me, it's about Cole. He's fragile, Chris. You don't know how fragile…"

Cole cringed.

"I know more than you think," Chris said. "Don't forget who you're talking to."

Her shoulders drew back and she poked her finger into Chris's chest. "I'm talking to someone who *didn't* see him put a shotgun to his head a day ago. You don't know what it's like…"

"Really? I don't?" Chris's voice rose angrily, but Cole didn't move. Bree could hold her own.

"You think you can help him, Chris, but have you ever put a gun to your head?"

"No, Bree, I haven't. But I did swallow a bottle of Vicodin once, and I washed it down with tequila. And you know who rushed me to the hospital to get my stomach pumped? Cole Caldwell. I spent a month in the psych ward after that little episode, and Cole's the guy who stood by me." Chris stepped forward, and she stumbled back. "So don't lecture me about my friend, lady. You've known him for about ten seconds, and you're already moving on. I've gone into battle next to the guy, and I'd do it again if he asked me to. Unlike you, I'm here for the long haul."

Bree's hand twitched, signaling this discussion was quickly approaching mortal combat.

"That's enough!"

His voice sounded harsh in his ears. They spun to face him, and the air was heavy with tension. He needed to get the hell out of here. "Chris, I'm ready to go. I called Nell and she'll watch Maggie for me."

Bree's face fell, and he could have sworn she looked hurt. "*I'll* take care of Maggie..."

He shook his head sharply. "No. You're making plans to take off, so there's no sense in Maggie getting any more attached." The dog was already sitting at Bree's feet, looking up at her with concerned brown eyes.

Bree exploded, arms waving wildly. "What the hell is going on with everyone talking about me leaving?"

She stepped forward as he descended the stairs. He was close enough to smell her spicy perfume, and to see the strain around her eyes. She looked frightened, and that pulled at him for a moment before he realized she was probably just upset they were on to her little secret.

"It's over, Bree. I heard you talking about going back to Malibu. Back to Damian. And that's exactly where you belong. In fact, I want you gone before I get back."

Her mouth dropped open, but no words came out. What could she possibly say to him now that she realized they knew about her plans?

"You heard me talking…" Realization dawned in her eyes, and she shook her head with a half smile.

"Seriously? Haven't I told you before that hearing only half a conversation leads to trouble? I'm not getting back together with Damian. In fact, I'm…"

"Come on, Bree, don't stand there and lie to my face! I heard you talking about kissing him." He hadn't intended to shout, but his words echoed around the hallway.

Her brief smile vanished. "Okay, I understand that sounded bad, and I'm sorry, but you can't really believe I'd go back to him, can you? My God, Cole, how could you possibly think I'd leave you for *anyone* after the past few days? After all we've been through together? How could you not feel what's happening between us?" She stepped forward and rested her hand on his chest, causing his heart to cramp. "How could you not know that I'm falling in love with you?"

The words hung in the air between them. She looked as surprised as he did, and he did his best not to take what she said to heart. She didn't mean it. Didn't even mean to *say* it from the look on her face. His fingers curled into fists and he forced himself to step away from her touch.

"I know what I heard."

"Oh, really?" Her voice went frosty. "You 'know what you heard,' huh? So you heard both sides of the conversation, right? Or did you just fill in the blanks from some crazy corner of your mind that has you convinced you need to push me away?"

"Whoa, Bree..." Chris started, but she spun to point her finger at him and he jumped back so fast he bumped into the door frame. Cole almost smiled. Her fury could do that to a man.

"Shut up, Chris! Your buddy fed you a line of bull. I'm not leaving. At least I *wasn't* leaving."

Chris gestured between Bree and Cole before heading out the door. "You two seriously need to figure this stuff out."

She turned back around, all puffed up and full of rage. But there was something brittle about her, like a sheet of glass about to shatter.

"All you had to do was *ask* me, Cole. I would have told you I'm not going back to Damian and we could have saved ourselves all of this. I called to tell him I was ready to sell him the beach house. That's why I'm meeting him in LA. He wanted a publicity favor in return. I wasn't making plans to leave. I was making plans to *stay*."

He wanted to argue, but no words came. He thought about what he'd overheard. Was it really just two people with a mutual history making a business deal?

"Of course, you've never asked me to stay, have you? You're just waiting for me to run. You've *always* been waiting for me to run. That's why you want to be the one to end us, regardless of how we feel about each other. That'll make you some kind of hero, right?" Her arms spread wide and he could see tears glittering in her angry eyes. Her voice was sharp as a whip. "The wise and magnificent Colton Caldwell, always willing to make the ultimate sacrifice. You're such a good little soldier, aren't you?"

Her words felt like a gut punch, and he stepped back from the force of it, sitting on the stairs because his legs would no longer hold him. He buried his face in his hands. He'd been wrong, and he'd hurt her. The anger and mistrust that was always simmering under his skin would make sure he'd keep doing it, too, unless something changed.

Her voice softened. "I just told you I'm falling in love with you, and you haven't even acknowledged it. Why is it you can't let yourself hear *those* words, but you're more than ready to hear that I'm leaving you?"

He winced. She was right. But more important, the guys were right. Her love wasn't going to be enough. He needed more than she could give, even though she was offering everything she had. He couldn't accept it. Not when he was going to keep breaking her like this. He stood with a heavy sigh and stepped forward, tugging her into his arms before she could react. He whispered his next words into her ear.

"I'm sorry, baby. Damn it, I'm always apologizing to you, because I'm always screwing up. You deserve better." She stiffened, but he didn't let her pull away. "I'm going to keep hurting you, keep pushing you away. But it's not you, sweetheart. It's *me*. I've got to fix me."

She looked up at him, her face soaked with tears. "I'll help..."

"No. You can't. This is *my* fight. You were right about me being a good soldier, and I'm doing the right thing here. I'm no good for you until I'm better for me." He rested his forehead on hers, staring into her shimmering eyes.

"You've helped me see what I need to do. I have to go away for a while."

"But Cole…" Her voice was strangled. "I *love* you…"

He shook his head and forced himself to step back, releasing her and raising his hands in defense. "Don't. Don't love me. Not now, not like this."

She angrily swept the tears from her cheeks with the back of her hand. "It's *love*, you jackass! I can't turn it off on demand. I won't stop loving you just because you tell me to!"

Ah, there was his feisty girl; the spitfire who'd rise to any challenge. He couldn't help but chuckle.

"I never could control you, Hollywood. But I can control *me*. And I'm walking away, for both our sakes. I don't want you waiting for me. When it's safe for you to leave Russell, I want you to go back to where you belong. Go live your life."

He didn't know if he'd ever be good enough to deserve her love, and he never wanted to hurt her again. "But first, let me do this one last thing…"

He stepped forward and put his hands on either side of her face and kissed her. It was a kiss that started slow and sad, but quickly grew into a flame of desire that nearly knocked him right off his feet. Her hands swept up and tangled in his hair, and she clung to him, kissing with all the passion she had. Her sweet body pressed against his, and *damn it*, he was going to miss this woman. He pulled back and dropped kisses on her closed eyes, the freckled tip of her nose and the top of her forehead. He released her and walked out the door without looking back.

After three combat tours, it was the single hardest thing he'd ever done.

Nell opened the front door twenty minutes later and found Bree standing like a statue in the hallway, right where Cole had left her. Hugging herself tightly and gritting her teeth together so hard it hurt, she was too stunned to speak. Nell took her hand and led her like a child into the kitchen, where she sat, staring at the table in front of her and wiping dampness from her cheeks.

Nell started to brew some tea then looked back at Bree and turned off the stove. She reached into the cupboard that held Cole's liquor and filled a juice glass with whiskey and ice before setting it in front of Bree. A few gulps of the burning liquid steadied her nerves enough to free her voice.

"I don't know what the hell just happened, Nell, but I'm pretty sure I got dumped. And I have no freaking clue *why*. Cole thought I was leaving, but even after I explained he was wrong…even after I told him I *loved* him…he left me."

Nell shook her head. "I knew something was going on when he called me to take care of Maggie, knowing you were right here in the house."

"He heard me talking to Damian about the house today and assumed the worst. When I called him out on it, he said he was always going to hurt me, so he was walking away to go fix himself."

Nell was silent while Bree sipped at the whiskey and replayed the past few weeks in her mind. From the moment she walked into The Hide-Away and looked into Cole's steel-gray eyes, her world had been upended. It wasn't just a matter of going from luxury to a simple country cottage. It wasn't about getting dirty and sweaty for the first time in her life. It wasn't even about falling in love with a man who twisted her in knots. She'd found her true self here, and she'd found peace, even in the midst of her fiery relationship with the hot farmer. She thought she'd found a forever home, but would that really work if Cole wanted her gone? Her eyes narrowed in frustration.

"You should have seen how proud of himself he looked when he told me I shouldn't love him. Like he was all noble and wise."

"Honey, pushing you out of his life saves him

from a situation that probably scares the day-lights out of him."

Bree sat back, rolling her shoulders and stretching. "Cole is as strong a man as I've ever known. What is there about me that could possibly scare him so much?"

"Oh, child, nothing terrifies a good man more than being loved by a good woman. Especially a man as vulnerable as Cole. And the fact that he loves you back really scares him." Bree looked up in surprise, and Nell just chuckled. "Of course he loves you. If he thinks he might hurt you or fail you somehow…well, even a man as tough as Colton Caldwell can be brought to his knees by that kind of fear. It might even be enough to send him running away."

Bree frowned. Was he dumping her because she scared him? Nell stood and extended her hand.

"I don't know what's going on in that boy's head, but don't give up on him just yet, girl. Why don't you come stay at my place tonight with Maggie? Things always look brighter in the morning's light, and a good night's sleep will help clarify your thinking."

# CHAPTER TWENTY

BREE TOSSED AND turned in Nell's guest bed for hours, but when she finally fell asleep, she stayed there until well after sunrise. Maggie was lying at the foot of the bed when she woke, as if she'd been standing watch. Her tail thumped happily on the mattress when Bree sat up.

"Good morning, Maggie Mae." She scratched the pretty dog behind her ears and looked out the window at Cole's farm. The first time she'd seen that house, she thought it looked cold, like him. But now she knew better about both. That old farmhouse was solid, filled with history and warmth. And Cole was the opposite of cold. He burned hotter than the sun. Sometimes he burned too hot and spun out of control, as he had that night by the river. His temper flared at the slightest provocation, and he was constantly on edge and ready to fight the world.

But he was more than his moods. He was fiercely loyal to family and friends. He could be kind and gentle. He could be loving and aware. She brushed a stray tear from her cheek with the back of her hand. She knew his explosive temper was the result of his experiences in the service. She'd seen his nightmares, watched his reaction to the death of a friend. If he didn't get help, he'd flame out. Just yesterday morning she'd wondered if she should leave so that he could work on healing his invisible war wounds. Was that why he was pushing her to leave, because he was thinking the same thing?

So much for the morning bringing clarity. Her mind was already spinning in circles, and her feet had barely hit the floor.

When she stepped out of the shower, she heard Nell talking downstairs. A man's voice answered. Her heart jumped, and she wondered if Cole had come back to tell her that yesterday was just a horrible mistake. Then she heard a teenaged giggle and realized it was Ty's voice she heard. He was here with Emily, and probably Tammy, too. She pulled on shorts and a T-shirt. Cole was still gone, but maybe his brother had news to share.

When Nell spotted her in the doorway, she quickly filled another mug with coffee and slid it across the table, gesturing for her to sit and join them all at the kitchen table. There was an awkward silence before Ty finally spoke.

"Nell told us what happened, Bree. I'm so sorry. I tried to tell Cole yesterday that you wouldn't just leave him like that, but I couldn't shake him from believing it."

"I'm sure you couldn't. He's always expected the worst of me. And to be fair, I was only supposed to be here for a few weeks, then back to—" she held up her fingers in air quotes "—my 'real life' in LA. I never planned on falling in love with your brother." Emily pumped her fist and hissed out a quiet "yes," but Tammy shook her head at her daughter as Bree continued. "I never planned on falling in love with this place. With all of you. I just don't know what to do now."

She took a bite of one of Nell's pastries and frowned. She felt like she was stuck in quicksand, with no way out.

"He called me last night," Ty said quietly.

"Did he say anything about…"

Ty shook his head. "When he and Chris got to the church service for Travis, Cole couldn't even get out of the Jeep. He described it as 'a bit of a breakdown.'" Bree closed her eyes tightly. She'd tried to tell Chris that Cole wouldn't be able to handle the funeral. And for Cole to admit to any kind of breakdown meant it must have been really bad.

"He told Chris to take him straight to Flat Rock," Ty said. "They had an opening and checked him in. They told him to expect to be there for at least six weeks."

"Thank God." He was getting the help he needed. As he'd put it, he needed to fix his shit, and this might be the answer. "Where is this place? When can I see him?"

Ty looked at her in sadness. "He doesn't want you there, Bree."

She felt as if she'd somehow left her body and was looking down at the empty shell of a woman with a broken heart. She pulled in a long, slow breath and held it before releasing it, trying to let her grief go with it.

"He needs to focus on himself," Ty continued. "You're a...distraction." She opened her mouth to protest but he raised his hand. "You're a beautiful, brave, loving distraction, but a distraction just the same. Cole doesn't have the capacity right now to worry about being the man you need while he's dealing with his experiences overseas. It's too much. Your brightness and his darkness are too far apart for him to be able to cope with right now. You've got to let him go so he can do this for himself."

Nell slid an arm around her shoulders. "If you love him now, then you'll still love him in six weeks, honey. I know it's hard, but let him do this. Let him heal."

Emily was sniffling as she leaned against her

mother. Nell wiped tears from her own cheeks then wiped them from Bree's face with a short laugh.

"Look at you, getting all of us crying just because you love our boy." Nell took her hands and squeezed them. "It's going to be okay. We'll take care of things here, and you'll take care of things in California. Then you'll come back to us and be ready to welcome him home."

Bree shook her head, summoning enough false bravado to speak firmly. "No. I won't be here waiting for him. He said he wants me gone. Until he says differently, I'll stay away."

Emily started to speak, but Tammy shushed her. Bree smiled at her precious friends. "I'm never going to stop loving Cole. But *he* has to make the next move. I'm not strong enough to have him send me away again. I won't survive losing him twice. When he's ready to accept my love and return it, he'll figure out how to find me."

By midafternoon, she'd moved to the porch swing with a glass of sweet tea. Nell and Tammy joined her while Emily sat at the produce stand. Ty was working on irrigation lines at Cole's place. Nell reached over and rested her hand on Bree's leg.

"What do you need, honey?"

She looked across the road to the big white

house. "I want him to come home. To be well. To be with me."

"And if that doesn't happen? What then?"

She considered Nell's question. Damian was buying the Malibu house. California would soon be behind her.

*Child, you're already home...*

The sky was bright blue and cloudless, and while it was hot, a steady breeze kept it comfortable. Shep groaned and rolled onto his side in the sunshine at the base of the porch steps. Maggie raised her head and looked up at Bree from her resting spot at her feet. A trio of hummingbirds buzzed around the feeder hanging from the corner of the porch. She could hear the cattle lowing behind the barn. A rusty pickup truck pulled up to the produce stand, where Emily quickly rose from her resting spot and walked over to greet the driver, a skinny young man with sandy hair who couldn't be more than seventeen.

This *felt* like home, but if Cole was going to push her away, what was the point? She could move to New York to be near her cousin Amanda, but that didn't feel right.

"I still want to start a foundation for veterans. Maybe scholarships for counseling programs, or housing or other things like the high-tech prosthetics." She glanced back over at Cole's house. "But I don't know where my home base will be yet."

"Bree, I'm telling you, that man loves you. He'll figure it out for himself eventually."

She stood and stretched. "Maybe. But he was right about one thing. I need to go back to Malibu to take care of things. I'm going over to the cottage for a bit."

Before she could move off the porch, a sheriff's car pulled into the driveway. A large uniformed man got out, and Nell and Tammy stood up behind her. Had there been an accident? Had Cole done something unthinkable? She tried to quell the panic that rose in her throat, and his name came out in a tight whisper.

"Cole?"

"Honey, don't even think that way," Nell said. "Let the man speak. This is Sheriff Langley. Tom and I are old friends from way back." She gestured for the sheriff to join them on the porch. Nell handed him a full glass of tea. "So, what brings you out to the farm?"

The man wiped the sweat from his forehead and thanked Nell for the tea. Then he looked straight at Bree. "Miss Mathews, I've got news about the person that's been stalking you."

Bree sat down, trying to corral her rattled nerves. *He'd called her by her real name.* Her

mmediate thought had been of Cole, not her
stalker. This wasn't the first time she'd forgot-
en why she was here in North Carolina.

"How do you know about that?" Her presence
here was supposed to be a secret.

"Miss Nell's daughter, Caroline, called our office when you arrived. She filled us in on what
was happening, and asked us to keep an eye out
for any suspicious activities, just in case the guy
found you here."

"And did he? Find me here?"

"No, but he was working on it." Everyone else
sat, and the wicker rocker groaned from the sher-
ff's considerable bulk.

"Are you familiar with someone named Mar-
in Kettner, ma'am?"

She shook her head. "I don't think so. Why?"

"He was part of the crew on that TV show you
worked on about women in Hollywood."

"You mean *Hot Hollywood Housewives*?"

The sheriff blushed and nodded. "Yes, ma'am,
that's the one. He apparently became obsessed
with you on the set after you said something
nice to him, and in his twisted mind, you two
were married as soon as you and that other fella
got divorced. They arrested him last night, and
found an entire room of his house wallpapered
with pictures of you. There was a bed in there

and other things…" He cleared his throat and looked away. "It appears he was intending for that to be *your* room. The walls were sound-proofed, the window was bricked off and he'd put a toilet and sink in there. The police chief told me Kettner planned on kidnapping you and holding you there as his…bride."

"My Lord…" Nell muttered, while Tammy shook her head in shock.

Bree was silent. All of this was set in motion by a random, forgotten man she'd once said a kind word to, and his mind had twisted that into a sick version of love.

"How did they find him? Was he arrested in Utah?"

Sheriff Tom shook his head. "He did go there, but he figured out pretty quick that it was a ruse, so he went back to LA and started following your agent, Miss Silverstein. He hacked her computer but couldn't find enough information to track you down. So he confronted her at the office yesterday."

"Oh, my God, is Sheila okay? Did he hurt her?" Bree was sick at the thought that this hiding game may have been dangerous for anyone other than her.

"They told me she's madder than hell but fine

otherwise. I take it she's a pretty tough lady, huh?"

Sheila Silverstein was in her seventies, and had been in the business forever, clawing her way to the top of an industry dominated by men. She didn't take any crap from anyone.

"Yeah, you could say that. What did she do to him?"

"He'd trashed her office then confronted her when she arrived, waving a knife and threatening her if she didn't give up your location. So she tasered the guy then locked him in her office and called the cops. The whole thing was captured on her security cameras. Apparently he didn't think a little old lady would be a threat."

She couldn't help but laugh. "He was a fool to underestimate Sheila. What happens now?"

"He'll be charged with harassment, criminal trespass and stalking, and maybe something along the lines of plotting a kidnapping. And then he's got breaking and entering at the agent's office, as well as assault. She assured the police she'll be pressing charges. He's going away for a good long while, Miss Bree." He looked at her and smiled. "You're safe now. You can go back home."

A flood of emotion overwhelmed her at those words. A tear-choked sob escaped her lips, and she was barely aware of Nell rushing to hug her.

Her reason for coming to North Carolina was gone.

Her reason for staying had walked away from her yesterday.

# CHAPTER TWENTY-ONE

DR. GRACE SINCLAIR stared at Cole over the top of her ever-present notebook. She was a couple inches shy of five foot tall, and her brown hair was pulled back into a tidy bun at the base of her neck. Her age was somewhere between 45 and 65, but he suspected she was closer to the latter. She lifted her chin and waited patiently for him to answer her question. He never would have guessed that the key to his recovery would be this relentless, ageless gnome.

Who knew it was possible for him to talk so damned much? Dr. Sinclair pushed and pushed at him. The past three weeks had been rough. Hell, it had been absolute torture at times, reliving every detail of his three military tours, especially the final episode.

"I'm still waiting, Cole. Tell me why your family hasn't visited when they're only a few hours away."

"I told them not to come." Seeing them would remind him of *her.*

"Care to share the reason for that?"

"I just wanted to focus on the healing process, Dr. Sinclair." He did his best to look sincere, but she didn't buy it for a minute and started to laugh softly.

"Yeah, my bullshit alarm just went to Def-Con Five, so let's try that again." Her head tipped to one side with an expression that took no prisoners. "Who or what are you hiding from?"

She didn't miss the way his body stiffened at her question, and her expression softened. "Look, we've spent all our energy talking about your service experiences, but it's time to shift our focus to what's going on in your home life."

"There's nothing to worry about at home, Doc. I live alone. I have friends and family around to support me. They're all working hard to keep my farm going and I don't want them taking time to come here. I talk to my brother every few days to make sure things are good, and they are."

Ty brought Bree up once in conversation, but Cole shut him down as soon as Ty said the stalker was caught and she'd left North Carolina. He'd told her to go, and she had.

*Breathe in 1-2-3. Breathe out 1-2-3-4-5. Breathe in 1-2-3. Breathe out 1-2-3-4-5.*

It was just one of the coping exercises Dr. Sinclair had taught him in therapy. It slowed his pulse, but it couldn't slow his thoughts. Just like that, he could see Bree walking into The

Hide-Away that first afternoon like she owned the joint, long red hair swinging and green eyes flashing with fire. He could feel her soft skin under his fingers and smell her spicy perfume.

She'd taken up residence in his heart, and he didn't know if he'd ever be able to evict her. He'd been a fool to think she might actually stay in North Carolina. But then, *he* was the one who told her to leave. He shifted in his chair. Yeah, that wasn't one of his more brilliant moves.

"Everything is fine with your friends and family. So it's a woman?" The smart little gnome could really be scary sometimes. "Look, this silent act isn't going to work. I can outwait you, Cole, and you know it. We've made great progress helping you deal with your combat experiences, but I need to know what we should address on the home front. There's no sense putting new tires on the car if you're just going to take it home and crash it into a tree. So start talking, soldier."

*Breathe in 1-2-3. Breathe out 1-2-3-4-5. Breathe in 1-2-3. Breathe out 1-2-3-4-5.*

He cracked at about the three-minute mark.

"A leggy redhead walked into my life last month, Doc, and she did a number on me, okay? I kept hurting her." He shook his head at the doctor's expression. "Not like that. I hurt her *heart*. I didn't trust her. I did things that frightened her. She fought to help me, and I chased her away. She said she loved me, but I thought she deserved better. She *does* deserve better. Now I'm going to have to go home to the house where we…"

Damn it, his hands were shaking. Maybe it was the aftermath of the exhausting session, or maybe it was just that he was finally confronting the truth. His house, Nell's place, The Hide-Away—they were full of memories of Brianna Mathews, and he was going to have to face it all when he left Flat Rock.

"Tell me more about this leggy redhead, Cole." Dr. Sinclair's calm but insistent voice was all it took for him to fold like a house of cards, and, despite the fact that they'd just ended a draining two-hour session, he found himself telling her everything.

THE SUN WAS settling low over the Pacific when Bree walked out onto the balcony of her Malibu home. By next week, it would belong to Damian, and she'd basically be homeless. As much as she wanted to go back to Russell, she'd promised herself she wouldn't do it without knowing where Cole's head, and more important, his heart, was.

Her phone pinged in her pocket with an incoming text. She swiped it open and grinned at the picture of Amanda's husband, Blake, sound asleep in a wing-backed chair with a tiny baby girl snuggled in his arms against his bare chest. Bree dialed her cousin's number.

"My God, Amanda, I don't know whether to hang that in my room as a pin-up poster of the hottest man alive, or put it with my collection of cute little puppy and kitten pictures."

Her cousin laughed. "I know, right? Mr. Uptight Executive has turned into a big pile of mush over our little Maddy. She misses her Auntie Bree already."

"I think she looks pretty content right now." Bree spent a week in Gallant Lake after Martin Kettner was arrested, arriving just in time to help welcome the new baby.

Since her return to Malibu, it had been a whirlwind of business meetings, press conferences and interviews with the police and the FBI. Because Kettner had crossed state lines with the intent to kidnap, he was being investigated for federal charges, too. The guy was going away for a very long time. And the foundation Bree was creating with the money from selling the house was beginning to take shape.

"You're closing on the house this weekend, right? Have you thought any more about our offer?" Amanda and Blake had invited her to stay with them in Gallant Lake until she knew what she was going to do. She might not have a choice but to take them up on it. Of course, her dad had offered to let her come home, but staying in California—and in her childhood bedroom—felt all kinds of wrong.

She looked down and watched people walking hand in hand on the beach in front of her. "I don't know, Amanda. I really have no idea what I'm going to do."

"You haven't heard from Cole yet?"

She sighed heavily and shook her head. Did he have any idea the power he wielded right now to grant her happiness or crush her hopes? Did he think about her at all?

"No. Ty said Cole still refuses to discuss me. It's like he's just excised me from his life. On the bright side, Ty says the therapy is helping a lot. He should be home in a few weeks."

"Are you going to be there waiting for him?"

"I'm not the type to sit and wait for my man like a good little girl, hoping he might want me. If he wants me, he's going to have to work for it a little." And if he didn't want her...

"I admire your determination, Bree, but are you really willing to let your pride keep you away from the man you love? Does he even know how much you love him?"

"I told him, but he refused to listen. But if I'm waiting there for him and he still doesn't think he's ready to have me in his life, I don't think my heart could survive it." She turned away from the blazing sunset to face the cluttered mess in the master suite and sighed. "I have to finish packing, Amanda. I'll be in touch."

Two mornings later she taped up the last of the boxes. Most of the furniture had been sold with the house, but there were personal items and artwork she wanted to keep. She didn't trust the movers with things like her mother's keepsakes, so she'd packed those herself. Her phone rang with a call from Emily, and she shook her head. She talked to the girl almost every day, and each conversation ended with a plea for Bree to "come back to Russell where she belonged."

She swiped her phone to answer. "Hey, kiddo, what's going on?"

"Oh, not much. I'm working at Miss Nell's and thought I'd call. Are you all packed?"

"I'm just finishing up. What are you helping Nell with?"

"I'm cleaning the house for her, and I'll run the produce stand today. Mom is out cleaning stalls in the barn, and then she'll be in to cook a few meals."

"Why are you doing all that? Is Nell away?"

"No, she's here, but she's in bed."

Nell was never in bed after the sun rose.

"Why is she still in bed?"

"She needs to rest and recuperate for a while, but it's okay. We're taking care of her place. And Uncle Cole's place. And the bar..."

"What are you talking about? What exactly is going on there, and don't make me drag it out of you, Emily."

"Oh, didn't Mom tell you? Miss Nell fell off the porch and hurt some ribs and her ankle, so she can't do any work."

Bree's heart jumped.

"When did this happen? How bad is it? Is she awake? I want to talk to her."

"She fell yesterday morning. She says it's nothing serious, but you know, at her age she can't take any chances. She's had a headache, too."

"A headache? Did she hit her head on something?"

"No. I mean, maybe. Hey, I think she's awake now. I hear her in the kitchen. Hang on, Miss Bree."

Bree sat in the nearest chair and listened as Emily slammed the screen door and called out to Nell. She could picture the girl and the woman in that bright country kitchen, and her eyes suddenly filled with tears. She missed the farm. She missed her friends.

"Bree, honey, is that you?" Nell's voice sounded faint.

"Nell? Are you okay? What happened? Why didn't you call me?"

"Whoa, slow down, girl!" Nell's voice came on strong, and it almost sounded as though she was laughing, then she faded again. "I lost my balance yesterday and missed a step. It was hot and I'd been out in the garden." Bree frowned. The woman worked too hard and was alone too much. "The next thing I knew I was on the sidewalk."

"How bad is it?"

"Nothing's broken, but I'm sore all over. But don't worry, Emily and Tammy and Ty are taking care of everything. I just feel bad because they're already stretched to the limit running Cole's place and The Hide-Away, and school starts up soon so Tammy and Emily will be gone during the day. I'll just have to dig deep, I guess, and push past the pain. How are you, dear?"

Bree didn't even think before the words were out of her mouth. "Nell, I'm coming to help you. I'll be there tomorrow."

"Are you sure, Bree? I'd love to see you, but I know you're busy."

"My work is done here. I just need to get this stuff in storage today and have dinner with my dad, and then I'll come work the farm for you until you're better." Bree thought about the one potential pitfall to her plan. "Cole's not…"

"Oh, no, honey, he's still at Flat Rock for another week or two."

That was good. She didn't want him to think she was running to North Carolina for *his* sake. This was just to help Nell.

"Okay. I'll fly into Charlotte in the morning and drive over." And this time she'd rent something more practical than the Mercedes. She couldn't keep the smile from her face. She was going back to Russell, if only for an emergency visit.

"Oh, honey, that's wonderful. We can't wait to see you!" Nell's voice suddenly sounded strong again, as if just the news of Bree's trip was enough to make her feel better.

"You go back to bed and rest, Nell, and I'll see you tomorrow."

# CHAPTER TWENTY-TWO

"SO THIS IS your last week at Flat Rock, Cole,"
Dr. Sinclair said. "How do feel about finishing
up a little early?"

He returned her smile and nodded. "I feel
good, Doc. I'm anxious to get back to the farm.
My brother's been shouldering a lot, and honestly, I miss the work. There's something about
working the land that's just good for the soul."
He chuckled when she raised her eyebrows. "Not
as good as therapy, of course. The farm alone
can't do it. I needed this."

"I'm glad you recognize that. Don't let this
work slide just because you're going home."

"I won't. I'll join Chris and the guys in their
group sessions at Bragg. And I'll work on the
exercises you've given me. I'm ready."

Her eyes narrowed and he braced himself.
That expression meant she was going deep.

"And are you ready to face a house that doesn't
have Brianna Mathews in it?"

Damn. The simple question made his chest
tighten. Just as with his combat memories, his

task wasn't to deny what happened, but to figure out a way to survive it.

*In 1-2-3. Out 1-2-3-4-5.*

"I'll be fine."

"And you still have no interest in speaking with her or knowing what she's doing?"

"None. She's back in California and that's where she belongs. I probably don't even cross her mind."

The good doctor set her notebook down, twirling her pen in her hand.

"Have you been online at all while you've been here, Cole? Watched any television?"

He tried to determine where she was going with this.

"I've watched some sports with the guys. I've been emailing with my brother and my parents. Why?"

Dr. Sinclair looked oddly conflicted.

"You fell in love with a very famous woman, Cole. You might want to look online and see what's going on in her life."

He couldn't imagine what Bree might be saying, or why he should care. He'd forced her to move on, and it was best for her. He stood and stretched, unwilling to take the conversation further today.

"I'll think about it, Doc, but don't hold your breath."

It was two nights before he finally succumbed

to his curiosity. Someone was bound to mention Bree when he got home, so he'd hear about it anyway. Better to deal with it now, with Dr. Sinclair standing by.

He went into the media room and pulled a chair up to one of the cubicles with laptops. His fingers floated over the keys for a long time before he finally typed Bree Mathews into the search window. It was almost more than his heart could take, seeing all the images of her.

She'd taken her hair back to its natural dark red again, and it had grown enough that it was sweeping her shoulders. She was wearing designer clothes, and makeup covered the freckles he hoped were still hiding there. This was California Bree. His eyes picked up some of the headlines.

*Stalker Chases Brianna Mathews Out of Hollywood.*

*Bree's Goin' Country!*

*From Reality Star to Philanthropist.*

He read about the stalker being arrested, and how he'd planned to kidnap Bree and hold her captive. The police had Kettner's journals, where he'd laid out his plans to torture Bree to "cleanse her" then kill her and himself in some twisted marriage ceremony. What if she hadn't come to Russell? What if this nut had found her? Cole stared off into space for a while. She'd told him her life wasn't in California anymore. After reading this, he could easily see why. Maybe she really had wanted to stay in North Carolina with him.

He scrubbed his hands hard over his face and swore. It was pointless to worry about that now that he'd forced her to leave. But then again, she said she'd never stop loving him. He pushed away from the desk, but one of the other headlines caught his eye. Why were they calling Bree a philanthropist? A video opened up on the screen, and he hovered the cursor over the play button. Was he strong enough to hear her voice tonight? He grunted. If he wasn't, then he might as well find out while he was still at Flat Rock. He might not be able to leave early after all. He pressed the mouse and held his breath.

"Yes," Bree was saying into a bank of microphones, "I've sold the Malibu house back to Damian." An off-screen reporter asked a muffled question, and Bree smiled warmly. His heart skipped a few beats at that smile. "Yes, I'm leaving California and 'show biz,' whatever that means. While I was in hiding, I found myself living on a small farm." She held up her hand and laughed along with the reporters. "I know it's hard to imagine, but it's true. I was actually *happy* there. Happier than I've ever been. That's the life I've decided I want. You guys will have to find someone else to pester." There was more general laughter, and another muffled question. "Damian and I have both moved on since our divorce. This was just a business transaction. I wish him only the best, but we are not reconciling now or ever."

Someone shouted out a question and Bree nodded in response. "Yes, that's true. I'm starting a foundation to help military veterans afford the care and supplies they need. I met several veterans while I was away, and their struggles affected me profoundly. The current VA system is good but overwhelmed, and some of these brave men and women need help finding the psychological care that works best for them, obtaining the best prosthetics, affording appropriate housing. The foundation will have a special focus on those dealing with post-traumatic stress syndrome, which can be debilitating to so many." She looked up and directly into the cameras. "These emotional traumas can leave good people unable to trust others, and unable to let people love them because they think they're too damaged to deserve it. People with PTSD can end up pushing away the very people they need in their lives. Somewhere out there right this minute is a truly fine man who's refusing to let love into his life because he's afraid. I want to help him and others like him find the courage to love and be loved. I hope others will join me in that mission."

Cole was suddenly having a hard time pulling oxygen into his lungs. Heat started spreading across his chest and throughout his body until his very skin felt flammable. He blinked rapidly and rubbed at his eyes, glancing over his shoulder to make sure no one was looking.

Cole slammed the laptop shut as if he'd just seen a monster ready to jump out of it. "Damn it to hell!" He jumped to his feet and backed away from the computer without taking his eyes off it. Bree had just spoken directly to him. She was telling him she understood. That she was still ready if he was.

He took his phone from his pocket and dialed. When his brother answered, he didn't bother with a greeting.

"Do you know where she is?"

"Cole? What the hell, man, it's almost midnight." He heard Ty rustling around and knew he was getting out of bed. Ty said something muffled. "Yeah, babe, go back to sleep." His voice got louder. "Cole? You still there?"

"Oh, yeah, I'm here. Why didn't you tell me about this foundation Bree was setting up?"

"Rewind that question for a minute, little brother, and think about it. You're the one who didn't want to hear anything about her, remember? I tried and you shut me down."

He didn't want to be confused by facts. "She sold her house so she could use the money to help guys like me. You couldn't tell me that? You couldn't tell me she still wanted me?"

"Uh-huh. And you would have totally listened to that, right?"

The phone fell silent.

"She never reached out to me once. She knows where I am, right?"

Ty sighed heavily. "That's on me, man. We wanted to give you a chance to get better. That's the priority for all of us, and she agreed to stay away. Plus, she was afraid you'd send her packing. She doesn't think she could deal with that again."

"It sounds like you've spent some time talking with her. She's called you?"

Ty chuckled. "Yeah, she called quite a bit from New York and LA."

"And where is she now?"

"Well, my guess is she's right where Tammy and I left her an hour ago, sitting on Nell's front porch drinking dandelion wine."

The room started to spin, and Cole sat on the sofa in the thankfully empty lounge with a thud. "She's in *Russell*?"

"Yeah, your niece and Nell cooked up a crazy

little scheme to get her back. She's staying at the cottage."

"I need to see her, Ty. I need to talk to her."

"You'll be home this weekend, and you can talk to her face-to-face. She thinks you're in for another week, so she's not expecting you." Ty hesitated. "I figured if we were keeping something from you, it was only fair to keep something from her."

Cole started to laugh. "And you also figured if I didn't know she was there, I wouldn't be able to tell you to get rid of her. I'd just come home this weekend and there she'd be, whether I wanted to see her or not. And we'd be talking, one way or another, because Bree is a force of nature and would never let me get away."

"And that's a bad thing how?"

"Holy hell. She's there, in Russell."

"Yes, Cole. She's here. Don't screw it up this time, okay?"

"I don't intend to, Ty. I don't intend to."

# CHAPTER TWENTY-THREE

BREE HAD NEVER seen this much rain. For the four days she'd been in Russell, it had been raining nonstop. The meteorologists explained that some hurricane was stalled off the coast, pulling in gulf waters that were soaking North Carolina. She fell asleep to the sound of rain on the cottage's tin roof every night, and she woke up to the same exact sound. The once-comforting noise was beginning to feel like torture. And now, on morning number four, it was…raining.

Maggie jumped off the bed when Bree got up. Even the dog was restless. "I think this is what they call cabin fever, Maggie." A rumble of thunder rolled across the sky. "Just be glad your daddy isn't here through all this."

She pulled her robe tighter and looked out the front window to Cole's farm, barely visible through the pouring rain. Would he be better about storms when he returned from Flat Rock? Or would they still set him on edge? She leaned her forehead against the glass, closing her eyes with a smile. The night of that first storm had ended pretty nicely, actually. She shivered as she remembered Cole pushing her up against the wall and kissing her desperately. He'd carried her upstairs and given her the kind of night that…well, it had been one hell of a night.

In another week he'd be home and she'd be gone. Despite Nell and Emily's plotting, she wasn't going to be waiting here to meet him. The teenager and the older woman had played her like a fiddle with their little matchmaking scheme. Nell really had taken a small tumble, but it was off the *bottom* step, not the top. She'd been bruised, but the woman certainly hadn't been injured enough to need all the help Emily claimed. It only took Bree a few hours after arriving at the farm to see that Nell was acting, and not doing a very good job of it. Sometimes she'd limp on her right foot, and sometimes she'd limp on the left. Sometimes her voice was feeble, sometimes it was strong and healthy. And when Bree caught her standing on top of the kitchen counter, reaching above the cupboards to pull down a basket she wanted, the game was up.

But she'd stayed anyway, happily settling into the cottage with Maggie, just to enjoy the company of her friends for a few days and do the farmwork that she'd been missing.

Later that afternoon she put the final touches on the introduction to the cookbook she wanted to write next: *Becoming Southern* by Bree Mathews. She was going to use Nell's recipes and a few others from Tammy and the neighbors. She'd write about the country life and why it was perfect for her. *Malibu Style* was last year's version of Bree Mathews, but from now on it was country all the way. She stood and stretched, setting her laptop aside.

If Cole Caldwell didn't want her around, she'd have to find her slice of country somewhere else. There was no way she could stay here and watch Cole live his life without her being a part of it. The sound of a tractor kept her from following that dangerous spiral of thought. She looked out the window and saw activity at the farm across the road. Her heart leaped, but Ty's truck was the only vehicle parked there.

He was on one of the big tractors, driving it quickly up the driveway and across the road to Nell's through the pounding rain. That was strange enough to make her reach for her hooded rain jacket hanging near the door. She tucked her jeans into her rubber boots and headed out to see what was going on, leaving an unhappy Maggie behind.

Although the rain was falling in sheets, she could still see Nell's house, where everything looked fine. Ty was driving the tractor behind the barn and up the hill, with Nell's truck following. Every muddy footstep threatened to suck her boots from her feet. The air was warm enough that she was sweating under the impermeable jacket. The rain wasn't letting up, so there was no way she could remove it. She broke into a jog, figuring she couldn't feel much worse.

By the time she reached them on the hill, the sky was growing even darker, and thunder rumbled in the distance. She was drenched in a mixture of rain and sweat, and her breathing was labored. Damn, she thought she was in better shape than this. She reached out and slapped a shaking hand on the side of Nell's truck, and Ty turned at the sound.

"What are you doing up here?" He shouted the words against the wind.

"I was about to ask you the same thing. What's wrong?"

Nell's window was rolled down, and her face showed nothing but worry. She reached out and grabbed Bree's hand.

"It's Trixie and Malibu, honey, and some of the other cattle, too. A big oak came down by the gully, and some of them are trapped between it and the fence line. We need to move the tree so they can get out and move down to the holding pen by the barns where there's a bit of shelter and I can get hay to all of them. I was trying to get the herd down there when I saw what happened. I was going to move it myself with the truck, but Ty stopped by just as I'd started. He didn't think it was a good idea for me to try it alone, even though I've been running this farm on my own for almost thirty years now."

Bree caught Ty's attention and nodded her agreement with him. He leaned into the truck and gave Nell a quick kiss on the cheek. "I need you to get back to the house and call Arlen. Tell him we need his help."

Nell scowled at them both, but she finally nodded and drove down the hill.

Bree and Ty walked past the idling tractor and examined the downed behemoth of a tree. She remembered it well, and it made her sad to think that the mighty oak would no longer grace the hilltop. The bulk of the tree had landed down in same gully where she'd help deliver Malibu weeks ago, but the spot was unrecognizable after four days of heavy rain. It was more like a whitewater river, and the tree's foliage was causing some of the water to back up even deeper behind it, where a dozen worried cows and calves peeked through the branches.

"Ty, did it land on any of them?" She hated the thought of an unfortunate animal being crushed beneath the tree.

He shook his head. "It's hard to tell, but I don't think so. Look, I've got a chain around one of the bigger limbs. I think the tractor will pull it aside far enough for the cattle to get up the other side of the gully so they can go around the tree and down the hill."

Bree nodded thoughtfully as if this was a situation she saw every day, trying not to show any panic as the dark water swirled below them.

"What can I do to help?"

He shook his head sharply. "Just stay out of the way and let me know when the tree is clear of the gully. Don't get between the tree and the tractor, in case that chain breaks loose. Got it?"

"Don't be ridiculous, Ty. I need to do more than that." She noticed a long board on the ground next to the tractor. "What's that for?"

"When Arlen gets here, I'll have him use that. Let's see if I can move this thing without it." He walked back to the tractor and put it in gear, but the tree's limbs were firmly anchored in the ground, and it was too muddy for the big tractor to get enough traction to budge the heavy oak. Ty climbed back down.

"We need leverage." He carried the long board over to the tree. Moving to the far side of the trunk, he jammed the board under it and pushed up. He looked at her and nodded. "You might be able to do this, at least until Arlen gets here. The 4x4 will act as a lever pushing the tree while the tractor pulls it forward. Which job do you want?"

She was distracted, staring down at the cattle below them. Some of the adults were belly deep in the swift water, and the calves were milling around on the rapidly shrinking patch of ground between the water and the tree. Malibu was there, staring at her mother and bawling loudly.

"Bree! Are you driving or pushing?"

"Neither!" She threw her hands in the air. "I can't drive the tractor and I sure can't push this tree. It must weigh a ton." She hated feeling helpless. Ty rested his hand on her shoulder.

"You're not going to be pushing the tree. You'll put all your weight on this piece of wood right here. A lever gives you superhuman strength. The tractor can rock the tree forward, and if you just keep pushing this farther underneath and push up on it, we might be able to get it moving. If not, I'll have to go find Cole's chainsaw and hope I can cut away enough to let them through, but we don't have a lot of time." He glanced to the west, where lightning flickered along the horizon.

"Damn."

"Exactly. Let's give this a shot, Bree. Show me you're a real farm woman."

She nodded with determination as she looked

down at Malibu's broad white face. Lives depended on her.

Nothing happened at first, no matter how hard she pushed up on the board. Her feet were sliding in the mud and she couldn't get traction. She fell to her knees in the goop, but she was back on her feet before Ty even noticed. And then it happened. Just a little bit of movement, but it was enough. She drove the wood farther under the trunk and pushed up against it with her shoulder. The tree shuddered and moved forward slightly. It was working!

She waved at Ty and pushed the board under the trunk again. The tractor roared and she gave out a yell, throwing herself against the 4x4. Suddenly the board moved dramatically, and the tree started to slide forward. She felt all-powerful as the board pushed up higher than it had before. They were doing it!

With a loud crack, one of the limbs that anchored the trunk in the mud gave way, and the tree rolled forward rapidly. The sudden movement caught her off guard, and she fell forward, sliding feet-first down the slope toward the cattle and the water.

She heard a shouted curse behind her and dug in her heels to stop herself. A strong arm wrapped around her waist and yanked her back against a hard chest. Hot breath blew across her ear, and her body froze when she heard an achingly familiar voice.

"You don't have to keep throwing yourself in the water to impress me, Hollywood. I already love you."

She spun in Cole's arms. His face was just inches above hers, and she couldn't think of anything other than how beautiful he looked with his rain-flattened hair falling into his warm gray eyes. She reached up and put her hands on either side of that wet face and smiled widely up at him. Now she knew where that extra surge of strength had come from. Cole must have grabbed the piece of wood behind her and thrown his heft into it.

"You're here." At the moment nothing else mattered.

"I am here. And so are you."

"Yes."

Ty cleared his throat nearby. "As fascinating as this conversation is, I'm heading down the hill. And I suggest you two do the same before that lightning gets any closer."

As if to support his words, a rumble of thunder rolled through the low-hanging clouds.

"The cattle..." Bree looked back, but the last of them were scrambling up the opposite side of the gully, which was passable now that the tree was moved. The tractor rumbled back to life as Ty headed off, leaving them standing in the rain.

"Do you really want to talk about the cattle, Bree?" Cole's warm voice made her melt, and she leaned into him.

"No. What I really want to talk about is what you just said."

"That I'm here? That you're here?" His grin grew wider, as if he couldn't hold it back and didn't want to try.

"No, not that."

"That you don't have to throw yourself in the water all the time?"

"No. That other thing you said."

He leaned closer and dropped a chaste kiss onto the end of her nose, causing a shiver to travel from her head to her toes. She sighed. "Don't tease me."

His lips hovered over hers.

"That I already love you?"

She closed her eyes in a futile attempt to control the adrenaline rushing through her veins.

"Say it again."

"Look at me first."

She opened her eyes, her tears mixing with the raindrops on her cheek.

He kissed her softly. "I love you." His strong hands cradled her face. "I love you." He pulled her close and just before his mouth pressed to hers, he said it again. "I love you, Brianna Mathews."

Now she knew how birds must feel. It was as if she could fly from the ground and remain airborne for as long as she wanted. He loved her.

She pulled away. "What happened before… all the misunderstandings… I'm sorry…" But he stopped her with another sweet kiss.

"Don't. It was me. I wasn't ready for you to love me."

"And now?"

A gust of wind blew her wet hair across her face, and he gently moved it behind her ear.

"And now I'm ready. Do you still…?"

Laughter bubbled up as her heart surged in joy.

"I absolutely love you, Colton Caldwell."

Despite the storm swirling around them, they had been very tender with each other so far. Fingertips touching skin lightly, lips brushing as gently as raindrops. But as they declared their love, staring into each other's eyes, the gentleness fell away. She threw herself at him and he lifted her into the air and spun her around while capturing her mouth with his. This. *This* was home for her.

They stood in the embrace until the storm gave them no choice but to dash down the hill to safety. They made it as far as Nell's barn.

As soon as Cole pulled her through the barn door, he closed it with a slam and pushed her up against it, kissing her deeply.

"God, I need to touch you, Bree. I need you. Right now."

She laughed against his mouth. "Your brother is right inside the house with Nell. And Nell called Arlen."

"No, she didn't. I pulled in just as she was heading into the house. I told her not to. And she and Ty both know better than to come into this barn right now."

An explosion of thunder made her flinch. She captured his face with her hands and frowned.

"You're better? The treatment was good? The storm isn't…?"

He kissed her long and deep then rested his forehead against hers. "I can't tell you I'm all fixed after six weeks, but I'm definitely better. Not cured, but better. It's a process. One of the exercises I learned was how to replace bad memories with good ones. And I happen to have a very good memory of one particular thunderstorm." He kissed her again and her knees buckled. With one smooth movement he swung her around and laid her on a soft mound of hay.

"I have some pretty good memories of that thunderstorm, too." She let out a gasp as his hands slipped under her shirt. His denim-clad leg slid between hers and he pressed her down into the hay.

"Only pretty good?" He kissed his way down her throat. "Sounds like a challenge to me."

She twisted her fingers into his hair, liking the fact that it was now long enough to do that, and lifted his head so she could look straight into his eyes. She didn't have to say it. He knew what she needed to hear.

"I'm back, Bree. I'm here, and I'm staying. And you..." He kissed her. "You are staying, too. And we're going to build a life together right here in Russell. A crazy life full of farming and children and friends and working to help other vets like me."

"You know about the foundation?"

He sighed and shook his head. "You really want to talk about all of this *now*? Yes, I know about your plans. Yes, I approve. Yes, I know you sold the Malibu beach house. Yes, I know you said you found happiness on a farm, which I assume means with me. Yes, I know we have a lot to talk about, and a lot of plans to make, and it won't always be easy and we'll both have to compromise and we'll learn as we go. We love each other and that's really all that matters. The other stuff can wait, but please, Bree, let me touch you and hold you and love you. I've missed having you in my arms so much. So much..."

His voice cracked, and emotion overwhelmed her. She laughed through her own tears and pulled him in for a long, hot kiss, where their tears blended together as closely as their bodies did. He'd come home to her.

Home to her in North Carolina. She smiled against Cole's warm, damp skin as his hands caressed her.

*Child, you're already home.*

\* \* \* \* \*

# LARGER-PRINT BOOKS!

**♦HARLEQUIN** *Presents*®

## GET 2 FREE LARGER-PRINT NOVELS PLUS 2 FREE GIFTS!

HPLP15

# REQUEST YOUR FREE BOOKS!
## 2 FREE WHOLESOME ROMANCE NOVELS
## IN LARGER PRINT
## PLUS 2
## FREE
## MYSTERY GIFTS

✻✻✻✻✻✻✻✻✻✻✻✻✻✻✻✻✻✻✻✻✻✻✻

### HEARTWARMING™

✻✻✻✻✻✻✻✻✻✻✻✻✻✻✻✻✻✻✻✻✻✻✻

*Wholesome, tender romances*

**YES!** Please send me 2 FREE Harlequin® Heartwarming Larger-Print novels and my 2 FREE mystery gifts (gifts worth about $10). After receiving them, if I don't wish to receive any more books, I can return the shipping statement marked "cancel." If I don't cancel, I will receive 4 brand-new larger-print novels every month and be billed just $5.24 per book in the U.S. or $5.99 per book in Canada. That's a savings of at least 19% off the cover price. It's quite a bargain! Shipping and handling is just 50¢ per book in the U.S. and 75¢ per book in Canada.* I understand that accepting the 2 free books and gifts places me under no obligation to buy anything. I can always return a shipment and cancel at any time. Even if I never buy another book, the two free books and gifts are mine to keep forever.

161/361 IDN GHX2

Name _____ (PLEASE PRINT) _____

Address _____ Apt. # _____

City _____ State/Prov. _____ Zip/Postal Code _____

Signature (if under 18, a parent or guardian must sign)

### Mail to the **Reader Service:**
**IN U.S.A.:** P.O. Box 1867, Buffalo, NY 14240-1867
**IN CANADA:** P.O. Box 609, Fort Erie, Ontario L2A 5X3

\* Terms and prices subject to change without notice. Prices do not include applicable taxes. Sales tax applicable in N.Y. Canadian residents will be charged applicable taxes. Offer not valid in Quebec. This offer is limited to one order per household. Not valid for current subscribers to Harlequin Heartwarming larger-print books. All orders subject to credit approval. Credit or debit balances in a customer's account(s) may be offset by any other outstanding balance owed by or to the customer. Please allow 4 to 6 weeks for delivery. Offer available while quantities last.

**Your Privacy**—The Reader Service is committed to protecting your privacy. Our Privacy Policy is available online at www.ReaderService.com or upon request from the Reader Service.

We make a portion of our mailing list available to reputable third parties that offer products we believe may interest you. If you prefer that we not exchange your name with third parties, or if you wish to clarify or modify your communication preferences, please visit us at www.ReaderService.com/consumerchoice or write to us at Reader Service Preference Service, P.O. Box 9062, Buffalo, NY 14240-9062. Include your complete name and address.

HW15

# LARGER-PRINT BOOKS!
## GET 2 FREE LARGER-PRINT NOVELS PLUS
## 2 FREE GIFTS!

**H HARLEQUIN®**

# INTRIGUE
## BREATHTAKING ROMANTIC SUSPENSE

**YES!** Please send me 2 FREE LARGER-PRINT Harlequin® Intrigue novels and my 2 FREE gifts (gifts are worth about $10). After receiving them, if I don't wish to receive any more books, I can return the shipping statement marked "cancel." If I don't cancel, I will receive 6 brand-new novels every month and be billed just $5.49 per book in the U.S. or $6.24 per book in Canada. That's a saving of at least 11% off the cover price! It's quite a bargain! Shipping and handling is just 50¢ per book in the U.S. and 75¢ per book in Canada.* I understand that accepting the 2 free books and gifts places me under no obligation to buy anything. I can always return a shipment and cancel at any time. Even if I never buy another book, the two free books and gifts are mine to keep forever.

199/399 HDN GHWN

| | | |
|---|---|---|
| Name | (PLEASE PRINT) | |
| Address | | Apt. # |
| City | State/Prov. | Zip/Postal Code |

Signature (if under 18, a parent or guardian must sign)

Mail to the **Reader Service:**
**IN U.S.A.:** P.O. Box 1867, Buffalo, NY 14240-1867
**IN CANADA:** P.O. Box 609, Fort Erie, Ontario L2A 5X3

**Are you a subscriber to Harlequin® Intrigue books
and want to receive the larger-print edition?
Call 1-800-873-8635 today or visit www.ReaderService.com.**

* Terms and prices subject to change without notice. Prices do not include applicable taxes. Sales tax applicable in N.Y. Canadian residents will be charged applicable taxes. Offer not valid in Quebec. This offer is limited to one order per household. Not valid for current subscribers to Harlequin Intrigue Larger-Print books. All orders subject to credit approval. Credit or debit balances in a customer's account(s) may be offset by any other outstanding balance owed by or to the customer. Please allow 4 to 6 weeks for delivery. Offer available while quantities last.

**Your Privacy**—The Reader Service is committed to protecting your privacy. Our Privacy Policy is available online at www.ReaderService.com or upon request from the Reader Service.

We make a portion of our mailing list available to reputable third parties that offer products we believe may interest you. If you prefer that we not exchange your name with third parties, or if you wish to clarify or modify your communication preferences, please visit us at www.ReaderService.com/consumerchoice or write to us at Reader Service Preference Service, P.O. Box 9062, Buffalo, NY 14240-9062. Include your complete name and address.

HILP15